Totally Bound Publishing books by Makayla Roberts

The Royal Gordanos
A Royal's Touch
A Royal's Pursuit
Craving a Royal

The Lucifer Brothers
The Devil is My Boss
In a Devil Bind

I0663216

The Lucifer Brothers

IN A DEVIL BIND

MAKAYLA ROBERTS

In a Devil Bind
ISBN # 978-1-83943-732-8
©Copyright Makayla Roberts 2021
Cover Art by Erin Dameron-Hill ©Copyright August 2021
Interior text design by Claire Siemaszkiewicz
Totally Bound Publishing

IN A DEVIL BIND

Dedication

A big thanks to Danielle L.
for your support and motivation.

Chapter One

Waking up in a stranger's bed was nothing new to Thorne Lucifer. At age eighty and some change, sex was one of the few things he had to keep from dying of boredom most days. If someone asked him to count how many lovers he'd taken in the past year alone — hell, the past month — he couldn't even give two names. They all came and went — pun intended.

On this occasion, however, he couldn't recall a day in his life when he'd awakened chained to a stranger's bed with a splitting headache and a bad case of nausea, having been stripped down to nothing more than his socks. With a grunt, he squinted his eyes open, sighing with relief when the only lights he could make out were from a handful of dim candles that had been placed on top of a wooden dresser. He didn't think his hangover would be very kind to him if he'd been encased in full illumination. A faint orange glow shone from the open door across from him — a bathroom, most likely.

He soon became aware of his other senses. Something smelled like mildew, piss and the very ass of hell. There was the sound of shuffling and scraping, though it was very light. It was distant, perhaps coming from another room.

Something cold and wet soaked one side of his head, so he turned a bit to spot a clear zipped bag filled with water, though the outside was coated in condensation.

Aw, his lover had been considerate enough to give him an ice pack for his hangover. *How sweet.*

With a snort, he waited until his vision cleared further before taking in his surroundings — moldy walls with chipped paint that had lost color long ago, a busted bubble-back TV, a crooked painting of a bland flower and furniture covered in stains that came from only-the-gods-knew what. Even the bed he was on was lumpy and uncomfortable, resulting in a deep ache in his lower back. A pile of sharp rocks would have been preferable.

He crinkled his nose in disgust. While he wasn't as particular about his sex partners as his uptight brothers were, he was damn sure not down with doing business in raggedy motel rooms. He was a classier dude than that. He'd screw his partner in a dark alley and send her on her way before bedding down in one of these shitholes.

What gives?

He frowned, images of the previous night coming back in bits and pieces. He'd gone to one of his favorite bars on the east side of town after leaving work. It had been a slow Saturday, so he'd wanted to go out for some drinks to pass the time. He was a big drinker, so throwing back shot after shot hadn't even given him a buzz. Instead, it'd put him in a horny mood, and he'd been scanning the crowd for the hottest woman to take home for a night of fun. If he were lucky, he would have found two of them.

It hadn't taken long before he'd spotted a petite blonde sashaying toward him. She hadn't been the only one interested, of course. Despite being a Lucifer, his devilishly handsome looks and easy smile always aided him in attracting the opposite sex. But that woman had been a nymph — his favorite. He'd sensed that right off the bat and wasted no time ordering a drink for her while they made small talk.

Everything went blurry from there. He vaguely recalled her leading him to the dance floor, grinding against his dick in tune with the music. Then they were outside and…everything went blank.

Frown deepening, he realized the wench must have slipped something into one of his drinks. He glanced down at his naked body, checking for any damage. *Nothing.* Not even a little nick from a needle drawing blood. He grunted, pushing himself up the musty pillows.

Well, damn. If she hadn't cut him open in his sleep, what the hell had she drugged him for? He'd already planned on screwing her brains out, so if she'd thought to use him for sex, it was pointless.

"Yo, nympho. You there?" he called, his voice rough from waking up. "You can unchain me now."

Of course, he didn't receive an answer. However, there was another collection of shuffling and thumping from the other room. He tugged on the chains binding his wrists in a way that made him look like he was being fucking crucified. A quick glance around showed a key on the nightstand next to him, and he sighed.

An ice pack and the key to free himself. *How freaking considerate of her.*

As he unlocked his chains, he grumbled a series of expletives under his breath, all directed at the vixen who'd caused this. While he didn't mind being used for sex, he'd be damned if he'd let it slide that someone had drugged him and left him in such a dank room. He didn't even know where he was. The blondie better pray he didn't find out her identity. He might be known as a pretty laid-back man, but he damn sure wasn't one to be crossed.

Freed, he stood and bent his body this way and that to inspect his backside for any blemishes. It wouldn't surprise him to find his back and ass ate up by bed bugs. He didn't see any, but he wouldn't hold his breath on that one. The longer he stood in the room, the grosser his skin felt.

He spotted his pants and shirt thrown over the back of an armchair and swiftly donned them, sneezing as a chill washed over him. *Great.* Not only were his surroundings filthy beyond repair, but there was also a draft. The top of his head felt cold as ice, despite the rest of the room feeling like a damn furnace. He pulled on his shoes and spotted his leather jacket tossed on top of the half-broken dining table. Next to it sat his cell phone and wallet, and a quick check showed that his battery had a little juice — and nothing was missing from his wallet, not even a single torq.

Before he could reach for his jacket, he paused at the sound of someone knocking — not at the front door but the one that connected his room to another.

Tensing in preparation to kick someone's ass, he strolled over and unlocked the latch, then threw the off-white panel open. "You have two seconds to explain what — "

Thorne stumbled backward as someone crashed into him. "Fuck," a female growled against his chest before shoving him away. Dressed only in a black bra and panties, she clutched the side of her head, her hand coming away with blood. "*Fuck*! I'm going to kill them. Ohhh, someone is going to fucking die tonight."

He stiffened when she looked at him, her dark eyes mere slits of coal. She bared her teeth like a wild animal. "Did you have something to do with this?" She flashed him her palm.

He cocked one eyebrow and jerked his thumb over his shoulder. "I just woke up tied to the bed, lady. Not sure what the hell's going on." He narrowed his eyes, taking her in. She wasn't the nymph, that was for sure. That woman had been blonde with sparkling green eyes and alabaster skin. The one before him was the total opposite. "Did *you* have something to do with this?"

She grumbled a curse and rushed over to his bathroom, dismissing his presence. Despite the strangeness of the circumstances and the amount of blood and dirt covering her, Thorne couldn't help the way his gaze dropped to her rear. Hey, he was a man, after all, and he'd always loved his women with bigger assets — special emphasis on the 'ass' portion.

The thong she wore was shaped against her like a custom fit, the lush globes jiggling with each step she took. Her lower back had two dimples, another thing he'd always liked on women. What bits of almond-colored skin he could see looked smooth to the touch, everything tight with lean muscles that spoke of a regular exercise routine. Her raven hair was parted down the middle and pulled into two thick braids that fell nearly to her waist.

His dick grew a bit hard while he followed from a safe distance as she entered the bathroom.

Snatching up a half-empty water bottle from the sink, she grabbed a washcloth and wet it, then began to dab at her wound with light touches. "Those motherfuckers," she jeered, wincing in pain when she applied pressure.

Thorne leaned against the doorjamb of the bathroom. "Do you have even the slightest clue what's going on here? I can't remember shit from last night."

She scoffed. "That's because somebody drugged you."

"No shit. I'm asking who did it—and why."

She tossed the bloodied towel aside before turning to face him. He tried to keep from gaping at her full breasts, which were barely contained by her lacy bra. She pouted, then planted one fist on her hip with no shame whatsoever at her lack of clothing. "Do you see this?" She pointed to her bleeding temple.

Forcing his gaze away from the breasts, Thorne grimaced at the deep gash struggling to knit itself closed. It was a wonder she was even conscious, given how much blood soaked her. A wave of nausea rolled through him. "Yeah, that's gross."

She twisted her lips into a grim line. "Those bastards are dead when I get my hands on them. Do you hear me? D-E-A-D." Before he could ask what she meant, she eyed him with caution. "You'd better get yourself checked. From what I know about devils, you guys can regenerate, but you can still catch an infection."

He frowned, doing everything he could to keep himself from throwing up. The bleeding had slowed to a stop, but the raw pink tissue lying beneath was what sickened him. "What are you talking about? I'm fine."

She lifted a brow, peering at the top of his head. "Sure, you are, Thorne."

With that, she slid past him and made her way back to her room. Thorne frowned after her. "How do you know my name?" He didn't bother trying to hide the suspicion in his voice. He'd be lying if he said she looked familiar. He'd come across so many women in his life that there was no telling who she was. Then again, there were few people who *didn't* know him. He was a Lucifer, after all. Their name was known far and wide as they sat atop the pillar of the Big Four families in Sheol. "Have we met before?"

She snorted in derision. "If you have to ask that, then no." She didn't even hesitate as she stepped over the threshold.

Thorne meant to follow her to get more information, but he paused at the sight of himself in the broken mirror. All the color drained from his face as he blinked at his reflection.

There, on the top of his head, was the worst monstrosity he'd seen since...since...hell if he knew. He couldn't even think of the proper words to compare it to, but it was disastrous.

His horns. His beautiful, six-inch, curved horns that held engraved patterns that were a proud sign of maturity and virility...

One was missing. Gone. Cut from his head, leaving him looking like a lopsided freak of nature. Like a fucking unicorn or something.

At the top of his lungs, he bellowed, *"What the fuck!"*

Chey would have fallen to the floor in a fit of laughter over Thorne's angry outburst, but the biting pain in her head wouldn't be forgiving if she did anything to further agitate it. Instead, she settled for a quiet chuckle.

She felt for the poor man. She truly did. Dismemberment was never a pretty sight, but damn if the bastard didn't look goofy as hell. Despite the murderous rage threatening to break the surface of her composure, the devil in the other room had looked ridiculous with only one horn on top of his head. She'd had to bite her tongue to keep from calling him all sorts of fitting names. 'Thorne the Unicorn' was just one of many.

Her amusement was short-lived, however, as her anger returned. It was her own karma for trying to be a good Samaritan. She should have left Thorne to suffer his fate alone. Instead, the ever-annoying honorable side of her that he didn't deserve had been persistent in warning him that the nymph from the bar had been up to no good.

The thought had her gritting her teeth in annoyance as she searched every inch of the disgusting motel room for her clothes. Like Thorne, she'd been drugged. Unlike him, however, whoever was responsible had figured that hitting her over the head would work much faster than waiting for the drug to work through her system. She'd awakened chained to the bed, though it was clear that of the two of them, her memory wasn't fogged with confusion. Perhaps it was because he'd imbibed too much alcohol beforehand.

She sighed as she recalled the dumbfounded look on his face when she'd said his name. The douchebag didn't even know who she was. *Figures*. Thorne Lucifer was the biggest bachelor in Sheol — and it showed. There wasn't a day that went by when he wasn't hooking up with some floozy, no doubt. She'd heard countless stories about the devil over the years, about how he left a string of broken hearts in his wake. Yet women still went after him like he was the rarest gem in the underworld.

How pathetic. Seriously, there probably wasn't a single woman in all Elysium he hadn't screwed.

Rolling her eyes, she scowled toward the front door. It was bolted shut, as were the windows in the room, so her only means of escape was through Thorne's side. If his door was sealed shut as well, then she'd have to rely on his brute strength to break it down. She was helpless until the pain in her head cleared and she was able to move without nausea rolling through her.

While her captors had been generous enough to leave the key to her shackles on the nightstand, they'd taken her clothes, leaving her to travel around only in her bra and panties. And she sure as shit wasn't about to wrap herself in the sheets that were covering the bed. She was positive that the itchy red bumps on her skin were from the insects inhabiting the dusty furniture.

Shuddering in disgust, she returned to the bathroom and picked up the bloody white towel. The mirror had been busted out, so she had to feel around with her fingertips for the opening of her wound.

Upon first waking up about two hours prior, she'd stumbled into the bathroom and taken note of the blood — her blood — staining the sink. There were even loose gauze pads littering the floor, as if someone had tried to patch her up before giving up the task. That's when she'd noticed the deep gash at her temple and had nearly lost her shit.

She wasn't a fan of letting people get the upper hand over her, and she sure as fuck didn't appreciate someone possessing the balls to kidnap her and drag her to…wherever the hell she was.

Grunting, she wrung the excess water from the rag. She placed it against her head and made her way back to Thorne's room. He was still in his bathroom, growling and talking under his breath as he poked and prodded the area around his missing horn.

She once again suppressed the urge to laugh before going for the front door. He caught sight of her in the mirror, then whirled around to face her. "Where are you going?"

She didn't break stride. "I'm not staying here."

He was standing before her in less than two seconds. Chey paused, taking a step back. Though she was pleased with her whopping five-feet-six frame, Thorne had a good eight or nine inches on her. And though she wasn't some weakling who couldn't take a punch, the man was stacked with bulging muscles that put her little ones to shame. Plus, he was a Lucifer, one of the most powerful demons in Elysium. He could probably flick her in the forehead and send her flying across the room.

"You can't leave yet. We still need to figure out what's going on."

Chey scoffed. "It's pretty obvious what's going on, dude. We were drugged and kidnapped. Doesn't take much thinking to figure that one out."

She tried to step around him, but he blocked her path, anger flitting across his features. "I can do without the smart-ass comments," he growled. "What I want to know is who did this and how I can find them."

Chey gave a helpless lift of her hands. "Your guess is as good as mine."

His nose twitched. "You're lying."

She jerked back, about to snap at him, only to realize it would be futile. She'd forgotten that his kind were able to sense everyone's feelings, even down to the most subtle of emotions. They could even tell whenever someone was lying, which was something she never did.

Well, most of the time.

Shit.

He bared his teeth at her, perhaps in an attempt to intimidate her. *Ha,* he'd have better luck picking a fight with a brick wall. Chey didn't scare easily. Instead, she admitted if only to herself that the man had a nice set of molars on him — so straight and pristine that his smile could be used for a lighthouse beacon on a stormy night. The thought made her snort.

"What the hell is so funny?" he demanded. He pointed to the top of his head. "I have to walk around looking like this for weeks. I'm in no mood for your games, so tell me what the hell you know before I lose my shit."

Chey didn't bother looking up at his missing horn, because if she did, she was going to burst into a fit of giggles. Instead, she scrunched her face into a deep frown to hide her amusement. "I don't know any specifics — or even who the people were." She made a dismissive motion with her hands. "And in case it hasn't occurred to you, this place reeks, I'm in an assload of pain and I'm about three seconds away from breaking off your other horn if you don't get the hell out of my way."

Of course, he didn't move aside. Instead, he clamped his hand around her wrist, tugging her into him. He leaned until they were nose to nose. "You indicated that there was more than just that nymph who caused this. Tell me what you know, woman, because it's a damn lot more than what I'm coming up with."

Chey froze. It wasn't fear that had her drawing in a sharp breath and desperate to put several paces between them. Being so close to him, to a male whose raw power and masculinity rolled off him in pulsating waves, caused her lower muscles to clench in response. *Gods below*. That was one of the few downsides of being a sex demon. The inevitable need to seek sexual release always came at the most inopportune times.

And being enclosed in a disgusting motel room with the one demon in the entire underworld who she despised with a passion *most definitely* counted as an inopportune time.

Thorne's nostrils flared as if he were able to smell her abrupt arousal. The golden flecks circling his irises darkened in response to her desire. It was common. Unmated men were susceptible to the pheromones of her kind. Not even the most reserved of creatures could resist the call of a horny succubus.

Not that she'd asked to be turned on or anything.

Chey grunted and took another step back, tugging her wrist from him. Well, she tried to, but the brute held fast. "Let go of me," she demanded. "I'll tell you what I do know, but not in this…shithole. I feel like my skin's crawling with every passing second."

Thorne nodded, eyeing her with a guarded expression as he released her. It was like he was just as put off by his reaction as she was. "Fine. We'll go to a clinic to get you patched up. We can talk on the — Why are you looking at me like that?"

Chey blinked, closing her gaping mouth. Damn, he'd caught her staring at his single horn, and by the thunderous look on his face, he was not pleased. "I can't help it. It's just…there." She gave a sharp shake of her head, turning sideways to avoid looking at him. "I'm not going to a hospital. I can stitch this up myself. I just need to get home."

Thorne grunted in annoyance. "Whatever, lady." He crossed the room and picked up a light leather jacket. None-too-gently, he tossed it at her. "Cover yourself up."

She scoffed but slid her arms inside the sleeves. The jacket didn't conceal everything, but it hid her necessities, so she was pleased. Plus, it was warm and didn't smell like sewage as the rest of the room did.

He waited until she had the garment zipped up before turning to the door. Like hers, it was bolted shut from the outside, but his superior strength had it opened after a few sharp tugs. When they stepped into the hallway, it didn't take long for them both to realize that this wasn't an ordinary run-down motel like they'd thought. The place was abandoned inside and out — dark, creepy and even more disgusting than the rooms.

"Stay close to me," Thorne commanded, keeping his voice quiet. "There's no telling who or what's lingering around here. And for hell's sake, if you get scared, at least wait until you give me my answers before running off into the dark and getting lost like those dumb broads in the movies."

Walking through an invisible spiderweb, Chey grunted. "Just don't do anything to piss me off until then. Otherwise, you'll be of luck and stuck looking like a fucking unicorn with no answers."

Chapter Two

As it turned out, no one else inhabited the abandoned building. The hallway was a straight shot from one end to the other, with one side holding boarded-up windows. About halfway down the far end, the walls were blackened and stripped down to the outer frame, while gaping holes made up the flooring. It didn't take a rocket scientist to figure out the cause for the abandonment. A fire had broken out, one that had engulfed a little over half the building. It was clear that the owners either hadn't had the funds for repairing it or they'd simply lost interest.

Judging by the ill-designed wall patterns on the section that was still intact, as well as the appalling décor in the rooms, Thorne was leaning more toward the latter.

Coming to a set of burned stairs that led down into an old lobby, he hesitated on the first step, judging the short distance between where he stood and the bottom. He could jump it with ease, but he feared his weight would just cause the pitiful remains of the floor to collapse. Then again, if he took the stairs, the damaged wood would likely give in under him.

Well, if his kidnappers had managed to drag the succubus and his big ass up the stairs without a problem, that was a sign that they were sturdy enough to support him again. *Right*?

Deciding to stick with caution, he descended with what he hoped to be light strides. The woman behind him wasn't as smooth, however, for she breathed a curse. He peered over his shoulder, scowling. "What is it now?"

She didn't bother looking at him as she held onto the railing with one hand to balance herself on one foot. She brought the other above her knee, and even in the dark, he saw the blood on her dirtied foot. "Stepped on glass."

Thorne rolled his eyes in exasperation and backtracked. "Why didn't you put your clothes on before we left the room?"

She made a rather unladylike sound of disgust. "For the obvious reason that I couldn't find my clothes. Gods, you're not the sharpest tool in the box, are you?"

Thorne gritted his teeth, two seconds away from just leaving her ass behind. Unfortunately, he needed her to give him at least some kind of explanation for what was going on. Her memory of the previous night was a hell of a lot better than his, and if she had a proper description of the nymph and her partner, it would help him.

"Come here," he grouched. He scooped her into his arms, groaning as his aching muscles protested. "Holy damn, lady. How much do you weigh?"

She growled and kicked her legs out. "No one asked you to carry me, you bastard. Put me down."

"If I do, it'll take another hour to get out of here. Hold still and be quiet so I can concentrate."

To his surprise, she cursed under her breath but stopped fighting. To be fair, she really wasn't heavy at all. He'd just wanted to be an ass. His muscles were sore from the lingering effects of the drug he'd been given, but it was fading with every passing minute. Plus, he'd be lying if he said her natural scent mixed with having her breasts so close to his chest didn't affect him. As it was, he was standing at half-mast, something that was entirely inappropriate given the circumstances. Despite his reputation, he wasn't so depraved that sex was all he ever thought about. He had hobbies and shit, just like everyone else.

Once again, he hesitated at the top step before deciding to just make a quick descent. Within minutes, he found the lobby's entrance with wooden doors that were, of course, bolted from the outside. They gave way after a few good kicks and he nearly fell to his knees with relief when a breeze of fresh air touched his skin. He wasted no time exiting the building and stepping out onto the cracked pavement of what used to be a parking lot.

As he took in his surroundings, he twisted his lips in distaste when all he could see was a large expanse of empty, untrimmed grass, dark trees from a dense forest and far, far off into the distance, a hill holding a faint halo of light that he hoped was the main city. He sighed. "I don't suppose you see a car sitting around here, do you?"

Though it was a rhetorical question, she didn't make a sound. He glanced down at her, only to find her scanning their surroundings with a calculating stare. "You have your cell phone, right?"

Thorne grunted a response. Still too weak to run, he settled for a brisk walk down the dirt path leading toward the trees. He'd feel even better the more distance he put between himself and the old building. "This is some real-life horror film shit."

"Really? What gave it away?" she asked, her tone dryer than the Sahara Desert. "Is it the creepy Overlook Hotel located in the middle of nowhere, the single dirt path leading into the Black Hills Forest or the fact that we just woke up in a scene that could be the entire setting for the next *Saw* movie?"

Thorne's lips twitched, though this time it was in amusement. He glanced at her in appreciation. "Fan of scary movies, are you?"

She shrugged. "There's just something about the mortals' perception of us and the 'paranormal' that gets me every time."

He chuckled. Somehow that bit of info was pleasing, because he, too, preferred horror movies over anything else. Nice to know that not all females were about romcoms and frilly dramas.

Then again, he'd long ago stopped trying to get to know women. No one held his interest for long, and these days he was only interested in one thing from them. Hey, he might be a dick, but at least he was upfront about it. It eliminated the risk of developing emotional attachments and heartbreak.

From their proximity, he studied the woman's face more closely as he continued to walk. She would have been considered pretty if not for the blood, dirt and smeared makeup caking her face. Her eyes were dark and beguiling, like the night sky above them. The cleaner parts of her skin looked as smooth as the rest of her felt, and her lips were full and wide. He wondered how they'd look wrapped around his —

"Stop right here." There was a small flare of panic that she'd been able to sense his dirty trail of thoughts, but then she said, "I need to sit down."

Biting back a sigh of relief, he obliged and set her down. She plopped onto the grass and began inspecting her injured foot. He left her like that for several minutes while he walked a few feet away, taking in the surrounding darkness. While he didn't sense anyone lingering around, he didn't want to take any chances by letting his guard fall. The entire situation was far too strange. The hotel was only two floors and it wasn't the largest, yet he and — *what was her name? Had she even told me?* — had been the only ones inside. He would have preferred to find the enemy outside ready to shoot them down, yet there was nothing. They had been left completely deserted.

He pulled his cell phone from his pocket and contemplated who to call. He had two percent left of his battery, so he didn't have much time. His father was a possibility, but he hesitated. As the current ruler of Elysium, Damien Lucifer would have a team ready to investigate at the drop of a hat. Thorne, however, would leave out the fact that he'd had his horn taken. That was just downright embarrassing. He felt emasculated, as if someone had stolen his very manhood.

And though he knew his brothers would long to seek justice as badly as he did, he would chew broken glass before he'd allow them to see him with a hole in this head. After all the times he'd poked fun at them and laughed at their most humiliating moments, they'd be more than eager to return the favor.

Plus, his father would just as well ridicule him for being so careless. Though his family weren't puritans who were against his casual encounters with women, they'd often said his dick would lead him into major trouble soon enough. He had no desire to prove them right.

Other good candidates to contact were either of his two chief operating officers, Colin and Bobby. There'd been a few times when he'd wandered somewhere lost, drunk and had needed a ride and they'd come through for him, but neither were very reliable at answering their phones while off the clock. Calling either one of them only to be sent to voicemail was risking using up the last of his battery.

Sighing in irritation, he dialed for a cab service. To his luck, the dispatcher answered on the first ring. He peered at the hotel and spotted a faded sign, and it took several moments of squinting to tell her the name of the place. Just before he could hang up, the phone went dead.

Thorne ran a frustrated hand through his hair and returned to whatever-her-name-was. "Help is on the way," he murmured. "It'll be at least an hour, though. We're pretty far from the city."

Once again, she didn't respond, nor did she spare him a glance.

He ground his teeth, annoyed that she continued to act as if he wasn't worthy of eye contact or even a simple nod of appreciation. "What's your name?" he demanded, crossing his arms. "And how do you know mine?"

She tilted her head to the side as if he'd asked her a philosophical question. "Hmm. What's in a name? What, actually, is a name? Is it *what* we are or *who* we are?"

Thorne blinked hard, pulling his eyebrows together in confusion. "What?"

"Do you mean my birth name? My nickname? My street name? My work name? My—"

"Good gods below, woman, just tell me what the hell I should call you."

Said woman's lips twitched in amusement, as if she'd intentionally tried to get a rise out of him. "Oh. *That* name. I'm Chey."

"Chey what?"

"Just Chey."

"Fine, *Chey*. Can you now tell me what the fuck is going on? And for the love of the gods, please leave off the dry-ass remarks."

Chey inhaled a deep breath, held it, then blew it out in a huff. She threw her head back, but not to look at him. Instead, she stared up at the stars twinkling in Sheol's permanently night sky. "Last night, I was in the same bar as you. I was just getting ready to leave when I saw that nymph slip some kind of liquid in your drink. Of course, I had zero intentions of stepping in, but—"

"Why the hell not?" At that, he crouched before her with a glare. "You were just going to let that shit happen?"

"Yep. You know how the saying goes. Stupid reaps what stupid sows."

"That's *not* the correct phrase."

"Luckily for you," she continued, ignoring him, "I'm not a complete bitch. I actually tried to warn you."

"But you failed," he grumbled. "Great fucking job at that."

Her fingers twitched, and if Thorne didn't know any better, he could have sworn she'd just prevented herself from slapping him. It almost made him laugh.

"So I did," she admitted with wounded pride. "Just when I made it outside behind you, some guy jammed a fucking needle in my arm." She shoved the sleeve of his jacket up her arm to show him the dark bruise circling a tiny hole in her forearm. "I'm not sure if it was the same shit you were drugged with, but I was lucid enough to see you get pushed in the back of an unmarked van. That's when the guy hit me over the head — and here we are."

She shook her head, her twin braids shaking side to side. Thorne caught sight of a black mark on the side of her neck, but he couldn't quite make out what it was. Not that he gave a damn, but now he'd have to purchase a new jacket since that one was stained beyond repair, thanks to her blood.

"I still don't get it," he murmured. "Why the fuck would they take my horn yet leave you intact?"

"Intact." Chey scoffed and turned her attention to the darkened sky. "The evident answer here would be that I was never meant to be taken — only you. For whatever reason, *you* were the one targeted and I just happened to get in the way." She paused, then added, "Well, I can think of a few reasons someone would do this to you, but that's neither here nor there."

Thorne glared at her, though he wasn't sure if he was so angry because she'd failed to warn him, because she'd risked her own life by volunteering to do something so reckless or because she continued to degrade him when he hadn't done a damn thing to her.

If he had a pinch of working brain cells left, he'd leave her ass to her own devices and go about his business. He'd been the one to call the cab, so it was just a courtesy that he was even giving her a ride home.

"Whatever. Why were you even at the bar?" he demanded.

"That's none of your damn business."

"Like hell." He sank onto his bottom, making himself comfortable in the damp grass. "I find it suspicious how you were there at the same time and claimed to have been drugged, yet you remember everything so clearly. For all I know, you could be working with them."

Another twitch of her fingers, but this time she curled them into fists, as if it took an even greater amount of effort to keep from attacking him. "I had nothing to do with this. If I did, I wouldn't have taken a big chunk out of my own skin, jackass."

"Then tell me why you were there."

She growled. Then, she sucked in a deep breath and waited several beats before releasing it. "I was working."

He cocked an eyebrow. "Working," he repeated. "You certainly don't give off any waitressing vibes. So, a call girl?"

"I work for SPD."

That surprised the hell out of him. "You're a cop?"

"A detective, actually."

Thorne stared at her for a good twenty seconds before the first chuckle escaped. Another followed it, then another until he fell out into a full fit of laughter. Perhaps the drugs in his system were making him loopy, but at that moment, he couldn't contain his amusement—not just with her revelation but with their entire situation.

"Gods below," he chortled, holding onto his side, "you are so full of it."

All the while, Chey watched him with a dark glare, but she didn't say anything. That only made Thorne laugh even harder.

"Wow," he said, finally calming down. "That was a good one. I'll give you that." He wiped the tears from his eyes. *A detective. Her.* Of all things she could have said, she chose to say a detective, as if he were dumb enough to believe that shit. "All right then, *Detective Chey.* Let me ask you again. How exactly do you know me?"

Her lips twisted downward, and he detected her flare of discomfort. Strange. "Everyone knows who the Lucifers are."

"Nah, try again. I told you that I can sense your lies."

"Damn," she grouched, shifting on the ground. "Let's just say we met a long time ago. It was brief and fleeting, nothing serious."

That time, it was hard to tell if she was lying or not. Perhaps it was a half-truth. "So, what? We've had a one-night-stand before?"

She snorted in derision, as if the very thought was ludicrous. Thorne was almost offended. Almost. "A five-minute hookup in a dusty broom closet is hardly worth the title of a one-nighter. Let's leave it at that."

If she'd thought to insult him, it worked. Thorne's annoyance once again reared its head, something that was becoming far too common around Chey. He was always cool-headed and laid back, yet two minutes in her presence threatened to toss his calm out of the nearest window.

Furthermore, a five-minute hookup? Not even his quickies were that short. Just the notion was a disgrace to his manhood.

He raked his gaze over her body, trying to place who she was — not an easy feat, if he did say so himself. After the first twenty years or so, women had started to look alike to him. It was hard to differentiate them all.

She was sitting at an angle in what he considered to be a 'mermaid pose', where her legs were partially tucked under her. His jacket was big and loose on her, but it showed a lot of leg.

Her skin wasn't perfect. She was dirty and covered in drying blood, but in the spots that were clean, she had a handful of tiny dark-brown scars that had healed ages ago. When she'd lifted her sleeve to show her arm earlier, he'd seen three round circles that he knew to be cigarette burns. He'd seen them plenty of times on mortals who'd died topside of domestic abuse.

Nothing immediately jumped out at him that helped him connect which of his ex-lovers she was. He shook his head. "I still have no clue who you are."

"That's because you're a piece of shit with no respect for women." She stood and turned her back to him. "Let's go. Our ride is here."

Thorne stood as well and followed close behind her as she limped toward the red cab that was driving up the dirt path. It wasn't the first time a female had been pissed at him. It was usually in the form of a broken heart, a friend's broken heart, him 'forgetting' to call them or any number of things along those lines. It wasn't his fault he couldn't remember all the women in his life. Hell, at this point he'd better start tagging them and keeping a logbook.

Whatever, though… He'd long ago stopped caring about the dramatic tears and whatnot. Yeah, he was a dick, but he now let women know ahead of time that he was not someone they should think about falling for. If they did so, they only had themselves to blame. He was *not* a one-woman man.

Chey was just another nameless face in the crowd. Whatever her reason for disliking him shouldn't matter in the least bit.

He thought that, but somehow it just seemed… wrong.

With a sharp shake of his head, he rose and followed behind her. He shook off the guilt and told himself it was nothing of importance. It was probably another lingering effect of the drugs in his system.

A detective, he thought again, biting his lip to keep from laughing. Now *that* was funny. Sheol's police force was composed of some of the toughest hardasses in the underworld, and while her sour personality could have fit the bill, the thought of her being a member of the more elite detective team was just...absurd.

Chapter Three

When Thorne had wandered off to make a phone call, Chey had assumed the devil would have had the sense to call a close relative or friend who would pick them up in a private vehicle — something with tinted windows at the very least. She was half naked under his jacket, covered in dirt and blood, while Thorne didn't look much better.

Instead, the daft man had called a freaking cab. *So much for discretion.*

Still, she wondered if he'd offered to pay extra for the driver to keep his trap shut, for the only time he spoke was to ask where they were going. Either that or Thorne knew the man personally. He didn't even spare them a glance in the rearview mirror, though the nervous twitching of his fingers on the steering wheel told her that he wanted to ask questions.

Chey shook her head and focused on remembering the route the cabbie was taking. She'd have to report back to HQ so they could investigate the motel. That was, unless Thorne's father got to it first. If so, they'd have to wait days, even weeks before they could do their own investigation. While not many people outranked the detectives of the Sheolic Police Department, Damien Lucifer and all the other head honchos of the underworld had their own secret services that could swoop in and take over any of SPD's investigations at any time.

However, she doubted they'd even find any useful information. It was clear that the motel had only been used as a place to stash Thorne. Instead of choosing any one of the many warehouses littered throughout the city, the kidnappers had gone out of the way to ensure he was holed up in one of the most remote locations possible.

She had to admit that it had been a smart move on their end. She was sure that cutting off a horn of one of Elysium's treasured boys would cause major repercussions for them if they'd gotten caught.

For a moment, she started to wonder who the nymph was and why she'd targeted Thorne, but then she shook the thoughts away, deciding it didn't matter. Her only guess was that the woman had been another ex-lover of Thorne's and had been seeking revenge. Chey knew first-hand that not all the women Thorne had slept with harbored lovey-dovey feelings for the bastard. Just the thought of her younger self falling for his ridiculous charm pissed her off.

Rolling her eyes at her own stupidity, she leaned her head back on the headrest when she began to recognize the main road they'd turned onto. It would take them to the intertwining highways that led to Infernal Regions, the capital city of Elysium.

After about an hour and a half of driving in silence, the cabbie finally began a slow crawl through one of the less-favored neighborhoods in the city. Though quiet, it was clear that this was the side of town only the poorest of the low-class would take up residence in. The area where she lived was a playground for gang-related activities. There wasn't a week that went by when the authorities weren't called to reconcile one crime or another. Half the time, they didn't even show up.

On one side of the street was an L-shaped apartment complex, every inch of the faded bricks tagged with graffiti. Adjacent from it sat a small corner store with its door and windows barred. They turned two more corners, where the street became lined with small homes that had been built some fifty years ago. More than a few times the cabbie had to swerve around potholes deep enough to flatten a tire or knock off someone's bumper.

They came to a stop sign, and Chey eyed a group of dealers watching the cab drive by. Instead of avoiding eye contact, she sent them a glare, satisfied when each of them turned away. In their neighborhood, newcomers were always prime targets for a home invasion. When she'd first moved in two years prior, they'd tried to get her, but she'd sent them on their way with a few broken bones and non-fatal bullet wounds. Since then, it hadn't taken long for news to spread to not fuck with her. She doubted they had yet to pin her as a member of law enforcement, but as far as she knew, no one had any interest in finding out more about her.

At last coming to a dead end, there were only two bungalow-style homes in the cul-de-sac. They were side-by-side with a vacant lot between them, both facing an open field that had once housed a fenced-in park. Now all that was left was untrimmed grass and weeds. It gave a nice view of anyone coming down the street.

Though both houses looked as run-down as the rest of the community, the vacant one was completely boarded up with signs preventing people from trespassing. Chey had never minded looking out of her window to see the raggedy mass of wood. Its exterior was so shabby that it tended to keep even the homeless from seeking shelter in it.

When the car came to a full stop before her house, she turned to the cabbie. "You were already paid for the drive, correct?"

He glanced at her through the rearview mirror and gave an eager nod. In a thick accent she couldn't place, he said, "Yes. Boss very good with pay. Jarvis tell no one." He made a motion of zipping his lips closed.

She smiled. "Thanks. Take care, Jarvis." She chucked the deuce at Thorne and opened her door. Carefully, she stepped onto the pavement, wincing at the pressure being placed on the healing wounds on her foot. When she heard the other door being opened and slammed shut, she whipped around to see Thorne stepping around the van to join her on the sidewalk.

He gave her a disbelieving stare. "*Take care, Jarvis,*" he mocked in a high-pitched voice. "Really? That's it?"

"I'm sorry?" she demanded, taking a limp backward. "What did you expect me to say to him?"

"I'm talking about *me*," he growled. "A peace sign is all you could do?"

She looked turned her head to glance to the left, then the right, then him again. "What, do you want a goodbye hug or something? I told you everything I know. Jarvis will take you home to your lair or nest or wherever it is you devils gather."

He clenched his teeth so hard that his jaw popped. "Gods, you are infuriating." He turned away to open the cab door.

Chey made a face, not sure what the hell he'd been expecting. She'd already given him the information he'd asked for, so his hunt for the nymph and her partner was his own problem from here on out. Hell, she shouldn't even have been dragged into *his* mess in the first place.

She turned away as well and made all of three steps before coming to a complete stop. When she tried to take another, her throat felt as though something was clamped around it, constricting with each tug. She reached her hands up, but all she could feel was her own skin.

Turning around to look at Thorne, she saw he was paused halfway inside the van. He kept trying to move, but it was as though the same effect on her was preventing him from moving any farther.

Chey frowned in confusion. There was about six feet of space between them, and nothing seemed out of the ordinary. She tried to take another step back, but her throat tightened again, cutting off her air supply.

However, now that she was facing Thorne, she could see the problem. Every time either of them tried to move away, a golden spark would flash in the shape of a string drawn taut. "Shit," she growled, dread settling in her gut. "No, no, no, no, no." She once again pulled away, but the golden thread continued to appear, tightening around her throat the harder she tried to move.

"What is it?" Thorne demanded, straightening from the cab. He looked as puzzled and frustrated as she felt. When Chey pointed to the space between them, she walked backward to show him the golden line that connected to invisible collars around both of their necks. His eyes flew wide with horror. "Oh, gods, *no.*"

He tried to jerk away, only to give a loud gag when the invisible string pulled taut. "Fuck!"

"Keep your voice down," she jeered, though she couldn't muster much anger into it. Her night had just become even more screwed up. Those bastards had placed a binding spell on her and Thorne, one that prevented them from moving more than six feet away from each other.

Depending on what kind of spell it was and who had cast it, she was now stuck with Thorne until they could break it—something that would be damn near impossible without a powerful sorcerer and an assload of money.

"You did this," he growled, storming toward her.

Chey held her ground, planting her fists on her hips. "Excuse me? Why the hell would I?"

"Oh, I don't know." He stopped directly before her, curling his lip in disgust. His eyes had turned red, a sign that he was *pissed*. "We fucked, I broke your heart and to get revenge you bound yourself to me and set up this whole thing. Crazy bitches like you are unpredictable as hell."

I'll show you a crazy bitch.

The thought growled in her mind a split second before she swung her fist with all the strength she could gather. Her knuckles connected to his jaw with a satisfying crunch. He stumbled, and Chey launched herself at him, knocking them both to the ground. He fell on his back with a grunt, and she wasted no time pressing one knee into his chest while placing her forearm to his neck. She was quite sure the sudden movements had stretched her wound open, but the pain was only a dull throb, thanks to her adrenaline rush.

Thorne blinked up at her more in surprise than anger, but she bared her teeth at him. "You never broke my fucking heart. Get that one straight. Second, you're the last person in the entire fucking world — here or topside — that I would bind myself to. You were never worth a second thought after we hooked up. And third" — she leaned down until their noses were nearly touching — "if you ever disrespect me like that again, I'll cut off your other horn and shove it so far up your ass that you'll be standing for the rest of your miserable life. Got it?"

All the anger in Thorne's body melted away in three seconds flat, giving way to a healthy mix of amusement and excitement. Perhaps a bit too much excitement, for his pants were growing far too tight for his comfort.

It couldn't be helped. Chey had one hell of a right hook. She'd knocked him on his ass, and he had no doubt that she'd deliver her dark threat to him. By all rights he should be livid. Yet, all he could do was lay beneath her with a straining erection after being punched in the jaw and a laugh threatening to erupt from his chest.

Yeah, he was definitely fucked in the head.

Giving his noggin a sharp shake, he stared into her eyes with the most serious expression he could muster. "Don't disrespect you," he muttered. "Got it."

With a disgusted noise, she shoved off him and stood, putting some space between them. Thorne rolled onto his belly and jumped to his feet. She eyed him as he ran a hand across his sore jaw. He didn't bruise easily, but he had a feeling he would after that punch. He turned his head to the side to spit out a bit of blood.

"Who the devil taught you to hit like that?" he demanded, moving his jaw side to side to make sure it wasn't cracked or broken.

She flashed a smug smile while crossing her arms. "Just don't piss me off again, Uno. I warned you back at the hotel."

Yeah, she had. He'd thought she was all talk, though. Now he knew better. He shoved his hands in his pockets, schooling his expression to be a scowl. "You caught me off guard, so I'll give you a free pass on that one." His annoyance with the binding spell came back. While he couldn't feel anything around his neck, the spell would tighten the invisible collar there that bound him to her. "What are we supposed to do about this?"

Her smile vanished, transforming into a frown. She glanced down one end of the street. "Let's discuss it inside." She looked past him and waved Jarvis away.

Thorne turned to see the cabbie had been there the entire time and had witnessed his embarrassing downfall at the hands of a woman who looked like a bunny compared to him. The driver gave a two-finger salute and drove off. When he was out of sight, Thorne turned back to Chey with narrowed eyes. "You're sure you had nothing to do with this?"

She paused halfway from turning onto the four steps leading to her front door. She brought her fist up in a threatening motion. "I'm not a liar," she growled. "Question my honor again and I'll end you."

Thorne gave a single nod, wise enough to hide his smirk. He didn't bother bringing up the fact that she'd lied about how she knew who he was, but he suspected that had more to do with protecting her own dignity. With another shake of his head, he followed her up the stairs onto the small porch that had seen better days.

Yeah, like sixty years ago, he thought with derision.

"Not exactly an upgrade from the hotel, now, is it?" he asked with no small amount of disgust in his tone.

Clutching one hand to her head, Chey felt along the panels of the outside wall until she was able to pull one away and take out a spare key. She shot him a glare over her shoulder. "What, hoping for a glamorous mansion and a butler to wipe your ass?"

He shrugged, refusing to feel an ounce of shame. "Just as long as he can brush my teeth for me, too."

She rolled her eyes. "Obnoxious prick." She made to unlock the doorknob, then paused. "That's weird."

"What is?"

"I thought I'd locked this." She hesitated, her back going rigid, as if suspecting someone would attack.

Thorne glanced around the yard for anything out of the ordinary, but with nothing but vacant space surrounding them, it would be impossible for anyone to hide out close by.

As if coming to the same conclusion, Chey relaxed and pushed the door open.

Steeling himself to be met with the smell of must and decaying wood, Thorne strode inside and was caught off guard by how...*new* everything was—new and beyond nerdy.

Under the shine of mounted LED lights, the walls were colored with a fresh smokey paint and the living room off to his right was decorated in endless framed posters of characters from several classic video games. Even the plush couch had a quilt from a popular fantasy show thrown over one shoulder, and a handful of gamer magazines adorned the glass coffee table. On the left side of the entrance was a small kitchen with a touch of sci-fi-themed décor.

Huh, Thorne thought, bewildered. Based on the tart personality he'd known her to have in the last few hours, he'd assumed he would find drab colors or even a pigsty.

As she continued leading him forward through a narrow hall, there were two doors across from each other and a small alcove holding a brand-new washer and dryer unit. Before entering one of the doors, she checked the one at the very end of the hall that he assumed led to the backyard. Satisfied that it was locked, she turned back to him and paused.

"What's that look for?" she demanded.

Thorne realized his mouth had been parted, making his shock evident on his features. "Is this your house or some sixteen-year-old boy's? It doesn't...fit."

She rolled her eyes. "That's because you don't know me." She moved past him and opened the bathroom door.

"How does everything look so—"

"I had this place remodeled a couple of years ago," she cut in, as if knowing what he was going to ask. "I left the outside the way it is to blend in. It keeps the thieves away."

"Right," he muttered, watching her. He'd expected her to slam the door in his face, but the bathroom was spacious enough that he had to step inside in order to keep the spell from choking them both. The scent of copper tingled in his nose, and he glanced down to see Chey leaving behind a trail of blood drops. "Are you bleeding?"

Chey ignored him and sat on the edge of the tub. Thorne took her wrist and made her look up at him.

"Let me go," she commanded, though there was no conviction in her tone—just exhaustion.

He narrowed his eyes, taking in the dark circles under her eyes. "You lost too much blood."

"Gee, you think?" She tugged her arm from him and turned on the water.

"Is it at all possible for you to go more than five minutes without a sarcastic remark?"

She paused and tilted her head as if to seriously consider the question. When she opened her mouth to say something, Thorne quipped, "Don't you dare."

She snapped her mouth shut, though a corner of her lips quirked into a small smile. "I don't know what they drugged us with, but it's interfering with my natural healing. The bleeding had stopped earlier, but tackling your giant ass only reopened the wound. I need to dress it while I still can."

Thorne shook his head and leaned against the wall, fingering a fluffy towel with a sewn *Star Wars* logo. "Seriously, what's up with all this geeky stuff?"

She turned her nose up at him. "If you don't like it, leave."

He snorted. "Trust me, princess. If I could, I'd be out of here faster than you could say hell bound."

"Hand me the first-aid kit that's under the sink."

"'Please' could go a long way," he grumbled, but did as he'd been told. He really wanted to hurry and head back out to carry on with his life, but doing so would be impossible if he had to drag Chey along. The being unable to move more than a few feet from her would be a major problem, especially since he had to go back to work. It would be hard to explain why she was tailing him like a lost kid.

When she started to undo the zipper to his jacket, she paused to glare at him. "Get out."

He lifted a brow. "In case you haven't noticed, I'm as far away from you as I'm allowed."

She grunted. "Then turn around. I need to bathe."

"Oh please, lady. I've already seen you in your bra and panties, and those left very little to the imagination." Still, his cock was hardening in remembrance of seeing all those lean muscles and gentle curves. The woman certainly had an attractive body — a little bit toner than he preferred, but still pretty sexy. When she only continued to glare, pressing her lips into a thin line, he rolled his eyes and turned his back on her. "Fine, whatever."

Moving to sit on the floor just a foot away from the doorjamb, Thorne listened as she unzipped the jacket and tossed it to the floor. After a few more moments, there was the faint wisp of what he assumed was her bra and panties. Then, there was the sound of her settling into the tub with the water still running.

She let out a soft sigh, and Thorne caught the scent of aloe vera soap. He inhaled a deep breath. Funny, that had always been one of his favorite fragrances. He hated the way women doused themselves in cavity-inducing sweet perfume. He put up with it, of course, but it always gave him a headache. If he was going to be stuck to her side, at least she'd smell pleasant.

He then found his mind betraying him as it conjured up the image of her sitting naked in that tub, lathering her body with soap. It was the first time a woman had been naked in his presence without them touching. Not that he saw Chey that way. The woman might have a rocking body, but her attitude left little to be desired. She was mouthy, rude and annoying beyond comprehension. He'd only met her a few hours prior — he didn't count their first encounter because he didn't remember that shit, if it even happened — yet in that short time, she'd become a fucking prick in his side, insulting him and speaking down to him like he was a damn invalid.

Never had he ever met someone, man or woman, who was so infuriating. Not even the craziest of his exes could hold a candle to her less-than-appealing personality.

Well, she isn't all that bad, a traitorous voice countered. *She's a fan of horror films, she has good taste in soap smells and she can knock a dude twice her size flat on his ass.*

Plus, at least by decorations alone, she appeared to be a gamer — a hobby he indulged in more often than sex.

Those were some redeeming qualities. It almost made her presence bearable. *Almost.*

When she sucked in a sharp breath, he turned, alarmed. "What is it?"

"Don't look," she barked, covering her chest with her arms.

Thorne rolled his eyes and went back to staring at the door. "If we've fucked, I'm not sure what you have to be so insecure about."

She was quiet for several moments, and Thorne could actually feel the tension in the air. "*If* we've fucked, huh?" she asked quietly. She made a *tch* sound between her teeth. "You really don't remember, do you?"

Thorne gave a careless lift of one shoulder. "I'm eighty-seven years old, cupcake. You'd have to have given me the best orgasm of my life to scratch the surface of my memories."

Instead of growling at him or giving an angry retort, she remained silent, for which he was thankful. It gave him time to think about what he was going to do after they left her house.

First things first, he needed to buy a glamour charm that would hide his demon features. While he typically only wore them when going topside, he'd be damned if he was seen in public with only one horn on his head. It was bad enough that the cabbie had seen it, and though he'd been sworn to secrecy, Thorne refused to allow anyone else to do so.

After that, he'd go to his brother Quin's to find a way to undo the binding spell. Quin would know how to break it if no one could. His brother was a wiz at these types of things.

He didn't know how much time had passed, but eventually Chey turned the faucet off. The only sound to be heard was the water draining. He sensed rather than saw her stand up and step out of the tub before reaching for the towel hanging on the rack above his head. Water droplets fell down his neck, but he ignored it, waiting for her to wrap herself. Only when the lid of the toilet sounded as she sat down did he face her.

He'd been deeper in his musings than he'd thought, for she'd washed herself completely, including her hair. Free from the braids and dripping water, she'd used a shorter towel to wrap the long mass of curls. Her face was clean from all the guck, and he'd been right in his initial impression that she was pretty — *really pretty, actually*.

There was a cute little mole above the arch of her left brow and her nose was a fine swoop with a slight tilt upward. Thick eyelashes lay across her high cheekbones while she gazed at the floor, casting long shadows across her skin. Her full lips held a natural pout, and though they curled in a way that made her look snooty, those were the type of lips that the gods made specifically to please a man.

A tiny snake tattoo curled around the back of her ear to rest its head just above her collarbone. The thick towel wrapped around her covered the important bits of her body, but it revealed long legs that had a collection of colorful jigsaw-puzzle pieces along her calf.

Odd how he hadn't noticed either before, but then again, he'd still been trying to shake off the effects of the drug and figure out what the hell was going on with him.

Still, even with the dorky tattoos and smooth almond skin, Chey looked appetizing with her fresh face and skin scrubbed clean. His dick actually jumped in appreciation, much to his annoyance.

He stood, shifting himself to hide his erection. "Am I allowed a shower or what?"

Without looking at him, she made a dismissive motion with her hand, as if she didn't care one way or the other. Thorne gritted his teeth and moved to the tub, thankful there were no blood stains left behind. He set the water to steaming hot and pulled the lever up to run the shower. Far less insecure than her, he pulled his shirt over his head and dropped it to the ground, then reached for the button of his jeans.

He caught Chey all but gawking at him and smirked. "Like what you see?" he demanded, flexing the muscles of his pecs.

"Hardly," she murmured, though she didn't take her eyes off him. They darkened with hunger, and Thorne could sense the arousal filling her.

With a grunt, he undid the button and shucked his jeans. When his cock sprang free, she licked her lips but averted her gaze, failing to hide her sudden excitement.

Ha! She could act high and mighty all she wanted, but there was no denying that she wanted him. The thought made him snort, but before he did something stupid like feel those lush lips on his skin, he stepped into the spray of the water and yanked the shower curtain closed.

Chapter Four

While Thorne showered, Chey stood in the mirror. She released her hair from the towel and placed the cloth between her teeth while she began to stitch her wound. A non-sticky Band-Aid had been the best the kidnappers could do to make up for the deep gash in her head.

Luckily, she was always prepared for this type of situation. She'd been in the streets long enough that she'd learned the basics of first aide and how to stitch lacerations. She wasn't a professional by any means, but she could do a much better job than a damn gauze.

When she finished, she smoothed a large bandage over it. So long as she didn't do something out of line to agitate it, she was good to go until she sated her cravings. Sex, of course, would speed up the process and close the wound.

Rewrapping the towel around her body, she opened a drawer around the sink counter and put her toothbrush to work, then brushed her hair.

She spent the whole time silently cursing whoever had placed the binding spell on her. Back in the hotel room, they'd woken up in separate rooms, yet whoever had cast the spell must have fixed it to where it activated once she and Thorne made physical contact or once they left the hotel grounds.

Of all people, it had to be *him*. She tugged the brush through her hair with far more force than was necessary and shot him a glare through the curtain separating them. She wished she'd used up all the hot water. She really hated that arrogant bastard.

He honest-to-gods didn't remember her. She'd already expected as much, but to hear him say it aloud and act as though she wasn't worth a second thought… It pissed her off. She hated everything about him, so much so that she'd purposely avoided ever returning to Elysium just to be as far away from him as possible. That was, until she had been reassigned to take up residence back in her hometown.

Despite that, her body acted as though he hadn't been the reason she'd…

No. I'm not going there, she thought, steeling her nerves. If Thorne Lucifer didn't remember her, then fuck it and fuck him. She really should have never even bothered trying to help him out back at the bar the previous night…or the night before. Hard to say when she had yet to check the date. However, even though it was always nighttime in Sheol, demons just knew what was considered night and day. As it was, she guessed it was nearing the evening. If they were topside, the sun would be sitting low in the sky, shining the last of its rays before disappearing over the horizon.

Finished brushing out all the tangles in her curling hair, she tossed the brush back inside its drawer and opened the medicine cabinet for a bottle of painkillers. Just as she swallowed three of them, Thorne cut the shower off and released a loud, pleased sigh.

Chey rolled her eyes and turned her back to him as he opened the curtain. "That was nice," he announced. "Don't suppose you have a spare towel?"

"Nope," she said. She did, actually, but she'd played the generous hostess long enough. The ingrate could catch a chill for all she cared.

"You're lying."

Chey gave a careless shrug. "I have them, but I don't have one for *you*."

He grunted. "Fine. I'll just take this."

Unprepared for his antics, Chey was caught off guard when Thorne fisted the part of the towel covering her back, and with one swift jerk, he snatched the whole thing away from her. "Hey —"

"As much of a douche as you want to be, I can be a bigger one," he jeered.

Chey half-turned, doing her best to cover herself with her arms. Thorne smirked as he gave his body a swift wipe-down, then wrapped her towel around his waist. "I hate you," she breathed, though she couldn't help her gaze from raking over his massive build.

He was just as tall and imposing as when she'd first met him thirty years before. Every inch of him was solid muscle, from his toned calves to the faint lines of his six-pack, to the large pecs holding a light dusting of dark hair. His lips were cocked into his signature grin, his eyes molten brown with bright golden flecks in the irises. His hair was dark brown shot through with blond highlights, and his nose was slightly crooked after being broken a few times. Not even the ridiculous single horn on his head diminished how drop-dead gorgeous he was.

Chey once again trailed her stare down to his abs where a thin line of hair started below his navel and disappeared under the thick towel that was barely hiding the impressive bulge of his excitement. She gave a hard swallow, her heart thundering in her chest.

Studying him, liquid heat pooled in the pit of her stomach and her nipples hardened in response to his evident arousal. Still smirking, he leered at her in slow appreciation, his smile widening when he no doubt sensed her inability to hide the dampness between her legs.

Chey tried to storm away. She made two steps before the collar activated, choking her as she tried to push past its limit.

"Stop it," Thorne commanded, moving toward her to slacken the thread. The pressure around her throat vanished, but to her dismay, the lust remained.

"*You* stop it," she breathed, wishing she could cover herself. Though she was far from insecure, she had too much pride to allow the devil who'd caused her nothing but misery and anger to get her all hot and bothered.

However, the heat of Thorne's gaze made her feel like a nervous young woman all over again. She despised her reaction to him. She hated that he could still make her feel this way after so many years. It was so damn embarrassing, more so because he *knew* his effect on her.

"What am I doing?" he teased, sounding far closer than he had a moment ago. So close that she could feel his body heat wrapping around her, sending goosebumps across her skin.

She moved forward as far as the spell would allow until she was standing out in the hall. "I'm a succubus. Your desire causes problems for me."

He chuckled, once more moving into her personal bubble. He slid a finger over the curve of her shoulder. "What makes you think I'm not responding to *your* desire? You aren't the only demon capable of sensing these things."

Chey drew in a shaky breath. The arrogant asshole had a point. As much as she wanted to continue denying it, she wasn't sure who'd been aroused first—him or her. In either case, one could have been responding to the other.

"Don't worry, though," he added, leaning to place his lips by her ear. She shivered when he whispered, "If you want it that much, I can take care of both our needs."

Chey closed her eyes and counted to thirty. When she opened them again, she turned her head to glare over her shoulder at him. "I'd rather fuck a valley troll than allow you to touch me."

Thorne's cocky smirk remained in place, but his eyes flashed with…something. Offense, maybe. *Good*, she thought. He deserved a blow to his ego.

Then he flashed those perfect teeth at her, though it was a bit strained. "Newsflash, sweetheart, I already did. You didn't seem to mind then."

Snarling, she whipped around to punch him in the gut. He let out a pained breath, but in the blink of an eye, Chey found herself pinned to the wall with Thorne's hand around her throat. Not choking her or causing any harm whatsoever, but it was a warning.

His eyes glowed red, a sure sign that he was either super pissed or super horny. Probably both, going by the raging boner poking into her belly. He leaned forward. "Keep your fucking hands to yourself," he growled.

Unafraid, Chey bared her teeth right back at him. "I told you not to disrespect me."

"It wasn't disrespect. It was the truth."

"How would you know?" she retorted, gripping his wrist to try and tug it away from her. He didn't budge, simply flexed his fingers to let her know he could squeeze the life out of her if he wanted to. "You don't even remember."

His smile turned mean. "It's obvious you enjoyed it. That's the only reason why you hate me so much." When Chey said nothing but continued to glare at him, he pressed firmly against her until she was stuck between his body and the wall. His erection rubbed against her, which in turn caused her muscles to clench. He drew in a deep breath, his body giving the slightest of shudders. "No matter how hard you might try to fight it, you want me. You want *this*." He rolled his hips into hers, extracting a soft sigh from her. "Go ahead, Chey. Tell me I'm lying."

They both knew very well that if she said it, *she'd* be the one lying. She wanted nothing more than to walk away and go back to pretending Thorne didn't exist, but her body was of a different accord. It wanted to feel his touch again, to have him take her right there against the wall as hard as he could. Her core was practically weeping to be filled by him.

While her mind screamed *no*, her body begged *yes*. It was a constant battle that had no intentions on finding a resolution anytime soon.

However, it wouldn't be long before her body won. Without sex — sometimes multiple times a day — she could die of starvation. Or she could turn into a lust-crazed zombie who would attack any male she came across. Neither was a pretty sight to behold.

Hell, with her fiftieth birthday just around the corner and no interest in any of the potential mates she'd dated, the latter seemed to be her inevitable outcome.

Gods, she was screwed. She needed to find release with a male as soon as possible before the cramps came. And Thorne Lucifer was one hundred percent out of the equation.

With a sharp shake of her head, she focused on a freckle on his shoulder, refusing to meet his gaze. "We need to break this spell," she stated in a flat tone, changing the subject. "There's no time for delays, so the sooner the better."

Still refusing to glance up at him, Chey could feel his eyes burning into her. It was hard to ever tell what he was thinking, but then again, she'd rather not know. She knew everything she needed to know about Thorne, that he was a heartless playboy who only ever thought about chasing ass. He screwed around so much that he didn't even remember the women he slept with.

Granted, she wasn't a damn virgin herself. Her blood could never allow it, and she preferred not to get to know her partners. She could sleep with one man tonight and walk right past him on the street without a second glance the next day. So, for her to say she hated him because of his lifestyle was hypocritical.

No, her dislike was on a much more personal level than that. His ignorance had cost the lives of good people.

With a small swipe of his finger across her jaw, Thorne released her and took a step back. "We need to plan our next move. I don't trust just anyone, and my brother Quin may be able to undo all this. However, there's no way in Tartarus I'm letting him see me like this." At that, he pointed to the top of his head.

Chey shook her head and walked toward her bedroom, thankful when Thorne followed instead of arguing. "I left my phone in my car back at the bar, but I'll reach out to Alber to have it towed here." It would be simple to take a trip to the office to replace her lost belongings, but they'd never let her past the front door without bombarding her with an assload of questions she wasn't ready to answer.

"Who's Alber?" Thorne questioned.

"A trusted friend and colleague." Chey stepped inside her walk-in closet and flipped on a light, then went to work selecting clothes. "Turn around."

He made a rude sound. "This again? I'm looking at you while we're both ass-naked. What's the problem?" When she only continued to glare, he rolled his eyes and turned his back to her. "Good gods, woman."

Satisfied, Chey dropped her hands and pulled on a black sports bra and spandex pants. Then, opting for something loose and airy, she pulled on a cropped T-shirt with a logo design and threw a jacket over it. She supposed Thorne's reaction to seeing her taste in décor shouldn't have been surprising. To most, their first impression of her was that she was a tomboy or perhaps a bit more on the edgy side. After all, she didn't bite her tongue and she cursed like it was a second language. However, while she didn't mind cute dresses and flirty skirts from time to time, her tastes tended to lean more toward punk casualwear—ripped jeans, leggings, leather jackets, so on and so forth.

"Do you have something for me to wear — or is this towel my only option?" Thorne demanded.

Chey almost told him to buzz off but changed her mind. If they were going to be stuck together, she'd rather he have a clean set of clothes instead of carrying around the musty scent from the hotel. She reached for the top shelf and grabbed hold of a pale-yellow bedsheet. "You can throw your clothes in the wash. Until then, here." She tossed the linen at him.

"What am I supposed to do with this?" he questioned, holding it out as if it would bite.

She shrugged. "Improvise." Then, she pushed past him and plopped onto her bed. She dug into her nightstand and pulled out a small white rock.

"Whoa, is that a — "

"Yep," she cut in. While modern technology gave way to the convenience of cell phones, Alber was old-fashioned. He preferred using magic-imbued crystals, the old way demons used to call each other over long distances.

"I haven't seen one of those in ages."

Chey ignored him and focused on remembering how to activate the crystal.

It was a bit different than using a cell phone, as there were no numbers to punch in. While she squeezed it between her fingers, in her mind, she conjured up Alber's face — well, what she'd always thought was his face. In truth, she'd never met him in person. When she'd been promoted to a detective, they'd given her the magical device. There had been a faint buzzing in her head that had refused to leave as she was going through orientation and given a tour around the HQ located in Asphodel. The buzzing had been present all day, and when she could no longer stand it, she'd voiced her annoyance to Lauren, the woman who'd been showing her around.

Instead of looking confused, Lauren had told her it was Alber trying to establish a mental link with her now that she had a higher rank. He was their head technical analyst, the go-to man if anyone needed something — whether it was to relocate homes, make a quick escape, get a rental vehicle or countless other things. After learning how to answer Alber's 'call', as well as how to reach out to him, Chey had had trouble relying on the faceless man.

These days, however, she trusted Alber far more than anyone and anything else. He'd saved her ass countless times, but more than that, she'd come to think of him as a friend, despite their having never met each other in person. So every time she needed to call him with the crystal, she used what she imagined he'd look like — a geeky computer boy who was wire-thin with stringy blond hair, wide-framed glasses hiding dull-brown eyes and favoring a dorky sweater-vest over his high collar shirts.

After several moments, Alber's voice — not deep and gruff like Thorne's, but still considered masculine — holding a slight Boston accent answered. *"Yes, Cheyenne?"*

Chey gave a mental grunt, speaking to him through her thoughts. *"I've asked you several times to stop calling me that."*

"Correction, you've told *me several times. Not once have you actually asked."*

She rolled her eyes. He was an even bigger smartass than she was, which was just one of many reasons why they got along so well. *"Yeah, yeah. Listen... I'm home. How soon can you get my car towed to me?"*

"*About an hour, hour and a half, depending on where it's at. Are you going to tell me about last night or what?*" His tone turned serious. "*I was worried when I couldn't reach out to you after you said you were leaving the bar.*"

Chey sighed, running a frustrated hand through her hair. "*I'm in a dilemma. I can't go to the station yet, so I need you to pass a message along for me to Shade. The wildest shit happened.*"

Alber grunted. "*Tell me.*"

And so, she did. She relayed the events of what had happened to her from the moment she'd spotted Thorne being drugged all the way up until her calling him. Of course, she left off the bits about the sexual tension between her and the devil, but she was sure Alber would connect the dots on that one. She was a succubus who needed sex every day in order to survive, yet with her prime approaching, she had so little time left to find a mate. Between busting her ass putting in overtime at work and seeking release from random men, there wasn't much room to sit for a coffee and get to know someone.

And there were those few men she'd managed to take a slight interest in, but they'd either stood her up or ghosted her after the first two dates, despite having shown an open infatuation with her.

When she finished, Alber remained quiet for several long minutes. She didn't need to see him to know that he was pacing. "*Shit,*" he breathed. "*You don't know who the guy or the nymph was? Did you at least catch a glimpse of them to get a description?*"

"*Do you even need to ask that?*" She snorted. "*I'd be shit at my job if I hadn't.*"

"*Good.*" Metal creaked in the background, as if he'd shifted to sit in his desk chair. "*Show me.*"

That was the beauty of magic and mental telecommunication. Chey didn't even need to sit down with a sketch artist to get an image of what her kidnappers looked like. She concentrated on the night of the bar and dredged up the best image she could of the nymph—gorgeous, blonde and dainty, with a thin nose and lips pumped with a bit too much collagen.

When Alber gave her the command, she focused on the accomplice. The man hadn't been very tall, yet he was stocky, with enough muscle to drag her and Thorne up a flight of stairs. He'd been bald with bulgy eyes and a discolored nose that had been shaped in a rather beak-like fashion.

"*Got it,*" Alber said. "*That's one ugly fucker, if I do say so myself. I'll run their faces through the system to try to get some names or an addy. In the meantime, I don't suppose you've caught a break in this C.S. case, have you?*"

"*No,*" Chey groaned.

C.S.—or the Cryptic Slayer—was a nickname the media had given to a serial killer back in Asphodel. Five years ago, there'd been a string of attacks on seemingly innocent victims—nothing fatal, but the beatings had been brutal enough to send them all to the hospital. Though those crimes had been too scattered to make the local news, Chey had pieced together that each of the victims had been attacked by the same assailant. While victimology had made them think the attacks were random due to the varying races and ages, they'd all been male with the carved initials of C.S. left on their bodies.

For a while, the assaults had died down and C.S.'s trail had gone cold. Then out of the blue, Chey and her partner had gotten another call about a potential victim. Only that time, C.S. hadn't left a living witness.

It hadn't been the first time Chey had seen a dead body, but the sheer amount of savagery and rage C.S. had poured into his victim had been...sickening. Even thinking about it now made her stomach turn.

There had been no explanation as to what had caused such an escalation in the attacks, nor had she gotten any closer to finding out who the killer was, yet the murdering hadn't ended there. It had only gotten worse. SPD had done their best to keep the deaths under wraps, but it had gotten to the point where her chief had deemed it necessary to make a public announcement to the residents of Asphodel. Though C.S. had only seemed to be targeting adult men, no one was safe.

Chey had lost a fair amount of sleep over cracking the case, so much so that the chief had ordered her to take a week off to recover. Add to the fact that her prime was so close and her hormones had been spiraling out of control, which only interfered with her work. It was with great reluctance that she'd agreed to return to her birthplace and find a mate before she lost herself to her needs.

While she'd been beyond disappointed to leave behind a case she'd worked so hard on, news had been revealed that C.S. was capable of traveling between regions. Not only that, but he'd left a trail of bodies in his wake, including a few in her new territory — Elysium.

The ability to travel between the four Sheolic regions was not an easy feat. Unlike traveling to a different country topside, moving from one district to another in the underworld took a grand amount of money, paperwork and documented support from one of the Big Four families. That narrowed the list down as to who C.S. could be — but not by much.

Chey was one of the very few lucky ducks who'd managed to travel due to working for the police department.

There was a faint buzzing in her head, bringing her back to the present. It took her several moments to realize that Alber was still talking to her.

"Sheol to Cheyenne," he barked. *"Are you listening to me?"*

She shook her head. *"I'm sorry. I got lost in thought."*

He sighed. *"You were hit so hard that you can't focus?"*

"Never mind that. Listen... I need a favor. Thorne and I are going to visit his brother to break this spell, but if anyone asks, I'll be working from home for a while. I know Shade will understand."

"Consider it done," he said. *"Speaking of, how's the dating coming along? Found any potentials yet?"*

Though he asked the question in a casual manner, Chey knew he was worried for her sake. Everyone knew what happened to unmated succubi when they reached their prime.

"A few," she lied. *"Don't worry about me, Alber. I won't let things get out of hand."* Alber was silent for a while, though it was clear he wanted to say more. Before he could, she said, *"Oh, and for the love of the gods, please don't tell Vaughn what's happened to me. He turns into a fucking drama king over stuff like this."*

Alber's laugh rang through her mind. *"It's too late for that. He's been blowing me up all morning asking if I've heard from you. At least you have a partner who cares."*

She snorted. *"A bit too much, if you ask me."* Even as she said it, she fought a smile. In truth, Vaughn wasn't all that bad. He'd been her partner ever since she'd first taken on the C.S. case, and though they'd gotten off to a rocky start—what, with their equal amounts of stubbornness — he was right along with Alber with the only few people she trusted. Even when out in the field, he'd shown her the utmost loyalty.

"I still don't get why you just won't mate with him," Alber drawled. *"Give me one reason at all why you shouldn't."*

"Are you sending the car or what?" Chey demanded. It hadn't been the first time he'd brought up the suggestion, nor would it likely be the last.

"Yeah, yeah, I'm sending it," was his grumbled response. *"It'll be at Big Daddy's Pizzeria in about an hour."* His playful tone vanished, turning solemn. *"Just take care, Cheyenne, especially when it comes to Thorne. After what he —"*

"I'll be fine, Alber. I owe you one." With that, she severed their connection and tucked the crystal in her pocket. She didn't need or want the reminder of why she hated the devil so much. There was no use dwelling on the past. It wouldn't change a damn thing. It damn sure wouldn't bring back the dead.

She glanced at Thorne, who had the bedsheet draped over his body toga-style, only to find he'd been glaring the entire time. "What?"

"Did you hear a word I said?"

"Nope." She stood and led him back to the bathroom. "Let's get your clothes cleaned. We have an hour to kill."

He grunted, stepping aside when she moved past him. She didn't need to look over her shoulder to see he was smirking when he said, "I can think of a few ways for us to kill time."

Without breaking stride, she retorted, "Not even in your dreams, One-Horn Willie."

Chapter Five

"Why do you get to drive?"

Already seated behind the wheel of her tinted car, Chey peered at Thorne through the rolled-down window on the driver's door. "My car, my rules. Besides, your license was suspended two years ago."

He sputtered, crossing his arms. "How the hell do you know that?"

She rolled her eyes and straightened in her seat. "I told you what I do for a living. Background searches aren't hard to do."

It was funny the first time she'd told him that she was a detective. For her to carry the lie this long was just annoying. "You can drop the whole cop charade," he grumbled. "It's getting old."

She narrowed her eyes and pursed her lips. "If I hit the gas and take off, do you think the spell's tension will break like a string or would it drag you along the highway?"

For a moment, Thorne thought she was joking, but from the serious look in her eyes, he decided he didn't want to find out. He wasted no time in cramming his large frame into the passenger side of the tiny sedan. "You know, for someone who just recently suffered some head trauma, it's a safety hazard for you to be behind the wheel. Think about the other people on the road."

Despite the lack of sunlight, Chey donned a pair of dark sunglasses and put the car in drive. "I could be paralyzed from the neck down and still wouldn't trust you to chauffer me a block over." With that, she turned the radio on full volume, perhaps hoping to keep him from arguing any further. The speakers blasted out a sick guitar solo, followed by a male singer taking the lead. After a beat, she began mouthing the lyrics.

Regardless of his constant annoyance with her, Thorne couldn't keep himself from smiling as he recognized the song right away. It was from one of his favorite bands, a rock-n-roll group that had been the highlight in Sheolic music over two decades ago.

Chey continued to surprise him. Once again, he marveled at how similar they were, despite having bumped heads the whole time they'd known each other. If he'd seen her for the first time from a distance, he couldn't even say what his initial assumption of her would be. She was dressed in a casual manner suggesting she was more of a tomboy, but from the looks of the outfits he'd seen in her closet, she had just about everything from old, ripped jeans to sophisticated pantsuits to flowery sundresses. Even her shoe rack had held a wide range from sneakers to stylish combat boots. The rock music added to her edgy-chic style, but the gamer tattoos and fandom posters making up her home décor revealed her inner dweeb side. It was hard to get a proper reading of her.

When the song ended and a commercial came on, he pressed the mute button and turned to her. "Do you know where we are going?"

She scowled, glancing between him and the volume knob. "Did you just touch my radio without permission?"

He paused, the question throwing him off before he shook his head. "I need to go to my place for a glamour charm. I'm not walking around with one horn on my head."

"Shadow Way Condominiums on Baldwyn Boulevard. Unit 666, as cliché as that is."

Thorne narrowed his eyes. "How the hell do you know that?"

"I told you. Background checks are not hard to do."

When he sensed the red flare of her lie, his suspicion grew. "Try again."

She was quiet for a moment, though the clenching of her jaw told him that she hated his ability to call her out on her BS. "We hooked up a long time ago, and I'd assumed your address hasn't changed since then."

That time she was telling the truth, but it only raised more questions. "Here's the thing," he said, studying her closely. "I've lived there for over thirty years. It's my comfort zone, the one place that has always been just for me. Not once—drunk or not—have I ever brought a woman over. *Ever.*"

That revelation surprised her, making her tighten her fingers on the steering wheel. However, he didn't miss the sounds of her pulse fluttering with unease before she schooled her expression. At the same time, the cellphone that had been sitting in the cupholder between them rang, breaking the silence.

He caught her muted sigh of relief before she picked up the device and answered with a curt, "Detective Wilcox."

Thorne snorted, though the more he thought about it, the more he wondered if perhaps she was telling the truth about her job. He hadn't sensed any deceit when she'd told him that she was a detective, not to mention that the way she studied her surroundings with acute surveillance wasn't something just anyone could pick up on.

Perhaps he'd be wise to do his own background check on her. He had plenty of connections around Sheol, plus his family had close ties with a local PI company. They were the best of the best. In fact, it was that very firm that had managed to uncover the truth about Remi—his sister-in-law—being the grand-daughter of Hades.

Though Thorne could make out a male's voice on the other end, the words were too faint for him to pick up on what was being said. Instead, he focused his attention on something else.

Like how the devil Chey knew where he lived. He was honest when he'd stated that he'd never brought any of his lovers to his condo. He usually rented a hotel room or went to their place instead. Or when that wouldn't do, he'd fuck them out in an alleyway or the nearest bathroom or someplace of equal convenience. For her to know where he lived was weird. What was more alarming was that he'd bought his condo under a made-up name, so even if she *had* run a background check, the address on file would have shown his father's mansion located on the far side of Elysium, nowhere near Shadow Way Condominiums.

Detective Chey Wilcox, he thought. Cheyenne Wilcox, if that was her full name. Why did that sound familiar? Once again, he studied her profile. While she had the cell phone up to her ear and sunglasses covering her eyes, he could still make out her profile while she spoke. The snake tattoo curling behind her ear didn't ring any bells, but the longer he stared at her, the more niggling the sense of familiarity became.

It frustrated him that he had no idea who she was. It shouldn't matter, yet it did. Chey's hatred of him ran far deeper than any other female who'd come after him with a grudge. He was used to finding angry letters, a flat tire or anonymous calls saying how much of an asshole he was. There had even been a few instances where he'd been stalked and confronted by ex-lovers who were pissed that he hadn't called them back or some shit.

Chey wasn't like that. She made her contempt for him *very* clear, but it was a quiet type of resentment. Whatever her issue was with him, she didn't want to tell him. In her mind, he should already know what he'd done wrong, and the fact that he didn't have the slightest clue irked her with every passing moment. He got the feeling that if given the chance, she'd do everything in her power to avoid ever running into him again.

Why that thought brought a bitter taste in his mouth was beyond him. He didn't care for the female. He didn't even like her. Enticed by her, for sure, but beyond his physical attraction, there was very, very little left to be desired.

"I'm afraid it won't be today," Chey murmured, jarring Thorne from his musings. "My hands are tied at the moment." She paused, and the man on the other end of the line gave a muffled response. "Yes, yes. I'm fine. I already spoke to Alber. I just have some— Oh, you talked to him? What did he say?"

When they came to a stop light, she used her free hand to pinch the bridge of her nose. "That rat," she growled. "I told him not to—" She winced and pulled the phone away from her ear when the other person's voice grew loud enough for Thorne to hear a series of curses. "Can you calm down? It's fine. I have everything under control."

A whispered curse and two eyerolls later, Chey shook her head and ended the call with, "All right, we'll talk later." She placed the phone back in the cupholder, though she didn't turn the music up right away. Instead, she stared ahead of herself, worrying her lower lip between her teeth.

"Boyfriend angry you didn't come home last night?" he asked in a casual manner.

He expected a snarky response, so he was surprised when she snorted with humor. "Worse. My partner gets butthurt whenever I skip a workday and don't tell him first."

"I would have pegged you as a lone wolf."

"I would have preferred working alone, but apparently that's a no-no for liability purposes." She shrugged.

The conversation ended there. Chey didn't strike Thorne as the quiet type, but it wasn't like there was a lot for them to even talk about. Up until that point, every sentence exchanged between them had been filled with either annoyance, disdain or colorful insults.

Instead of trying to force it, Thorne glanced out of the window and settled for listening to the radio the entire drive. Not once did Chey ask for directions, nor did she use either of the GPS navigators on her phone and built into the car. However, he didn't question it further. He'd already made up in his mind that her extensive knowledge of him was odd, and to counter it, he'd have to dig up some information on her once he got free.

The high-rise apartment building sat on its own block, surrounded by acres of manicured lawn. A separate, smaller structure connected to it made up the parking garage, and Chey wasted no time in pulling into a spot. The two of them exited the car.

Thorne drew in a deep breath, wishing he at least had a hood attached to his jacket. It was after hours on the weekend, so the lobby would be closed to loungers and anyone looking to loiter. However, there was always the possibility of having to share the elevator with other tenants who were either leaving or entering the building, visiting the pool, working out in the on-site gym or anything along those lines. Even after living there for years, most of the residents didn't know who he was, yet there were a handful of employees and others who would know. Having any one of them seeing him with just one horn on his head would be beyond embarrassing.

Shoving his hands in his pants pockets to feel for his keys, he heaved a sigh and turned to Chey. She was bent over on the opposite side of the car, digging through the backseat for something. When she straightened, she slung a backpack over her shoulders. Then, she pulled her jacket's hood over her head, fastened the drawstring and pushed her sunglasses up her nose.

She met him on the other side of the car, frowning at his disbelieving stare. "What?"

"What's with that getup?" he asked, his tone accusing. There was no mistaking her intentions to hide her identity. However, he wasn't sure if she was embarrassed to be seen with him only having one horn—or just him in general. Either way, he was beyond insulted.

Instead of responding, Chey tucked her thumbs under the straps across her shoulders, then glanced all around. "Let's hurry up and get inside."

Grumbling under his breath, he led the way inside the main building. As expected, the lobby was still lit, but the front desk and lounging area both had signs informing everyone that they were closed until Monday. In the distance, he could hear the evening cleaning crew vacuuming and buffering the floors. Being sure to avoid them, he rushed down one hall toward the bank of elevators.

He pushed the button multiple times, still looking around to make sure the coast was clear. "Come on. Please be empty. Please be empty. Please be..."

Thorne trailed off as his gaze landed on Chey for a moment. Her head was turned to the side, her lips parted slightly as she stared off at a door across the room. It was a supply closet. Frowning, he wondered if perhaps she'd heard something he hadn't.

"Hey," he muttered, waving his hand in front of her face.

She jumped in surprise, snapping her mouth shut. "What?"

"You just..." The elevator dinged, making him shake his head. "Never mind."

Without another word, they stepped onto it, and Thorne blew out a deep breath of relief to find it was empty. However, he didn't relax completely. There was still the matter of making it to his floor without being seen.

He cast a curious glance at Chey. She was clutching the straps of her backpack even tighter than before, her lips set in a grim line as she peered down at her feet. Forcing his senses into focus, he became aware that it wasn't anger or even embarrassment that made her seem so disturbed. The longer he studied her, the clearer it became that she was practically brimming with apprehension.

Something wasn't right, but hell if he knew what it was. Ever since she'd gotten off the phone with her partner, her mood had shifted. She'd gone from biting out snide remarks and bossing him around to being this forlorn, quiet creature.

The sudden change in the atmosphere around her was dark, and he didn't like it one bit. Quite frankly, it was starting to freak him out. He almost wanted to say something stupid just to get a response out of her.

Before he could, the doors slid open on the top floor. He peered out to check both ends of the halls before stepping out. "Thank the gods below," he sighed, pulling out his keychain as he approached the door to his condo. Unlike the other floors, the top one only had four apartments—two on each side of the large hallway.

Thorne rushed to his door, but he gagged when his throat tightened and he couldn't take another step.

With a grunt, he whirled around to snap at Chey for halting their progress, but once again, he paused.

She was stopped dead in her tracks, her jaw clenched as she stared at the door to the condo right next to his. Her grip on the backpack straps was so tight that her knuckles had changed colors. The anxiety he sensed within her was even greater than it had been downstairs, making him frown. "Chey?"

Chey didn't answer, didn't so much as flinch.

Hesitating momentarily, he moved to nudge her with his elbow. She jerked away from him, her shades sliding down to reveal her startled gaze. "What?"

His frown deepened as he watched her. "Are you good? You look...lost."

At that, she visibly shook herself, as if trying to dislodge an old memory that kept resurfacing. She pulled her glasses off and let out a small sigh. "Yeah. I'm..." She glanced at the door again, her tone becoming stiff. "I'm fine. Let's go."

She urged him toward his door, her face settling into a familiar dour expression. Thorne hummed to himself, both annoyed and relieved that she was back to normal — well, whatever was normal for her. It was hard to say when he couldn't get a clear reading on what type of person she was.

Shrugging it off, he unlocked the door and stepped inside, flipping on the light. He waited for Chey to enter before closing and locking it behind her. "First things first," he murmured, leading the way past his living room to the kitchen. He dug in one of the drawers and pulled out a thin, thread-like chain. Within seconds, he had the necklace fastened around his neck.

There wasn't so much as a tingle to indicate whether or not it was working, but a quick glance at his reflection on his phone confirmed that his horns were no longer visible — *correction…horn*. The necklace was a common glamour tool that hid demonic features, designed specifically for whenever a demon needed to venture topside.

Grunting, he turned to Chey with his arms splayed. She gave a snort in derision, though she couldn't hide the twitch of humor in her lips. "Better," she muttered.

Satisfied, he dug through another junk drawer and pulled out a long black cord to charge his phone. "I'll need to get some juice on my phone before we head out." He hesitated only a moment before meeting her blank stare. "Do you mind if I use yours to call my brother?"

As expected, she wanted to argue. "Can't we just drive to his place?"

"No. My brother isn't a fan of pop-ins. Even if it's an emergency, he wouldn't let us through the gate."

With a small grunt, she handed over her cell with great reluctance. Thorne flashed her his most charming smile. She flipped him the bird in return.

Chuckling, he punched in Quin's number and leaned his hip against the counter. His brother didn't answer the first time, but when he hit redial, Quin answered on the third ring with a groggy, "Who the hell is this?"

"That's no way to answer the phone," Thorne drawled.

There was a short pause. Then, "Thorne? Do you know what time it is? And why the devil are you calling me from an unknown number?"

Thorne absentmindedly drummed his fingers on the countertop. It wasn't even eight o'clock yet, but Quin had always been an early bird — first to go to bed, first to wake up in the morning. "Long story short, I need your help involving magic — like, *now*. We're on the way."

Quin did quite a bit of incoherent grumbling as he presumably sat up. He yawned. "Don't bring any strangers to my house. Where are you?"

"My place." Thorne glanced at Chey, only to find she'd turned her back on him as she studied her nails. He couldn't keep his gaze from trailing down her backside. *No panties. Nice.*

"What kind of magic? If this is another one of your childish pranks — "

"It's not. I swear. It's..." He sighed and ran a hand through his hair. "I need you to undo a binding spell. Like I said, it's a long story."

Chey snorted in derision. "That's an understatement."

"Fine," Quin murmured, yawning once more. "I'm coming to you and I'll be there soon. Just know that you owe me for interrupting my sleep."

"Yeah, sure, man. No problem." Hanging up, he passed the phone back to Chey. She grabbed it between her thumb and forefinger, then wiped the screen on her pants leg as though it was contaminated. "Really?" he demanded.

"Devil germs," she murmured with a shrug. "Can't be too careful."

Rolling his eyes, Thorne grabbed his charger and led her toward the living room. "My brother is on the way. Might as well get comfortable." He waved his hand toward the plush U-shaped couch. The dark color was complemented by red, black and white pillows.

Chey waited for him to take a seat before moving as far away as the spell would allow. Only when it was at its limit did she take a seat. He resisted the urge to make a face. While he was just as pissed about the spell as she was, at least he'd tried to be amicable. There was no need for either of them to be so hostile, yet she seemed dead-set on keeping as much space between them as possible — literally.

Without looking at him, she slid her backpack off her shoulders and sat it on the floor. Then, she shrugged out of her jacket. The sleeveless cropped shirt revealed a tantalizing strip of toned skin — just barely below her belly button. He peered at the black-and-white design on her shirt featuring a multi-headed beast playing a guitar. "Scylla's Wrath?"

At her questioning look, he nodded at her shirt. Then, a small smile tugged at one corner of her lips. "One of my top ten favorites. It's a shame they went their separate ways. I'd give anything to see one more performance."

"Ditto. It's hard to find good music like that. These days, everything's become...soft."

"The authenticity is gone. Everyone's pushing out records to sell, rather than crafting songs with actual meaning." She shook her head in disappointment.

Thorne leaned forward with his elbows on his knees. It was the first time since meeting her that they'd carried on a real conversation. Granted it wasn't long, but for just a few fleeting moments, he got to see the casual side of her, complete with a smile. He didn't hold his breath on it lasting very long, but for the moment, it was...nice.

He cleared his throat, considering his next question. He knew she was going to snap at him or go back to her hard-assed, no-nonsense mood. However, he was curious about her reaction upon entering the building. That wasn't normal.

Before he could utter a word, she beat him to it. "There are only four apartments on this floor. Are you close with any of your neighbors?"

That was…random.

Thorne continued to eye her. She was leaning back against the couch with one leg crossed over the other, giving off an uncaring vibe. However, the nervous tapping of her fingers against her thigh and the way her eyes shifted all around the room — everywhere *but* him — gave away her false nonchalance. *Interesting.* "Why do you ask?"

She lifted one shoulder in a stiff shrug. "Just trying to pass the time."

The red flare of a lie sparked again. His senses were far too great to be misleading. However, instead of calling her out on it, he humored her. He'd be lying if he said he wasn't interested in her sudden curiosity with him. And he didn't dare think for one minute it was because she was *actually* fascinated with getting to know him.

He tilted his head, pretending to be lost in thought. "No one else has lived on this floor for quite some years. Some of them used to be pretty cool."

She finally met his gaze, her expression confused and shocked. "Used to?"

"I'm the sole renter of all four apartments…for personal reasons."

Earlier in the afternoon, she'd pulled her damp hair into a tight ponytail. Now that it was drying, several strands had managed to free themselves to frame her face in loose spirals. Every so often, she would shove them behind her ear in frustration, only to have them stubbornly pop back out of place. He wasn't sure why, but it was...kind of cute.

"You—" She broke off her own words with a small grunt, apparently losing all interest in conversation at that moment. "Never mind. How long before your brother gets here?"

Chapter Six

"Whoa," Chey murmured as Thorne's brother stepped inside the condo, bringing with him the smell of eucalyptus and some kind of antibacterial product.

The two devils were identical to each other, though Quin looked to be older by some years. There was a certain...maturity about his presence that was rather lacking in the younger Lucifer. He seemed more reserved.

Quin's dark hair wasn't as long, instead stopping just long enough to curl under his chin. His eyes were also lighter than Thorne's and his lips were fuller, but Thorne's jaw was a bit stronger. Even with the subtle differences, they could have been mistaken for twins.

Two gorgeous, masculine brothers who oozed so much testosterone that had Chey's mouth watering and her core dripping.

Damn, but it was past time for her to seek release. The cramps had already begun to twist her insides into knots, and the pain would only grow worse each passing minute she didn't take care of her needs. Had today been an ordinary day — as in, she hadn't woken up in some dank hotel bound to Thorne — she would have sought out a male two or three times by now to satiate her lust.

Quin's nostrils twitched in response to her pheromones, but he clenched his jaw as though trying to ignore it. Likewise, Thorne grunted under his breath and shoved his hands inside his pockets. However, he wasn't able to fully hide the darkening of his eyes. "Quin, this is —"

"Cheyenne," she interrupted with a flirty smile. "It's a pleasure to meet you."

Thorne narrowed his eyes at her. "Cheyenne, huh? Yet all I got was Chey."

Ignoring him, she extended her hand. However, Quin merely regarded her outstretched appendage with a look of poorly disguised revulsion. "Forgive me," he murmured, taking a small step back. "I don't do handshakes."

Chey's smile fell. "What the fuc —?"

"He's a germaphobe," Thorne rushed to say. He must have known she was taking offense to Quin's comment. "Don't take it personal."

Quin nodded in apology. "It's not you, I promise. I won't even let my brothers touch me."

"Huh," she muttered, her annoyance fading. She cast Thorne a side-eyed glare. "Trust me. I know the feeling all too well." His lips parted, but before he could give a retort, she returned her attention to Quin. "Whatever then. Do you think can undo this spell or what? I've got things to do."

"I get the feeling you two aren't quite getting along," he drawled, following them into the living room.

"On the contrary," Thorne replied, his tone chipper, "we're pretty good friends. Like fire and dry wood."

Chey snorted at the sarcastic words. "What do you need us to do?"

"Show me what happens when you two try to separate."

At once, she and Thorne faced each other and backed apart until the golden line sparked between them. Digging through his bag, Quin pulled out a small booklet and began turning through the pages. Every so often he'd look up at them and jot down notes.

Chey waited and watched patiently as he strolled forward. He waved his hand through the six feet of space, as though to check whether or not the spell was tangible. Next, he circled Thorne, using the butt-end of the pen to feel for the invisible collar connecting them. He poked and prodded his brother for several more minutes before shaking his head and stepping away.

"It's a simple binding spell, but the layers of magic are intricate." He placed the notebook and pen in his bag, then pulled out a bottle of hand sanitizer. As he spoke, he put it to use. "Whoever cast it did not want it to be broken."

That explained the smell of disinfectant, Chey thought as she watched him with curiosity. The longer she eyed him, the more traits of his OCD she detected.

The fitted white polo didn't have a single speck of dust or a wrinkle to be seen, and his khaki pants were ironed to perfection. His hair was brushed neatly behind his ears, and every time some of the smaller strands escaped, he'd swiftly tuck them back in place. His face was clean-shaven and smooth, and even his nails were trimmed and clean.

At first glance, he merely looked like a well-dressed man who took care of his appearance. Now, however, she knew better. She wondered if he'd always had the disorder, or if perhaps something in his past had traumatized him into picking it up along the way.

"But it *can* be broken, right?" Thorne demanded, snapping her out of her musings.

Quin shook his head and zipped up his bag, then slung it over his shoulder. However, he still held the bottle of sanitizer. "Unfortunately, the magic involved is more than what I can handle. The fastest and easiest solution is to find the person who cast it in the first place. Any idea who that could be?"

Chey couldn't halt the cocky smile twisting her lips as she crossed her arms and faced Thorne. "What an excellent question, Quinton. Do you?"

"It's just Quin," he grunted.

Thorne glared at the ceiling. "This cannot be happening."

"Lucky for you, there are two other options." Humor lit his eyes, an impish twinkle that Chey couldn't decide whether it was good or bad. "The first might be easier, but..."

"But what?"

"It's going to require flowers, chocolate and quite a bit of ass-kissing."

Chey frowned at the two brothers when Thorne's expression flickered with realization, followed swiftly with dismay. "What is it?" she asked, annoyed to be the odd one out.

He heaved a deep sigh and ran his fingers through his hair. "Remi. My other brother's mate is a djinni with the power to grant wishes, but only if we go topside."

"Seriously?" Then, she gave a soft gasp. "Oh! The goddess, right?"

Both of them turned to her. "You know?"

"It was all over the news two years ago. Hades' long-lost granddaughter mating the eldest Lucifer. I forgot all about that."

Quin snorted with humor. "That's her. I'd advise you not to bring up her being a goddess should you meet her, though. She still likes to pretend she's normal." He turned his attention to his younger brother. "And *you* better get your speech prepared to sweet talk her into helping. She doesn't give out wishes for free."

"Why wouldn't she help her own brother-in-law? This is a serious matter."

Instead of responding, Quin chuckled. Thorne rubbed the back of his neck. "Yeah, about that... She hasn't been too happy with me ever since I crashed her wedding. Gods below."

Chey rolled her eyes and breathed a rather unladylike curse. "I swear, if I'm stuck with this pain in the ass for the rest of my life, I'll—"

"You think I'm happy about it? I'd rather be castrated."

"If you had been in the first place, we wouldn't even be in this shit."

He snapped his teeth, baring them in anger. "Says the succubus."

She glared right back at him. "A succubus who doesn't have a string of psychotic exes pulling crap like this."

"You...might have a point." He sighed in defeat, his seething expression losing its effect.

Quin watched their bickering, his visible amusement unwavering. "There is one other option, which will probably require some time. This is fae magic, so your best bet is to find a fairy, nymph or someone along those lines who's earned a degree in the Summoning Arts. They would have been taught all manners of binding spells, so they would possess the knowledge and magic to undo it."

With a scoff, Chey shook her head. "Right, so we're supposed to just go around asking random fairies if they've majored in one specific — and quite un-popular — program?"

"Actually, I know just the man for the job," Thorne said, relief causing his features to relax. "I have an employee from Abyssia who boasts about his college years. We can catch him tomorrow morning before his shift starts."

"Well, there you go," Quin said with a pleased nod. "Problem solved."

"Problem *not* solved," Chey fumed. "I'm not staying the night here. Why can't you call this guy now so we can hurry up and get this over with?"

Thorne rolled his eyes, exasperated. "For the simple fact that I'm not buddy-buddy with all my employees. I don't have his number, and I'm not making a trip to the office this late just to dig up his file. By then, he might even be asleep, and I'm not so much of an asshole to disturb someone's rest."

"Well, just fuck me then, huh?" Quin groused.

Chey was about to snap and unleash an entire essay of colorful curses, but her phone's ringing made her hold her tongue. She pulled it free from her pocket, glanced at the caller ID and answered. "Detective Wilcox."

"How are you holding up?" Vaughn asked, his deep voice full of concern. "Did you manage to get the spell undone?"

She grunted in annoyance. "Not yet, but we have a plan. Unfortunately, we can't move forward until tomorrow."

There was a brief moment of silence. Chey liked to call it the calm before the storm. As much as she valued Vaughn as a partner, his hot-headed temper was even worse than hers. Not only that, but the standstill in their case had put them both on edge. The delay in her being unable to return to work for days was stressing him out.

Before he went on his venting rant, Chey covered the speaker and turned to Thorne. "I need to take this in private."

She could tell he wanted to say something sarcastic, but instead, he nodded and led the way toward the sliding glass doors of the balcony. Muttering a reluctant thanks, she stepped outside and closed the door.

"All right, you wanna tell me what the fuck is going on, or should I be the one to deliver news of another fuckup to Rhys?"

Thorne grunted at Quin's casual threat. "Saturday night I went to a bar downtown like always. Saw a nymph, danced a little — typical shit. Next thing I know, she drugged me and I woke up chained in some abandoned, creepy ass hotel room in the middle of nowhere." As he explained the rest of the night's events — leaving out his missing horn, of course — Quin's expression remained blank.

When the story was over, he folded his arms, looking as though he was struggling to absorb everything. "None of that makes sense. So, you're saying Chey was at the same bar as you. Then, when you woke up, she just so happened to be there too, and now you're bound together."

"It sounds suspicious, but I can sense her lies. She was telling the truth."

"Right," Quin murmured. "That gauze on her forehead is from that guy hitting her, right? Are you hurt, too? Is that why you're wearing a glamour charm?"

Thorne swiftly waved that aside, refusing to reveal the truth. "Nah, different story."

Clearly his brother didn't believe it, but he let it go. "Detective Wilcox. Please tell me she works for a private company and not SPD." At Thorne's guilty silence, Quin shook his head in exasperation. Then, he gave a sinister chuckle. "Gods below, you'd better hope the media doesn't catch onto this. After that last incident you had with the police—"

"I know. I know," he groused, not wanting the uncomfortable reminder of the near life-destroying encounter he'd had some years ago. "No need to bring it up."

He moved to lean against the wall near the glass door. Every so often, the spell would tighten around his throat as Chey absently walked around his balcony, only to realize she'd gone too far. When she met his annoyed look, she flipped him off and continued speaking on the phone.

Quin chuckled once more. "I've seen rabid hellhounds treat people nicer than she does you. What's up with that? You two have some history?"

With a shrug, he replied, "She fucking hates me, man. Like *really* hates me. According to her, we hooked up once a long time ago, but that's it."

"You don't remember?"

Thorne rolled his eyes and fixed Quin with a dry look. "Do you remember any of the chicks you slept with thirty years ago?"

"I do, actually. I remember all of them. Even if I didn't, I doubt I'd ever forget an ass like *that*." He shot a pointed look toward Chey, who had her back turned to them while she leaned over the railing, still on the phone.

That was...not the answer he'd expected. Even with the severity of his OCD, Quin was still attracted to women. He just didn't act on his most basic needs anymore. He was a look-but-don't-touch kind of man.

Thorne's gaze lingered on Chey a bit too long before he managed to glance away. She really did have a nice butt. "Trust me. A hot body doesn't guarantee a nice attitude."

"I thought she was just delightful," Quin said, smiling. "Funny as hell, too. You ever think maybe *you* are the problem?"

Thorne narrowed his eyes. "Whose side are you on? If you like to play with hellcats, by all means, take her off my hands."

"Whatever you did to her has caused her quite a bit of grief, brother. That's what I'm picking up from her."

Taken aback, Thorne straightened from the wall. "What do you mean whatever *I* did? I don't even remember her. For all I know, she could be pissed because it was just a one-time thing."

Quin shook his head in pity. "For a man who spends so much time with women, you really don't know a damn thing about them. Have you even fully opened your senses to look at her? I mean *really* look at her. She might dislike you, but she's filled with grief that flares every time she looks at you. *You* did something to cause that pain. I can't say what it is, but hers isn't the kind of grudge you hold for thirty years over not getting a call back from a stranger." He shook his head once more and turned away. "I'm out of here. Call if you need anything else. And for the love of the gods, please try to stay out of trouble."

Thorne waited until his brother was out of the door before returning his gaze to Chey. He'd used his powers to read her before, but he realized he hadn't put much effort into it. He'd only checked the surface, a half-assed attempt to try to figure her out.

Mulling over Quin's words, he eyed Chey, though it took more effort than he was willing to admit to keep his gaze from falling to her bottom. For devils, they read the auras of the people around them. Most of the time, they were able to connect a certain color to an emotion — though the colors were translucent due to the ever-shifting feelings. For instance, if someone was lying, there was usually a streak of red that flashed. Warm yellow and orange shades generally signified happiness, darker hues represented negative emotions, so on and so forth.

Each time he'd used his powers on Chey, he'd been met with a boring gray sight with the occasional swirl of annoyance and anger. However, he cranked his senses up another notch, looking past the hypothetical cloud. Quin had been correct. Beneath that neutral façade she liked to use, her aura was full of grief and pain. The colors were dark and dense, as if they'd been festering for a long time.

Thorne frowned and closed his eyes, essentially shutting off his powers. All that time he'd been convinced that Chey was just a bitter ex-lover, but evidently that wasn't the case. While most of his exes tended to hold a grudge, none of them had any deep-seated pain like Chey's. They were fleeting emotions, usually gone after a few days or weeks.

It bugged the hell out of him that he had no idea what was up with her. He still didn't like Chey much, but his original impression of her was gone. She was angry, sure, but he knew now that it was forced. She might dislike him, but it wasn't pure rage that pushed her to treat him the way she had.

Then again, why did any of that matter? What did it matter if she did or didn't like him? He didn't owe her shit, nor she him. Once they found a way to break the spell, both of them would be on their separate way without looking backward. He didn't give a damn what she thought of him.

Well, he shouldn't.

When Chey stuck her phone in her pocket and slid the door back open, Thorne refused to acknowledge the lie he'd just told himself. Instead, he took note of her annoyed expression. "Boyfriend troubles, again?"

She rolled her eyes but didn't look at him. Instead, she focused on a distant object hanging on the wall across the room. He wondered if she'd been refusing to meet his gaze all this time so he wouldn't detect the pain looking at him gave her. "I don't do boyfriends. I was discussing a case with my partner." After a beat, she added, "Don't say a word."

Thorne snorted but didn't comment further. As many times as she'd mentioned her being a detective, not once had he sensed her lying about it, yet there were other instances that had proven she wasn't able to hide her deceit from him. The realization only made him wary. He was an asshole most of the time, but he wasn't a criminal. However, having one of SPD's finest literally tailing him all day wasn't the most comfortable experience of his life.

Shaking his head, he shoved his hands inside his pockets. "I know neither of us are happy about this arrangement, but we're stuck together at least until the morning. Can we call it a temporary truce? I'm starving, my back is killing me from that lumpy mattress and I just want to forget about last night without worrying about waking up to find a knife sticking out of my chest."

As expected, she made her suspicion known as she met his gaze with pursed lips. "Personally, I would have chosen a pillow to the face. Less mess to clean."

Hiding his amusement to show he was serious, he added, "We don't even have to talk to each other. We can throw a movie on, sit on separate ends of the couch—whatever it takes. I won't say a word unless you address me first."

"Somehow I doubt that," she muttered, her gaze once again trailing away from his. "Do what you want. I'll try to make this work...for now."

Well, I suppose that's the best I'm going to get from her.

Chapter Seven

Chey was dying.

Not literally, but it certainly seemed like it. As it was, what had been mild, ignorable cramps in her abdomen turned into a hundred razor-sharp needles stabbing into her from her womb to the bottom of her pelvis. The pain was accompanied with nipples beaded into tight points and her clit swollen to the point where she had to sit perfectly still or else the tiniest of movements would undo her.

On the other end of the U-shaped couch, Thorne was impervious to her suffering as his gaze remained fixated on the wall-mounted TV.

After agreeing to a temporary truce, he'd kept his word by the two of them just relaxing. To her surprise, not only was he a horror film lover like her, but he'd also chosen to order seafood—her favorite dish. However, she didn't let him know he'd done a good job in deciding both.

Unfortunately, she hadn't been able to eat more than a few bites before the discomfort of her needs had decided to worsen. And so, after waiting for him to finish the last bit of food on his plate, she stood. Moving too swiftly, the soft material of her pants smoothed across her damp flesh, making her release a soft moan before she was able to fully stifle it.

Thorne shot her an alarmed look. "Are you all right? You look pale."

Gritting her teeth, she did her best to shield her face from him. "It's the shrimp," she lied. "Can I use your bathroom?"

Of course, he didn't believe her. He sensed the lie for what it was, but he didn't argue, much to her relief. Instead, he stood and headed for the short hallway where a private gym and a bathroom faced each other. Without another word, she ducked inside the door on the left and slammed it shut.

"Dammit," she murmured, her voice hoarse. Walking had made it so much worse. Shaking, she slid one hand down the front of her pants. Her fingers met naked flesh that was already soaked, but when she applied pressure to her clit, there was...nothing, not even a faint tingle.

She worked at the swollen nub, squeezing her eyes shut as she willed her body to react to her own touch. However, it was pointless. The cruel twist of being a sex demon was that no matter how much they needed the release, they lacked the ability to bring pleasure to themselves.

Even knowing that, she kicked her shoes off and shucked her bottoms before continuing the attempt to pleasure herself until her hand became cramped.

With a groan of frustration, she gave up and glared at her reflection in the mirror. Gone was the dark brown color of her eyes, replaced instead with a golden ring. Her face was pinched with pain and sweat formed a line across her forehead.

"Damn," she breathed again, running the sink water. Several cold splashes later, she checked her face once more. She growled at the sight and fisted her hands on the vanity.

I fucked up. That was the only thought in her mind as another wave of lust rolled through her, bringing with it more sharp pains as her core clenched with the need to be filled. It was growing to an unbearable point. It wouldn't be long before she caved in and went searching for someone — anyone — to take the edge off.

A sharp rap at the door made her jump, reminding her that she wasn't alone. Before she could bark at Thorne to buzz off, he pushed the door open.

"Chey, are you — Oh shit."

She glared at him, yet through the growing haze causing her to have tunnel vision, all she could focus on was the fact that he was exactly what she needed — male, unmated and exuding raw sex appeal. And he was horny. She drew in a deep breath through her nose, biting her lip at the delicious scent of cinnamon spices and something darker. Something...powerful. The kind of power only a devil could claim.

Thorne drew in a short gasp, his eyes turning red in response to her pheromones perfuming the air. A quick glance down south revealed that he was just as hard and aching as she was. All it would take was a quick snap of a button and a single move to have him buried inside her, satisfying the unforgiving desire raging through her.

It was that thought that had her taking a step backward, shaking her head with a bit too much force. "Take me outside," she commanded through clenched teeth.

Confused, he followed her, but hesitated when she shuffled away again, stumbling and nearly falling over in the process. "Outside? Why?"

She held her hands up, silently urging him to stay back. There was only a thin, tentative hold on her control, and if he came too close, she'd be powerless to stop herself from launching toward him. While it would fix her problem right away, she'd never forgive herself for breaking her own vow — a vow to never, ever lay with the devil who'd caused nothing but pain where she was concerned.

"I need...someone. *Now.*"

A low sound rumbled deep within his chest as he took another step forward. "Chey, let me — "

She shook her head so sharply that her ponytail swished side to side. Her knees buckled, forcing her to catch herself on the edge of the countertop to keep from doubling over. "Not you. Anyone but you."

With a growl, his lips curled in a snarl that showed a flash of those pristine teeth. "Look at you! You can barely stand. You said I didn't break your heart, so what's the problem? Why the fuck do you keep treating me like I kicked your puppy? You clearly need sex, yet instead of using me — who's right here willing to help you — you would rather go out of your way and suffer more to find some random guy on the street. What could I have possibly done to make you hate me so much?"

Chey snapped her gaze to him, doing her best to glare, though she couldn't bring her eyes to focus. "You. Ruined. *Everything.*"

Ignoring her hands, he marched up to her, invading her personal bubble. "Whatever happened between us is in the past. I'm not coming on to you. I'm trying to help."

When she didn't respond right away, he took her wrists in light hold. She stiffened, but the warmth of his palms prevented her from tugging them away. "It doesn't have to be personal, Chey. Just think of me as a tool. You have needs, and I have the proper equipment. It won't mean anything."

Of course it won't, she thought, annoyed with the entire situation. She hated Thorne more than she hated anything or anyone else. Despite how attractive he was — *and gods below, is he attractive* — just looking at him repulsed her. He was a selfish, arrogant, careless bastard who didn't give two shits about anyone besides himself and his dick.

And yet, he was right about one thing. She was only going to suffer more if she continued to drag it out. She'd pushed herself too far as it was, having gone without it since the morning before she'd tried to intervene with Thorne's kidnappers. Even if he did follow her outside and she grabbed a random man from the street, she wasn't at all comfortable being screwed with Thorne as a bystander just six feet away.

Just the mere thought of letting Thorne touch her was revolting…and yet far too tempting. As she stared up at him, she was reminded all too well of how good his touch felt.

Granted, it really had been a five-minute hookup, but it had been the best orgasm of her life. She remembered being bent over and coming so hard that her knees had gone weak, with only his arms around her keeping her upright. She recalled the feel of his lips pressed against the back of her neck as he murmured a slew of soft compliments about how good she felt to him.

The memory made her shudder, temporarily pushing aside all thoughts about how much she was going to regret this. *Again.*

Gritting her teeth, she tugged her wrists free from his hold and fisted his shirt instead. "Fine," she breathed, her voice shaky to her own ears. "Just this once, but we do it *my* way."

Thorne nodded in acceptance, his eyelids growing heavy as he watched her.

"*Impersonal,*" he'd said. Chey could do that. Everyone else in her life had been merely passing through. Thorne shouldn't be any different.

Except, in a way he already was, but before the warning thoughts could take form, she pressed herself against him.

Chey didn't bother with foreplay or teasing as she groped Thorne through his jeans. He didn't mind, however. As much as she pissed him off, there was no way he could deny how much she turned him on. Despite the constant insults and glares and sneers she threw at him at every possible turn, his cock continued to perk up with excitement every time she stood too close or walked ahead of him or...anything. From the moment he'd first sensed her arousal back in that hotel, a part of him had been eager to get a taste of that fire, even if he got burned.

A good fuck would clear that right up, and he was more than willing to test out that theory.

"The couch," she commanded, her voice nothing short of a sexy growl.

Thorne grinned. Snaking his arms around her, he picked her up, making her circle her legs around his waist for balance. And damn the gods if her heat didn't feel so good, even through his jeans. In a few short strides, he carried her back to the living room.

Chey dug her nails into his shoulders when he set her on her feet. She went on the tips of her toes to glare at him. "Do that again and I'll knock those teeth down your throat."

As much as he wanted to laugh, he bit his tongue to hide his amusement. He had no doubt she'd try to act out her threat, but at the moment, he couldn't find it in him to care. She was just too cute, but more than that, he was aroused more than he'd been in ages. The scent of her lust was sweet as it tickled his nose, clouding his senses and making his cock swell until it was borderline painful.

Unable to wait any longer, he tore open the button of his pants. He'd gotten them pushed to his knees before she shoved him onto the couch. She wasted no time in straddling him.

"Don't say a word," she huffed.

Thorne was unable to do so anyway when his tip met the damp heat of her pussy. Before he could draw in his next breath, she descended onto him.

"Fuc—"

Chey's breath hitched as she slapped her palm over his mouth, silencing him. "No words," she half-said, half-moaned.

Hell's bells. She felt better than he could have imagined. She was tight and wet as her core clasped around him, gripping him in a vise. She went up onto her knees before slamming back down, as though to punish him.

And damn the gods below if it wasn't a punishment he'd endure for the rest of his life if he could.

With her hand still over his mouth, he gave her palm a little nip, eliciting a hiss of pleasure. He watched every movement, adoring the expressions she made. Sometimes she'd hold her breath to try to keep from making a sound. Sometimes she'd let out a tiny whimper. Her eyes were squeezed shut as though to block out the sight of him, yet her parted lips and knitted eyebrows told him she was floating on the same cloud of ecstasy as he was.

He needed to see more. He reached for the edge of her shirt, but when she slowed, he worried she was going to stop him. Instead, he swallowed his frustration when she pulled the garment over her head and tossed it to the floor. Next went her bra.

Unable to stop, Thorne groaned at the sight of her fully naked as she rode him. The dark peaks of her nipples pointed at him, begging to be tasted. He obliged, drawing one into his mouth. Chey fisted his hair and held him against her skin as he sucked on the sensitive flesh. When he flicked his tongue across the beaded tip and rolled it between his teeth, she arched her back and hissed. He switched his attention to the other nipple, going back and forth to shower them both with equal affection.

Perhaps sensing he was close to coming, Chey threw her head back and palmed his shoulders as she rolled her hips faster against him. Needing to occupy his own hands, he roamed them across every smooth inch of skin he could find.

When his fingers grazed a rough patch of skin on her sternum, he sent it an absent-minded glance. It was a scar, a jagged lump of raised skin that wasn't quite a perfect circle. He brushed his fingers across it again.

It was fairly old, having healed over years ago, yet there was no uncertainty over what had caused it. There had been hundreds of thousands of mortals Thorne had guided to Sheol who had perished from gunshot wounds. Chey's was located almost dead center under her breasts, barely missing her heart.

As he eyed it, he spotted a similar scar lower, just above her navel. He frowned and wondered why he hadn't noticed either when she'd been half-naked in the hotel room — or even fully naked at her house. Though old, both were so prominent that they should have been impossible to miss. He'd still been full of confusion and anger, so it was likely that the shock of their situation had made him overlook it.

Curious, he peered up at her in question, but the pain in her golden eyes halted him from asking the queries pressing on his mind.

After a beat, Chey's expression shifted into frustration. She grabbed both of his wrists and pinned them to the couch. "Don't," she bit out, still grinding against him. Then, on a whisper he barely heard, she added, "Please."

Thorne sighed and silently accepted that now was not the time. Instead, he leaned his head back on the couch and settled for watching her through half-cast eyes. Her features relaxed as she focused on the rolling movements of her hips. Within moments, he forgot all about the scars as his pleasure took over.

Without warning, Chey jumped off him and stood. Before he could utter a complaint, however, she nudged his legs apart and stepped between them.

Turning her back to him, he stared in wide-eyed amazement as she once again lowered herself onto him.

"Shit," he dragged out when she started to ride him in a reverse fashion.

Chey's breathing became short pants as she palmed his knees for balance. Thorne gripped her hips, both to aid her and keep from tearing through the couch with his bare fingers. His dick swelled, a warning that his orgasm was lingering so close. Fucking Chey felt so damn amazing that he didn't want it to end, but if there was one thing he knew about succubi, it was that they were physically incapable of coming before their partners. As much as he wanted to satisfy her first, delaying his climax was only going to cause her more pain.

And despite all accusations, he wasn't that much of a prick.

He peered down at where their bodies were connected. Watching her ass bounce over him caused a memory to flicker in his mind. He remembered having her in a similar position, bent over against a wall while he pounded into her from behind. He'd had one hand fisted in her hair while the other muffled her moans.

A split second later, Thorne stiffened and shifted his hips upward. He heaved a choked curse as his climax exploded, shockwaves of pleasure rippling through him until he had to squeeze his eyes shut to keep from passing out at the sheer bliss of it all.

At the same time, Chey threw her head back and cried her own release, the curly ends of her hair brushing his lap. Feeling her core spasm around his cock damn near made him come again, a feat he didn't think was possible in any circumstance.

With his heart still beating in erratic pulsations, he sank into the couch with a sigh of contentment.

Chey didn't move for a good two minutes, though that had more to do with her legs still trembling against his than her actually wanting to sit there. His assumption was confirmed when she tried to push herself upright, only to have her arms give out.

Without a word, he lifted her by the waist and shifted her so that she could take a seat next to him.

As they both wound down from the exhilaration, the awkward reality of what came next set in. At this point, Thorne would normally already be dressed and heading out the door without a backward glance. However, he and Chey were bound, so there was nowhere for either of them to go. In all honesty, he had no idea what to do or what to expect.

Thankfully, Chey didn't say a word to him. Instead, she reached for the remote and continued the movie where they'd left off, filling the room with the sounds of classic horror music. She then picked up her discarded T-shirt and bra.

Thorne had to bite his lip to keep from groaning in disappointment as she got dressed. He rather liked seeing all that smooth flesh on display. When she sat back down, he glanced at her out the corners of his eyes. She merely stared straight ahead at the mounted TV, unwilling to look at him. He supposed he should have been glad she wasn't showing him any attention. After all, he was the one who'd stated that the sex would be impersonal. For her, it was nothing more than a means of masturbation — a tool to satisfy her needs.

And he'd meant those words.

However, that memory toppled with the earth-shattering orgasm made him feel...conflicted. He still didn't fully remember her, only the act of them fucking in some closet a while back. It had been just as she'd claimed.

Ever since waking up in that hotel room, he'd been indifferent about who she was and just exactly how she knew him. Now, he was curious to know more. It shouldn't matter one bit, yet upon realizing he'd done something to hurt her in the past, it's been bothering him not to know.

He'd been a hotheaded, temperamental youth back in his younger days, but he couldn't recall a day in his life when he'd gone out of his way to cause someone grief. Well, there was that *one* time, but his actions had been justifiable.

Wait a minute...

Thorne narrowed his eyes at Chey. He recalled the strange way she'd acted upon entering the building, including the odd sorrow that had filled her eyes as she'd stared at the vacant apartment next door to him. Chey had said they'd hooked up thirty years prior. Around that same time, he'd bought out all four suites to prevent anyone from moving in near him, all because of one neighbor — the one who'd lived next door.

He wondered if the two events were connected in some way. If so, he didn't understand how or why Chey would hold a grudge against him. He'd barely even known his ex-neighbor, as he'd done his best to keep a low profile upon first moving into the condominiums. Could that be how Chey knew him? Was she friends or perhaps even related to the woman?

That somewhat could have explained why she would have hated him at one point, but to hold a grudge for thirty whole years?

Shaking his head, Thorne returned his attention to the movie. Nothing about Cheyenne Wilcox made sense, and he was only going to burn himself to the ground if he tried to figure it all out in one night. Besides, come morning, they were going to find his employee and get rid of the spell. Then, there would be no sense in trying to get to know her.

He told himself that, but it was a false reassurance that did nothing to quell the discomfort sliding through him.

Chapter Eight

Chey didn't remember the exact moment she'd fallen asleep, but she recalled very clearly curling into one corner of the couch as far away from Thorne as she could get after they'd both gotten fully dressed.

As she blinked away the last remnants of sleep, Chey soon realized that she wasn't where she was supposed to be. At some point in the night, either she or Thorne — or both — had shifted into a position where he was lying on his back with one leg stretched out, the other bent so that his foot rested on the floor. She was nestled between those long legs, her head resting in the shallow valley between the hard planes of his pecs. His heartbeat was slow and steady against her ear, a soothing drum that almost lulled her right back to sleep.

The next thing she noticed was a heavy weight settled over her. Tilting her head a fraction, she spotted one of his arms draped across her hip, resting on top of the warm fleece blanket she didn't recall using.

Chey blinked again to clear her foggy thoughts. As sculpted as Thorne was, he made an excellent body pillow. It had been a long time since she'd slept so comfortably, and even longer since she'd been cuddled. Most days she woke up multiple times through the night drenched in sweat and shaking after a night terror involving the faceless enemy known as the Cryptic Slayer.

It wasn't so much that she feared another demon. Growing up in the unforgiving streets of the city had hardened her at a young age. She didn't scare easily anymore. What disturbed her sleep was the guilt over not catching the man in that first year. Each day that passed where he wasn't in custody was a reminder of the victims she'd failed, along with the taunt that more would fall before she could stop him.

If she could stop him.

Sighing, she urged the thoughts from her mind and eased into a sitting position, careful not to disturb Thorne. It took a grand effort to banish the memory of the sinful deed she'd committed with him. She hated the part of her that wanted to curl into him and drift back off into slumber, the part that longed to relieve the morning wood popping a tent in his jeans.

Disgusting, she chided, annoyed over her reaction. She chanced a peek at his sleeping face and scowled. He was even more gorgeous when he wasn't fixing her that arrogant half-smile he seemed to favor. He should have looked ridiculous with his hair disheveled and his lips slightly agape as he breathed light snores. *He doesn't deserve to appear so peaceful, dammit.*

As she glared at his sleeping form, she absently fingered the scars on her torso. Even through the material of her shirt, she could feel them. They were so old that most of the time she forgot about them, yet each time she noticed, she was reminded of why she despised Thorne Lucifer with every fiber in her being.

There were times when she could still feel the sharp bite of the bullets entering her flesh — one becoming lodged so deeply inside her that the surgeons had been unable to remove it. She could still hear the resounding booms, followed by ringing in her ears that had resulted in damaged eardrums for days afterward. Sometimes she still feared she'd wake up in the hospital again, disoriented and confused as her body fought to survive those near-fatal shots.

Thorne stirred, making her blink back to reality before she sank too far into the past again. She used the heels of her palms to wipe her eyes, frustrated at the tears that had formed. Thirty years later and that piece of history continued to haunt her. It was as though even in death the angry spirit of her dear friend wouldn't allow her to move on.

Refusing to let him see her in a moment of weakness, she grabbed for the remote control and turned the TV on.

"Morning," he murmured.

Chey cringed at the sound of multiple bones popping as he stretched. "How soon until we find this employee of yours?"

"Not a morning person, I see," he grumbled as he checked his cell phone for the time. "We still have about an hour to spare. If we make it there by seven-thirty, he should be clocking in. We can catch him before he goes topside."

Surprised, she glanced his way. "Topside?"

He yawned and ran a hand through his tousled hair. If it was at all possible, the action only added a boyish charm to his good looks. *Curse it all.* "He's a reaper." Taking in the confused look she gave him, he elaborated. "I run the Field Division at Elysium Underworld Corp. Our reapers are the ones who fetch mortal souls."

"So, they get a free pass topside every day? *And* get paid to do so?"

Thorne snorted at her incredulous tone. "It's not like they're on vacation. Humans die every day around the clock, but we only send so many reapers out at a time."

Unable to contain her curiosity, Chey faced him on the couch. "If mortals die that often, how many reapers do you send out? Is each human assigned a specific reaper? What about employee hours?"

Blinking, Thorne cocked an eyebrow. "This is…interesting to you?"

"By far the most interesting thing you've said since the hotel."

Instead of grunting an insult under his breath as she expected, he surprised her by chuckling. "We only send thirty to fifty reapers topside at a time, depending on the death rate. Basically, they're given a list of mortals on the brink of death. They travel all around the world to collect souls, constantly going back and forth to drop them off with the charons. After they work a fixed number of hours a day, they clock out and the next shift takes over. We're the only division that works overnight."

"Wow," she murmured, trying to imagine what it was like to be one of the elite runners. "What about the charons? What do they do?"

"They're the guys who transport souls to their destinations. It's like this. After the reapers collect the souls, charons deliver the new ones to the processing unit — Quin's division. Their life's deeds are collected and passed over to the Soul Distribution Center. That's where Rhys — my other brother — and his mate decide what to do with them afterward. Good souls go straight to our sister corp, Infernal Meadows, to await resurrection, while the not-so-good ones go to our other destination, the Center of Eternal Punishment."

"The Meadows or Asphodel," she murmured, nodding in understanding.

He tipped his head in confirmation. "Yes. For the heavy sinners, the severity of their over-indulgences determine how long their sentence is, but once they've served, they get assigned a new life. The charons once again pick the souls up from either region and bring them back to the reapers, who in turn deliver the newly cleansed soul to their body."

Every demon knew what Elysium Underworld Corp was. Children and teens went to school up until age eighteen, and history was one of the more vital subjects to learn. Elysium had started out as a vast region with the earliest line of Lucifers, who were charged with handling mortal souls. Over time, massive cities had been built all throughout the region with EUC at its core, though there was no greater contribution to the economy and lifestyle of Sheol than the soul-collecting industry.

Chey had never cared to learn the inner workings of it all, but she'd never thought there were so many different divisions and steps to go through for the life-and-death cycle of humans. Such wasn't the case with demons. There was no such thing as reincarnation or an afterlife. Death was death, and that was all there was to it. It was part of the reason why they'd been created to live such long lifespans and could recover from most wounds that would be fatal to mortals.

She shook her head in amazement. "It sounds like such a...bizarre process."

He snickered and folded his hands behind his head as he leaned back into the cushions. "It's a piece of cake compared to the old way the Lucifers kept up with souls. Back then, they didn't have technology, nor did they have the sense to hire others to help with tracking. It was only a thousand years ago when my father and his siblings decided to change things by building EUC. Hell, even after that it was hectic until IM and CEP were created. Now everything runs in a busy, yet balanced flow."

While she was still occupied soaking in all the information, he turned to the TV. His eyes flew wide in shock. "Whoa, turn that up."

Chey blinked and aimed the remote without looking. There were a dozen more questions she wanted to ask.

" – *authorities have been calling the Cryptic Slayer has struck a bit closer to home here in Infernal Regions. We're here at the crime scene where police were called after a local shop owner discovered the body of an unidentified male. Though the cause of death is unclear, the male was reported to have had the initials of C.S. carved onto his torso, a trademark that had been present on the bodies of a dozen other victims in the last five years. The detectives of the Sheolic Police Department have yet to release a statement regarding the presence of a serial killer in our city, but it's safe to say – "*

Chey muted the TV and snatched her phone off the coffee table. "Shit," she breathed upon seeing she had over twenty missed calls. The ringer was turned on loud, but she hadn't heard a thing in her sleep.

"What's wrong?" Thorne asked, sitting up.

She ignored him and dialed her partner. Vaughn answered on the first ring. "Chey, where the hell are you? We've been blowing you up all morning."

"I know, I just—"

"Stop fucking off with that devil bastard and get your ass down here *now*. I'll text you the address. We got a shitstorm coming our way."

He hung up, making Chey curse again. She stood and two seconds later, Vaughn's text came through. "Come on," she said to Thorne. "I need to get downtown fast."

Still looking confused and a bit alarmed, he rose as well. "Can it wait? Once my guy goes topside, we won't be able to catch him until his shift ends, which can be unpredictable."

After tugging on her shoes, she grabbed the keys and slung her backpack over her shoulder. "Sorry, but this is more important right now. I can deal with you for a few more hours."

He didn't even bat an eye at her words. "Chey, what is going on? Is this about the news?"

Sighing, she tapped her foot in a rapid motion. Patience wasn't her strongest suit, especially not when it came to her career. "I'll explain in the car. Can we go? Now, please."

Thorne frowned, though he didn't argue. Instead, he reluctantly tucked his phone in his pockets. "Fine, but can I at least brush my teeth first?"

Chey rolled her eyes, but the two of them made quick work of fixing their appearances one at a time in the bathroom. Minutes later, they were out of the door, down the elevator and striding through the parking garage toward her car. She was so anxious that she'd forgotten all about her previous reluctance over being seen with him. It wasn't so much that she'd been embarrassed, but that the shame she'd felt from being anywhere near him — especially inside his apartment building — had been unyielding.

When they neared the car, she explained, "Five years ago, there was a series of random attacks on men back in Asphodel. The victims had been beaten, but nothing major at first, and since none had been able to give a description of their attacker, it was just one of those cases SPD could never get a firm grip on. After the first year, the attacks grew more violent to the point of hospitalization, and just over a year ago, we had our first murder. I...was taken off the case, but the trail of bodies has since made it here." She almost let it slip that she'd once lived in another region.

"So, those attacks were connected to this killer? How do you know? It could have been — "

She shook her head. "He leaves his initials carved into his victims. While we don't know what C.S. stands for, the media named him the Cryptic Slayer. His MO is always the same. It's the one thing that has connected all the victims." Approaching the driver's side, she opened the door. "We've been trying to keep the media out of this since we haven't gotten a solid lead, but it's too late now. Our only clue is that he fishes for his victims in social gatherings — clubs, bars, that sort of thing."

"So, when you said you were working at the bar the other night, you were — "

"Undercover. Yes." As she slid into the seat, she frowned when Thorne stopped dead in his tracks and fixed her with a look of disbelief.

"What? If this guy is as violent as you say, why the hell would you risk your life like that?"

Chey wasn't sure why he sounded so pissed. "C.S. only targets men. I was merely there to observe and report if I saw anything."

"Bullshit," he snapped, his expression turning thunderous. "What if he found out you were watching him? Just because he's only attacked men doesn't mean he won't be less hostile with you."

She grunted and gestured toward the passenger seat as she cranked up. "I'd like to get there *today*, if that's okay with you."

Though it was clear he looked like he wanted to argue, he shook his head and rounded to his side of the car. Once he was seated, she pulled off.

"Did you at least have backup there?" Thorne asked, turning to her.

She glanced at him out the corner of her eye. "Is that relevant?"

"Hell yeah."

Returning her attention to the road, she considered her words before responding. "There are more than three dozen bars in this city alone. That doesn't include nightclubs. We simply don't have the numbers to double up if we're to find this guy."

Without looking at him, she could practically feel the seething rage in his eyes as they bore into her. "That's such bullshit." Instead of commenting further, however, she was thankful when he turned away from her. With his arms crossed, he was silent for all of three seconds. "Why keep this from making the news? The city needs to be alert with some raging lunatic on the loose."

Chey didn't bother correcting him. C.S. wasn't a lunatic. He'd managed to elude them for five years. Not only was he skilled enough to have kept multiple victims from identifying him, but he stalked and hunted his victims until he found the perfect moment to strike when they were secluded. Such a feat took a grand amount of cunning and patience, something a madman on a killing spree wouldn't have.

"In Asphodel, news of these brutal attacks had spread so quickly that the people were in an uproar. The tip line was ringing off the hook as people reported any and every individual who they thought looked suspicious. It impeded the investigation and slowed their search. It wasn't until the first body showed up here that we learned he was capable of traveling between regions." She shot him a pointed look. "You know what that means."

He grunted a curse. "Then he has close ties with either my family or one of the other ones."

She nodded in agreement. "Now that the word is out, it won't take long for people to figure out he has that kind of political power to back him up. They'll start throwing accusations at everyone with a decent standing in society, which in turn will cause us to have an assload of lawsuits on our hands. The sooner we catch this guy, the sooner we can prevent chaos from ensuing."

Listening to the GPS's audio, she followed the directions as it guided her onto the interstate, and back off four intersections later. Thorne was mostly silent the rest of the ride, though she could sense he was still fuming.

She didn't speak to him, though. The silence gave her time to gather her bearings before approaching the crime scene. C.S. had everyone in the department on edge, but none more so than her. The fact that she hadn't been able to solve shit about it in five years was a failure she couldn't get over.

A half-hour later, Chey eased the car to a stop. She groaned upon seeing multiple vans bearing the logos of different news stations. Vaughn was right about the shitstorm brewing. It was already too late to keep the media from running their stories, so her only hope was that they could find C.S. before things got worse.

"Look…" she said on a sigh. "When we get out, keep your head down and don't say a word. Any questions you have, I'll answer after we get back in the car. Just…please don't draw any attention to yourself. My job is riding on the line already."

When his lips parted in question, she scowled, making him pause. Then, he nodded in reluctance. "You got it."

Grudgingly trusting his word, she got out and walked toward the scene. There was caution tape sealing off a wide alley between a small bakery and an antique shop. The crowd of reporters and other onlookers was tough to get through, but she forged on. A handful of officers in uniform were keeping guard, and with a short nod, they lifted the tape to allow her and Thorne to pass.

Vaughn was already at the back of the alley with the forensics team. Though his back was to her, he must have sensed them approaching when he turned. His hard gray gaze landed on her. "It's about damn time," he said, his lip curling upon seeing Thorne. "Why is he here?"

Chey grunted. "We didn't have time to break the spell, since we came straight here. Catch me up."

Despite the death glare he was receiving from her partner, Thorne merely stood with his hands in his pockets, appearing nonchalant as he stared right back at Vaughn. "Victim is an incubus — no wallet, so no identification. Cause of death was blunt force trauma to the head, but he took a beating prior to the killing blow." He moved to crouch near the body, and with a gloved hand, he peeled back the white sheet covering the victim.

Chey made sure to keep her expression blank as she looked over the face that was so badly beaten that it would be impossible to identify him from looks alone. The white T-shirt he wore was stained with blood, though his killer had sliced it open to reveal his chest. Still red, the initials were carved right between his pecs.

As Vaughn continued to fill her in on the details, she followed him around the alley toward each of the markers on the ground. Every bit of blood splatter was tagged, including the small pool that had a footprint in it. She rounded back to the victim and went on her haunches to inspect him closer.

She had to force back a grimace. There was something different about this crime scene. Quite a few things, actually. For one, C.S. had never before used a weapon. Instead, he'd strangled the victims — after using them as a punching bag. She turned a frown up at Vaughn, who stood over her with folded arms. "Have you recovered the murder weapon?"

He jerked his chin over toward a nearby dumpster. "Crowbar. Must have tossed it before taking off."

Chey rose and circled back to each marker of blood. More than once she cast her gaze to the corpse, taking in the angles. Her frown deepened. "C.S. has been clean all this time. Violent, but with minimum bloodshed." She returned to them.

"You think he's escalating?" Vaughn asked, peering down at the body.

"No. If that were the case, he'd be getting better." She glanced at the footprint, then the other markers. "This was sloppy. Rushed, like he was...desperate."

"Looks like the victim put up a fight," Thorne said, breaking his silence. He nodded toward the body's hands peeking out from under the sheet. "His knuckles are bruised. A big guy like this wouldn't go down easily."

"Stay out of this," Vaughn snapped, clenching his jaw. "We know how to do our job."

"Yes, but good eye pointing that out," Chey murmured, distracted. "That could explain the mess, but" — she shook her head — "this guy is wearing gym shorts, running shoes and a plain tee. These aren't the clothes you wear to get a drink or go dancing. He looks like he was going for a jog."

"So, this was a chance encounter," Vaughn said, catching on to her train of thought. "I get that, but why—?"

"C.S. hasn't had any *chance* encounters thus far. He's meticulous. He has a routine and sticks to it. All this time, we've pegged him as being a thrill seeker, but it doesn't look like he's killing for the media's attention. It just seems like these kills are...personal." She indicated the body. "Especially this one. Something triggered him to snap like this."

She spoke aloud to herself, but after a few beats, she aimed her next statement at Vaughn. "There's no wallet, no phone. Has anyone filed a missing person's report on him yet? Once we identify him, we might be able to find a connection between him and the suspect."

"Unfortunately, no. Shade's coming down to give a statement to the press. We'll get an image of his tattoo out to see if anyone might recognize it, but other than that, all we can do is wait."

"Tattoo?" she asked. She walked toward him when he bent down to pull the sheet back even lower, revealing a half-sleeve shaded tattoo of a lion with a flaming mane. She drew in a sharp breath, her blood running cold. "I know this man." Glancing up at Vaughn, she did her best to keep her tone steady as she said, "Alexius...something. We met at the bar the other night."

Vaughn straightened and fixed her with a stern frown. "You're certain?"

"Yes." Peering down at the body, she shook her head. "We had an entire conversation about his tat being a tribute to his mother. We exchanged numbers to meet up for brunch, but..." She grunted and sent Thorne a narrow-eyed look. "I got caught up with other matters."

"A date, huh?" Vaughn drawled as he tugged the sheet back over the body. "I didn't know incubi were your type."

She snorted and nudged him in the side. "It's not like I can afford to be very picky now, can I?" When he scoffed and muttered something under his breath, she fished inside her pocket for her phone. She hadn't truly checked through her numerous missed calls and texts upon rushing to get there, but as she scrolled through, she checked the one text message from a number that hadn't been saved. Confirming that it was from Alexius, she dialed Alber.

"You know something?" he said without so much as a greeting. "I'm starting to believe none of you respect me. I give out the crystals for a reason, yet not a single one of you ever use it unless you lose or break your cell phones."

Chey hid a smile. "Forgive me, Exalted One. I have a phone number I need you to run. It belongs to the victim."

There was a series of loud clicks and tapping as Alber worked his technological magic. Then, he said, "Too easy. Alexius Barios, Elysium born and raised. Only one living relative, an older sister. And no, she hasn't reported him missing. I'm guessing with him being dead for only a few hours, she hasn't even noticed."

Pinching the bridge of her nose, she heaved a deep sigh. "Poor girl. We're going to have to bring her in for questioning. That's the worst part of it all."

"I don't envy you," he replied in a solemn tone.

"Can you find his phone's location? It's possible he was just going out for a jog and left it at home, but if there's a chance C.S. stashed it away, we might be able to find some prints. It's a long shot, but at this point we have to try everything in the books."

"Don't worry. This bastard can't hide from us forever. I'll call you back if I get a hit."

As Chey ended the call, she frowned down at Alexius. She'd forgotten all about agreeing to meet with the handsome incubus. After spending several hours scoping a few bars in the area for anything out of the ordinary, she'd reported that she would be turning in for the night. However, Alexius had approached her at that point, offering to buy her a drink. While it was true that she didn't really go for the male equivalent of her species, she'd accepted, and they'd struck up a conversation, one that had revealed they'd had a lot in common—including a similar interest in dating to mate.

They'd exchanged numbers with arrangements to meet the next day, but of course, she'd gotten caught up with Thorne and his drama.

A selfish part of her found sick humor in the dark twist of fortune. She'd first complained that her potential dates thus far had been jerks for either standing her up or ghosting her, but her latest one had wound up dead. It was as though the fates were determined to have her turn into a sex zombie. If such was the case, whichever bastards were in charge didn't have to start taking lives to keep her single.

Shaking her head in dismay, she sent a silent apology to Alexius. Then, as though some cruel cosmic joke was just itching to mock her even more, she felt the first light stab of a cramp working its way through her abdomen. She clenched her jaw and willed it to go away, but she knew from recent experience it would only grow worse in the coming hours.

"Fuck," she whispered as she zipped her jacket and shoved her hands into her pockets. She did her best to apply some kind of pressure to soothe the slow mounting pain, but it was a failed attempt. The men around her didn't even have to be horny. The lack of mating scent on some of them filled her senses until she had to force herself to focus on doing her job.

Vaughn was the first to notice, being closest to her. His eyes darkened in response as he licked his lips. "You're killing me here," he murmured, shifting himself in his jeans. A collection of pale brown scales formed on his neck and crept up his jaw, revealing his naga blood — a species of serpentine demons who could take on a cobra or humanoid form.

"There's no on or off switch," she sighed, moving away from him. Like Thorne, Vaughn was all rugged good looks and raw sex appeal, but she'd never crossed that line with him. After graduating from the academy, she'd taken a personal oath to never sleep with a coworker. While there were no strict rules against fraternization, she'd known early on that she'd wanted to climb the ranks as a professional, a feat that would have been difficult had there been rumors floating around about her fucking her way up the ladder.

As though reading her mind, he once again stepped toward her and lowered his voice to where only she could hear. "Don't push yourself too hard. I know how you feel about mixing business with pleasure, but if it comes down to it, you know I'm willing to lend you a hand. It's got to beat fooling around with that bastard over there."

Chey snorted and shook her head. It wasn't the first time they've had that particular conversation, nor would it be the last. "I'll be fine. Let's just focus on getting through this 'shitstorm', as you put it."

As she walked away, she didn't hear the entirety of his grumbled response, but she caught another side-eyed glare he aimed at Thorne.

Chapter Nine

It had been one headache of a day. After hours of speculation, processing, interviews and still getting nowhere with the case, all Chey wanted to do was down a bottle of wine and hide under her bedsheets as she and Thorne drove away from the office.

She supposed that the only positive about the day was that he'd been good on his word and had done his best to stay out of the way, though more than once, each time he spoke, Vaughn had something slick to say about it. It'd gotten to the point where she'd had to tell her partner to back off, which in turn had landed her getting reprimanded by their boss, Shade. The man had sent her on suspension until she got her shit taken care of.

She'd known she would face consequences for bringing an outsider to a crime scene, but damn if her ears weren't ringing from the tongue-lashing she'd received. Not only that, but the cramps from her neglecting her needs had grown to where she could no longer ignore them.

With a heavy sigh, she parked the car in an empty lot, away from the nearest streetlight. Still gripping the wheel until her knuckles turned white, she gritted her teeth against the pain in her abdomen.

Next to her, Thorne was silent, though he had a knowing look in his eyes as he took off his seatbelt. Without a word, he undid the button of his pants.

Closing her eyes, she slid her own off. As reluctant as she was to use him again, a part of her quivered with excitement, proving she wasn't as repulsed as she wanted to be. Gods below, both times she'd had sex with Thorne had been mind-blowing. The noises he made, the rough touch of his hands, the orgasms that literally took her breath away—it was everything a succubus could want.

More than that, when she wasn't focused on her hatred of him, she'd learned he was actually...kind of decent. He'd been laid-back and casual ninety-five percent of the time since she'd been stuck with him. He hadn't done much complaining, nor had he freaked out every five seconds as anyone else would have done. Even when they'd been deterred from finding his employee, he'd been patient and mostly well behaved as she'd worked. And whenever they'd have a normal conversation, despite her insulting and belittling him, he took everything in good humor.

It made it difficult to remember why she shouldn't be enjoying his presence, why she shouldn't want to know more about him.

Gemma, a cruel voice reminded. *Never forget Gemma.*

Swallowing hard, she forced back all thoughts and worries as she reached to take Thorne's dick in her hand. He drew in a short breath, releasing it on a soft moan as she stroked him.

Those molten brown eyes watched her, his lust teasing her senses. *This doesn't mean anything*, she warned herself. It was just sex, a fruitless means to take the edge off her hunger.

Thorne clenched his jaw, turning his face away from her. "I know," he said in a quiet voice. There was an edge to it, an odd sort of annoyance she couldn't dissect.

Then, she realized she'd voiced her thoughts instead of keeping it inside. As embarrassing as it was, she didn't apologize, nor did she try to take back the words. There was no point. They both knew what this was, and neither should have had an issue with it.

Refusing to acknowledge the lie, she leaned over the center console and took him in her mouth. He held his breath as she drew her lips downward, taking in as much as she could before going back up. Then down. Then up. She swirled her tongue around his swollen head. On her next descent, she relaxed and took every inch of him until she felt the tip touch the back of her throat.

Thorne choked out a curse and placed a tentative hold on the nape of her neck. When she started to move faster, he tightened that hand, tangling it in her hair in silent encouragement. It wasn't until she felt she'd drenched him enough that she sat up and climbed to his side of the car.

As he scooted the seat back as far as it could go, Chey straddled him while he angled his dick upward. Gripping his shoulders, she sank onto him, wasting no time rolling her hips.

Minutes later, they were both panting at the sensation of him sliding inside her. As though unable to help himself, he wrapped his arms around her, pulling her as close as possible as he buried his face in her neck.

Chey moaned at the feeling of those sinful lips, kissing and nibbling until she started to make little mewling sounds of need.

"You feel so good, Chey," he murmured, the slick warmth of his breath fanning her damp skin. He slid his hands down to palm her ass, squeezing handfuls of her flesh.

Groaning in response, she rode him faster. He threw his head back, the thick veins in his neck straining with how close he was to release.

She dug her nails into his shoulders, leaned forward and bit his earlobe. He stiffened and erupted inside her, his climax coaxing her to come a split second later. By the time her breathing settled, he was gently rocking into her, still hard. His hands were everywhere as he stroked her back.

When his fingertips grazed the scar where one of the bullets had gone straight through her, she went still, a fresh surge of that old pain resurfacing. She none-too-gently climbed back into her seat and shoved her legs into her pants.

"Chey," Thorne started, placing a light touch to her arm.

She snatched it away, banging her hand on the window in the process. "Fuck off," she bit out, refusing to look at him.

He growled, a rough sound that made her finer hairs stand on end. Faster than she could react, he reached over and jerked the key out of the ignition, shutting the car off. "I'm tired of playing this game with you. I want you to tell me exactly what it is that I did to you all those years ago. You can threaten or insult me all you want, but we're going to stay right here in this spot until you tell me."

Snapping a glare at him, she curled her hands into fists on her lap. "You wanna know so bad? Thirty years ago, there was a girl who lived next door to you. Her name was—"

"Gemma," he said, interrupting her with a roll of his eyes. "The psycho. Why did I know it had something to do with her?"

Chey reeled back. "Psycho? Have some respect, you son of a bitch."

Thorne shifted to face her, his face set in grim lines. "Have some respect? She stalked me for a year before I got a restraining order on her, and even then, she wouldn't leave me the hell alone."

"Liar," she snapped, though the tremor in her voice revealed her uncertainty.

That…was new. Lying was the one thing Thorne didn't do. He was always brutally honest to the point where it made him seem like an asshole. He didn't give a damn about impressing other people or even telling white lies to comfort someone. If he didn't believe in his own words, he wouldn't bother saying them.

However, even knowing that, Chey didn't want to believe him. She *couldn't* believe him. Instead, she kept a hard expression and demanded, "What are you talking about?"

Thorne scoffed. "Exactly what I said. I always thought she was a nice girl—the shy, quiet type. Never really said more than two words, but she was polite. That was in the beginning." He shuddered, scrunching his face in disgust as though an ugly memory had resurfaced. "I started to get these little...trinkets outside my door. Handmade bracelets, keychains — just random things. After a while, they turned into letters from a secret admirer, talking about how we were destined to be together and all kinds of weird shit."

Chey grunted, dread sinking to the pit of stomach. "That doesn't mean it —"

"I knew it was her," he cut in with a glare. "Every time I'd step out of my apartment, she just so happened to be doing the same. When I went down to the gym, she was there. Same goes for the pool, the garage...all that. Eventually I got sick of it and told her to knock it off, but that didn't do shit but make it worse. She started following me everywhere, harassing me and telling everyone I knew — including my father — that we were engaged, she was pregnant and an assload of other shit. At the end, I finally filed for a restraining order, which forced her to move out. Not long afterward, she violated the order by destroying my car and breaking into my apartment. The police literally had to drag her away kicking and screaming. I've never seen or heard from her again, but for years I was judged and looked at like *I* did something wrong — even by my own family."

He tilted his chin to an annoyed angle. "Is that why you're so hellbent on treating me like I'm some kind of insect? Let me guess... You were friends with that crazy broad and she told you all kinds of bad stories about me."

Feeling like she'd just been dropped into a pool of ice water, the rage that had filled her while he spoke disappeared in a single moment. It left her numb on the inside, yet endless thoughts and questions ran through her mind at a hundred miles per hour.

Gemma had been her best friend since preschool. They'd lived next door to each other all their lives, had celebrated every birthday and holiday, had gone through all the trials and adolescent troubles during their middle and high school years. Despite having come from two different backgrounds, they'd always been close. After graduating, they'd gone to separate colleges and walked different paths of life, but their friendship had always endured.

Until Thorne had come along. She'd always believed that his careless flirting and seducing Gemma had been the cause of her becoming unhinged, but if what Thorne was saying was true, she'd been wrong. She'd gone thirty years despising him all for nothing.

She just couldn't accept that, not after everything that had happened — and certainly not without proof.

Without looking at him, she held her hand out. "Please give me the keys."

Thorne grunted in response. "So, it's true then," he said, sounding disappointed. Then, he scoffed and dropped the keys in her hand as if too disgusted to touch her. "You know what? Fuck you and everyone else who's always got an opinion of me without actually knowing me. Let's just go."

Chey didn't comment further. Instead, she clutched the keys in her hand and started the car. Thorne pulled one of her moves and blasted the car's radio to fill the silence.

However, not even the blaring music could block out the tormenting thoughts threatening to tear her apart.

Neither he nor Chey spoke a word the entire drive back to his place. They'd only stopped by her house for a few minutes for her to pack an overnight bag, and even then, they didn't so much as glance each other's way. Besides, what was there even to talk about? All this time he'd struggled to figure out why she couldn't stand him, yet the truth was that she merely disliked him because one of her friends had spoken ill about him. Her entire attitude toward him had been built on senseless gossip and falsehoods.

It wasn't anything he hadn't endured before. Countless other people had tried to slander his name, whether it was an ex-lover or someone close to them. Then, of course, there were the political scandals that had erupted a handful of times where his family had been targeted through him. All because he didn't go around wearing suits and ties, he enjoyed casual nights out and he spoke his mind freely, that somehow painted him as a rebellious delinquent.

No, his disappointment in Chey was…conflicting. They hardly knew a thing about each other, and if not for the fact that they were bound, he doubted they would have ever met. Well, met again. She didn't owe him a damn thing, nor he her.

Despite that, after seeing through her for the first time, something in him had changed — not anything drastic, but the small type of switch that made him realize he didn't really dislike her presence anymore. In fact, it had made him worry that he really had done something horrible to her in the past that had caused years of pain.

Yet, the true problem was so damn basic and childish. It infuriated him that he'd expected more from her.

With a soft sigh, he unlocked the door to his condo and stepped inside, waiting for Chey to close it before moving forward. She held the communication crystal in her fingers, and the soft glow from it told him she was talking telepathically to someone on the other side.

Uncaring, he went upstairs, glad when instead of being stubborn, she followed him in silence. He had no intentions of lingering there. The bathroom downstairs was much smaller than the one connected to his bedroom, meaning he could shower in peace without her needing to be inside.

With that thought in mind, he grabbed a change of clothes and returned to the main floor, then entered the bathroom. Still, Chey didn't say a word—not even a grumbled curse or a roll of her eyes.

He supposed he should have been glad she wasn't nagging his ear off, but as he stared at the closed door, a cold feeling of longing started to worm its way through his chest. Rather than dwell on it, he stripped and stepped into the shower, not minding the biting chill of the water before it warmed up.

When he finished and let Chey inside, he made himself useful by ordering a pizza for them. As much as he wanted to ignore her existence, he wasn't *that* much of an asshole. They'd both gone the entire day without eating and adding hunger on top of the tension between them wasn't helping one bit.

While he sat outside the door waiting patiently for her to finish, he scrolled through his Fangsbook feed to pass the time. Nearly an hour later, she stepped out of the bathroom, a cloud of steam surrounding her.

Thorne spared her a minute glance. For several moments, he forgot all about why he wanted to ignore her. She hadn't washed her hair, instead choosing to pull the thick mass of curls into a high messy bun, though a few loose tendrils framed her face. She wore an overly large T-shirt and loose pajama shorts, complete with socks that were two different colors. If he hadn't known her, he would have assumed she was a college freshman getting ready for a girls'-night-in sleepover. It was positively the most non-sexy getup he'd ever seen.

And yet she looked so damn innocent and adorable that he just couldn't find it in him to turn away. The more primitive side of his genes begged to rip the whole outfit apart and take her right there against the wall, while the more logical part of his brain continued to rationalize why he was supposed to be upset with her.

In the end, stubbornness won, because as much as he wanted to fuck Chey until her voice went hoarse from screaming in pleasure, he just couldn't get over the fact that she'd gone thirty years hating him for no reason other than idle gossip. After all the shit he'd been through in life, he had nothing but contempt for people like her—especially someone who was close friends with a woman who'd made his life hell.

With her bag thrown over her shoulder, she peered up at him and opened her mouth to say something, but she paused when the orb in her free hand started to glow. "Erm…can I step outside to take this?"

Thorne rolled his eyes. "It's a telepathic link." Even as he grumbled, he led her toward the patio.

When she stepped outside and slid the door closed, he leaned against the wall and once again pulled out his phone. However, he couldn't bring himself to focus too much, for against his will, his gaze kept trailing toward Chey.

"Fuck," he muttered, running a frustrated hand through his hair. Never before had he been so distracted by a female. As many times as he'd picked on his eldest brother when Rhys had first met Remi, he supposed what he was experiencing toward Chey was payback. He wanted to argue that these circumstances were different. Rhys had been an uptight workaholic who'd been drowning beneath the weight of the world. When he'd met Remi, the total opposite of what he was, the two had balanced each other out. It only made sense that both would fall head over heels.

Thorne, however, lived his life carefree. He was content and happy. Not once had he stopped to wonder what it would be like to develop an attachment to someone, because he'd never had a desire to do so. Hell, even now he still wasn't interested in taking a step in that direction, but in the brief time he'd spent with Chey, he couldn't keep denying that he'd developed some kind of attraction to her that went beyond the physical sense. He just wasn't sure how to proceed, certainly not now after learning the truth about her.

There was a knock at the door that stirred him from his musings, and he called for the deliverer to enter. The young man's mouth was agape as he stared in awe around the condo, making Thorne snort with pride. "You can set that on the coffee table."

He did as told, still entranced by his surroundings. Thorne paid and gave him a generous tip, then waited for him to leave before turning to the patio. His stomach growled, and he was prepared to tell Chey to wrap up her conversation or bring it inside.

However, he froze at the sight of her sitting on her bottom, her knees drawn up with her arms wrapped around them. Alarmed, he opened the door and stepped outside. The scent of her tears hit him a split second before her sorrow did. It was suffocating.

"Chey," he murmured, moving to sit next to her, while still maintaining a safe distance. Even while crying, he wouldn't put it past her to lash out at him for being too close.

She didn't answer right away, just continued to cry into herself. He was patient and quiet the entire time. When her quiet sobs turned into scattered sniffles, she drew in a shuddering sigh. "I didn't want to believe you," she whispered, her voice filled with an agony that made him want to wrap her in his arms.

Instead, he watched her from where he sat. "What made you change your mind?"

Raising her head but not looking at him, she indicated the crystal on the floor a few feet away. "I had Alber dig up your case."

At that, Thorne couldn't leash the irritation that once again rose. "Because my word alone isn't good enough, right?"

"I had to be sure." She blew out a shaky breath and used her fingers to wipe her face. "Gemma and I were closer than sisters. We'd known each other our whole lives. After college, she had so much going for herself. She'd just started a really good internship, her parents spoiled her with a brand-new car, this condo, her schooling—everything. She was really living every young adult's dream, while I had moved to the other side of the region. We hadn't seen each other for a while, so one day when I'd saved up enough sen, I decided to visit. Even by plane it was almost a full day's trip. That's a long time for a young succubus to go without sex."

She turned to him with a pointed look and waited for him to give a slow nod of understanding before continuing. "By the time I got to the lobby, she'd been just making her way home from work. I don't know if you sensed my pheromones or if we were just two horny demons near each other, but I turned around and there you were—just a devil across the room with this goofy, cocky grin on your face."

As she described it, a scenario popped in Thorne's head, a distant memory from the most forgotten crevices of his mind. A blurry figure came into focus, a woman he'd seen from across the room that he hadn't been able to take his eyes off of. Those tell-tale golden eyes had filled him with a hunger right on the spot.

"The janitor's closet downstairs," he murmured, recalling the way she'd zoned out the other day after looking at it. The memory of him first seeing Chey shifted to where he'd had her bent over against the wall. Just that brief flash was enough to turn him on.

"Yes," she said, looking away from him. "That's where it happened. I never knew you were the crush Gemma was giddy over for weeks, so you can imagine how awkward it was when we stepped out and she was standing right there."

Thorne snapped his fingers. "I remember that."

"Do you?" She fixed him with a dry look. "So, you remember slapping me on the ass and saying thanks before walking off?" At his guilty silence, she shook her head. "Back then, I didn't know why she'd started acting differently. All of a sudden, she told me she was too busy to see me that day, never mind the fact that I was supposed to be staying with her. I had to get a hotel room. Afterward, she wouldn't speak to me, never returned any of my calls or texts and blocked me from all social media."

When her shoulders sagged, Thorne grew bold enough to sidle closer to her. She peered at him, but thankfully didn't argue against it. "Did she ever explain why she cut you off?"

Chey turned her head away, shielding her face from him. "No. That probably went on for over a year. Then one day, I got a call from a random number."

"Gemma, I'm assuming?"

She nodded. Her voice began to shake, so it took several attempts to clear it before she spoke. "She was in town and had asked me to meet her somewhere. I knew something was wrong. I could hear it in her voice. I thought maybe she was in trouble or she'd gotten her heart broken or something."

Thorne grunted. "Sounds like you still cared, even after she'd ghosted you."

"Of course." She brought her elbows up to rest on her knees, then buried her head in her hands. "You don't just let go of a friend you've known all your life. I rushed to meet her that same day. Looking back, I was so stupid for going. I should have known something was off. It was so late at night and the park we'd agreed to meet at was creepy, even by Sheolic standards. When I saw her, she looked so…different, like she hadn't been taking care of herself."

When she fell silent, Thorne placed a hesitant, light hand on her back. Her shirt was so thin that when he stroked her in a soothing motion, his fingertips grazed that raised scar. He almost dreaded to hear the rest of the story, because her sorrow combined with how crazy Gemma had turned out to be, he could almost guess its ending.

"She started accusing me of ruining her life. She'd lost everything because of me. You two were in a happy relationship until I came along and stole you away, and... It was a lot. I just stood there completely clueless. I'd felt so guilty over screwing her boyfriend, but even when I apologized and tried to tell her I had no idea, she wouldn't listen. Next thing I knew, she pulled a gun on me. She didn't even hesitate as she fired away."

Chey's voice broke once again as she caved into herself, though she didn't have a sobbing cry. Hers was quiet, the only indication of her holding it back was the sight of her fingernails digging into her own skin. It was almost like she was trying to physically hold herself together.

All Thorne could do was throw his arm over her shoulders and pull her into his side. It was an awkward position for them both, given that neither were the comforting type. However, he didn't mind one bit when Chey relaxed into him, clutching his shirt as though afraid she'd drown if she let go.

Minutes later, she released a soul-deep sigh. "I...I really thought I was going to die that night, terrified and alone. Her eyes glaring down at me as she watched me bleed out is the last thing I remember. It took weeks for my body to heal enough for me to leave ICU. One of the bullets had gone straight through, but the other one had become lodged, just barely missing my heart. By the time I was able to maintain consciousness, I'd learned that Gemma had taken her own life the same night that she shot me — and that was that."

They sat like that for a long time, him rubbing a soothing hand up and down her arm, her leaning into him as she fought to regain control over her emotions. He didn't need to know much about her to assume that she wasn't someone who allowed herself to be vulnerable. She was too proud, too independent to need someone to lean on. The fact that she was opening up to him about such a critical part of her past filled him with a startling amount of appreciation. He relished in the fact that she trusted him on such an intimate level.

It also opened up a new world of feelings that terrified him to his core, yet he didn't want to push it away anymore.

He sensed the moment Chey finally managed the gather her bearings. She sat up, but she didn't move away, for which he was pleased. "All this time, I blamed myself for Gemma going off the deep end, and when that wasn't enough, I shifted that resentment toward you. Do you know that if you type your name in Boogle, you'll find a bunch of articles and blogs about how the youngest Lucifer is the ultimate bachelor? That, mixed with what Gemma had told me, was what led me to believe that you'd initiated contact with her. And had it not been for you, she wouldn't have..."

Thorne didn't take offense. Not anymore. While he had been livid that Chey had believed someone else's words over finding out for herself, given the circumstances, he could understand why.

She turned her gaze up at him. Her eyes shimmered with unshed tears, making the dark color twinkle in the most beautiful way. "I never thought I'd say this but...I'm sorry for the way I treated you. It was — "

He cut her off by pressing his lips against hers. It was intended to be a soft touch, a barely-there brush of the lips to silence her apology. He'd never been a kisser. His encounters had always been a quick wham-bam —

no kissing, no unnecessary touching, no intimacy whatsoever.

With Chey, however, he couldn't find it in himself to pull away. Despite her being hesitant and stiff as if the act were just as foreign to her, her lips were soft and damp, making him lean into the kiss.

When he pulled back, her eyes were wide with surprise. Slowly, she reached up and placed her fingertips to her lips. A touch of uncertainty waded through him. He had no idea what her reaction would be. She was so unpredictable that he wasn't sure if she was going to close herself off to him and kick his ass or what.

To his utter relief, a flicker of gold lined her irises. "Do it again," she whispered.

Chuckling, he took her chin in a light hold and leaned forward, kissing her once more. It was another timid, slight touch of the lips, but only for a moment. When she let out a soft sigh and melted into him, all caution was tossed over the balcony. He deepened the connection by prodding her lower lip with his tongue, circling the soft flesh until she opened up for him. Their tongues met, both of them taking turns exploring each other like pre-teens sharing their first kiss.

However, the lust that erupted between them felt far from pubescent. There was nothing innocent about the way he wanted to have her dripping wet and writhing against his tongue or the way he wanted her legs over his shoulders while he slid inside her until he became completely buried. The very thought made him groan.

Thorne damn near started to turn those desires into reality, but he refrained. It had nothing to do with the slight chill in the air and everything to do with the fact that he wanted to take Chey somewhere comfortable.

This time, his goal wasn't a quick fuck to ease some tension. There was no telling what was going to happen after they broke the spell the next morning. It was entirely possible they'd both end up going their separate ways and put this entire ordeal behind them. As painful a thought as that was, if such were to be the case, he'd gladly send her off with a memory that permanently replaced the first one she had of him.

Breaking contact, he smiled at her sound of impatience. "How about we take this upstairs?"

Chey gave him a half-smile and stood. "Fine, but you —"

Whatever she was about to say was replaced by a squeak of surprise when Thorne grabbed hold of her thighs and buried his face between her legs. The material of her shorts was so thin that when he touched his tongue to her pussy, he could feel the dampness already soaking through. He swirled and teased until she tangled her hands her hands in his hair, then pushed the cloth aside to finally taste the sweet scent tickling his nose.

Another squeak sounded, followed by a drawn-out moan. "Gods below," she whispered, tightening her hold on his head.

Thorne pulled away, eliciting another groan of exasperation. He rose and placed a hand on the back of her neck. "It isn't any of the gods you should be praising for this," he growled before slamming his lips to hers.

She had to go on the tips of her toes to wrap her arms around his neck, pressing her body flush against his. He made to backpedal her inside, but when that became too slow of a process, he pulled away enough to pick her up and toss her over his shoulder.

The breathy laugh ringing through his ear went straight to his groin as he carried her upstairs to his room. He gave her ass a nice slap before tossing her onto the bed. When he took his shirt off and made to cover her, she gave a saucy smile and rolled him onto his back.

"Oh, no you don't," he chuckled. "You did all the work the last two times. It's my turn."

Those golden eyes pierced right through him, the impish twinkle making his cock jump with excitement. "Maybe I like taking control." To prove her point, she finger-walked up his chest before placing her hand to his throat. She squeezed ever-so-slightly, smiling when she sensed the flare in his desire.

A rough growl rumbled through Thorne's chest before he rolled on top and pinned her wrists above her head. "Yeah?" he taunted, leaning forward to take one beaded nipple between his teeth. Just like that, through her T-shirt. "Not this time. Give yourself to me."

Chapter Ten

Chey groaned and gasped as Thorne teased her nipples. "No," she breathed. Still holding her wrists in one hand, he brought the other down to squeeze her breast. She arched in encouragement.

Leaning forward, he placed his lips to her jaw. "I will drag this out for days if I have to. Succumb to me." He gave her breast another squeeze, then pinched her nipple. The electric sensation zinged through her body and tingled at her very core. "I won't ask you again."

Chey sucked in a sharp breath, biting her lower lip when he nudged her legs apart to settle between them. "Make me," she gasped, raising her hips to grind into his.

He paused and lifted his head, shooting her a stunned look. "What did you say?"

Opening her eyes, she peered at him with a lowered gaze. "If you want me to submit to you, you'll have to earn it. So... Make. Me."

His dick twitched against her thigh, as if the thought of dominating her was exciting. Those sinful lips curved into a sexy grin, and to her dismay, he lifted off her. Her annoyance was short-lived, however, when she suddenly found herself flipped onto her belly with his weight straddling her upper thighs. She pushed up on her forearms, but he placed a hand between her shoulder blades to keep her from fighting.

He rocked into her in a way that had his erection sliding between the cleft of her ass. "I'll make you, all right," he growled in her ear. He smoothed his hands over her hips, up her back and under her torso to cup both of her breasts.

The feeling of being trapped and unable to do anything more than accept his touch had Chey aching from the depths of her soul. It was a sweet ache, though, the kind that could only be soothed by having him fill her until their bodies became one.

He took the end of her shirt and slid it upward, so slowly that it was on the tip of her tongue to tell him to get on with it. However, she could tell he wanted to take his time, and if she were being honest, so did she. Without the self-hatred and disgust filling her for enjoying his touch, she was at last able to revel in the experience. Oh, the guilt was still there, and perhaps it would take a long time for her to forgive herself for driving her friend to do such horrible things, but opening up to Thorne had allowed her to begin the final stage of grieving she'd avoided for thirty years. Acceptance.

As Thorne pushed her shirt ever upward, she jumped at the feel of his lips on her lower back, first toying with her dimples before trailing his tongue the same path up her spine. He tossed her shirt to the side and planted wet kisses back downward, all the way until he made it to the edge of her shorts. He didn't slide them off, though. Instead, he pulled one leg hole aside and lapped at her flesh.

Chey jerked, but he placed a hand to the middle of her back to keep her still. She couldn't help it as she raised her hips a little higher, giving him better access. With a groan of approval, Thorne continued to pleasure her as he inserted one finger into her pussy, right down to the knuckle.

Her breath hitched and she bit into the pillow. She wanted to come so badly. It was already there, hovering right at the edge, but it would never take that final leap into oblivion until Thorne had his release. It was unfair and utter agony in the best of ways, but such was the life of a succubus.

Turning her face to draw in a deep, gasping breath, she begged, "Thorne, please."

Thorne laughed against her. With one final kiss to her folds, he released her and sat up, giving her ass an affectionate pat. "That's all you had to say, Cheyenne."

Without giving her the opportunity to turn over, he once again jerked her shorts to the side and entered her in one smooth motion. Chey cried out in ecstasy. His rigid length filled every bit of her — and she loved it.

"Hell's bells," he hissed, stroking his hands across her back. He leaned forward, angling himself even deeper inside. He wrapped one arm under her chest and used the other hand to take her chin in a firm hold. Then, angling her head as far around as she could, he kissed her while rocking into her.

As a demon who fed off her partner's sexual needs, Chey liked to believe she'd experienced all there was to explore in the bedroom. From toys to food to bindings and everything in between, she'd tried it all at least once in her life. Each time she and Thorne had done the deed, it had been fairly tame compared to her more taboo adventures. However, it was the raw emotions she had toward him that made sex with him rock her world each time. No matter if he'd been a stranger across the room or a man she'd hated, a piece of her had gotten attached to him that very first day. She just thought she'd done well at removing that bad weed long ago.

"Whatever you're thinking about," he murmured against her lips, "stop it. Just relax."

"I wasn't—"

He nipped at her chin. "Don't lie to me."

Smiling to herself, Chey closed her eyes and focused on how good he felt sliding in and out of her. His movements were slow, though every so often he'd slam back inside with enough force to draw a gasp from her lips.

He planted his free forearm against the pillow near her head, half-caging her in. With each stroke, he'd let out a soft curse against her ear, which in turn sent shivers through her. Her climax was still so near, so ready to be unleashed that everything from the hardened peaks of her nipples to her swollen clit started to buzz with need.

Much to her relief, she could sense Thorne getting close too. Still, he refused to move more than that damnable turtle pace. She dug her nails into the comforter and raised her hips in tune with his gentle strokes, hoping he'd take the hint.

He did. Planting a line of kisses along the curve of her shoulder, he withdrew and pulled back enough to allow her to shift onto her back. Settled, he hooked an arm beneath each of her knees to spread them both wide. He didn't enter her right away, though, much to her chagrin. He merely flashed another cocky smile and peered down at her. "You're so wet," he purred in delight. "I could spend all night sitting here, just staring."

"Please don't," she breathed. "You're killing me."

Thorne laughed at that, the sound breaking off into a choked cough when she reached down to slide a finger through her folds. She parted them with her thumb and pinky, then used her middle and forefinger to rub her exposed clit in a circular motion. Of course, she didn't feel a thing, but she relished in watching Thorne's throat work on a swallow and his eyes darken to coal.

"I should be saying that," he rasped. He fisted his cock, still glazed with her dampness, and angled it at her slit. Mesmerized, he teased it a few times, pushing just the tip in before withdrawing. Then, his gaze became fixed on her hand as she dragged it up to her lips to taste herself. His arm trembled against her thigh.

The scent of his lust becoming unhinged slammed into her before he lunged inside her pussy.

Gone was the tender, unhurried man at her back, replaced by a fierce, wicked devil. There was nothing sweet about the ominous hunger burning in his eyes or the veins straining from his neck as he slapped hard strokes against her at a rapid pace. The glamour chain around his neck shimmered with a silver glow, growing brighter as he leaned forward and stretched her legs higher. His rhythmic pumps shifted to wild, furious thrusts of demand.

All Chey could manage were breathless gasps. She curled her hands over his waist, digging and scraping her nails into the slick skin. When she threw her head back and moaned his name, that silver chain shattered from the force of his raw power. His single horn came into view, and his irises were swallowed by a red ring, making him look every bit the ferocious demon pounding into her.

He made a choked sound and buried his face in her neck, pulling her sensitive skin between his lips. He didn't bite, for all she felt was rough suction and tongue as he latched on and exploded inside of her. She felt each delicious pulsation of his dick as it finally coaxed her orgasm. Arching forward, she cried as she came undone, digging her heels into his back as if it were possible to push him any deeper.

They were still a quivering mass of loose limbs tangled together minutes later. In that brief time frame, neither had looked away from the other. Thorne held her gaze as if the underworld would end if he blinked.

Likewise, Chey was just as transfixed. She couldn't find it in herself to look away. That...that wasn't just sex. Nothing about the emotions rolling through her made her feel like this was just another casual encounter with him.

At last, they both let out a deep breath at the same time. Thorne lowered her legs and relaxed, not quite laying on top of her, yet still nestled between her knees. He laid his head between her breasts, his ear pressed to her scar. For a while, she wasn't sure how to proceed. She'd stopped all the cuddling business long ago when she'd first given up on dating, along with the post-sex pillow talk and tender gestures. The intimacy of it all unnerved her the point where she wanted to bolt.

Perhaps sensing her rising panic, Thorne spoke in a mellow tone. "There's pizza downstairs. It's probably cold now, but we can eat and throw on another horror movie if you'd like."

Thankful for the distraction, Chey smiled and let out a quiet sigh. "That would be great."

Chuckling, Thorne sat up. He didn't move off the bed right away, though. Instead, he stared at her — specifically, her scars. Despite having accepted that he wasn't directly responsible for Gemma's actions, the pain behind her dearest friend attempting to murder her was still fresh. It was so hard to let go of years of self-loathing and regret in just one night. As wonderful as sex with Thorne was, once the excitement had died to embers, she was back to being filled with uncertainty and reluctance.

The only difference was that she no longer knew who to point the finger of blame at. It had always been herself and Thorne. Not once had she sat back and thought about holding Gemma accountable for her own acts. With the way everything had gone down, Chey hadn't wanted to believe that the innocent, sweet girl she'd known all her life could become so dark over a crush on some guy. She'd believed that had it not been for Thorne being unfaithful in a relationship — as well as Chey's own ignorance for sleeping with a taken man — Gemma wouldn't have broken.

And yet with the truth having been revealed, Chey's heart was torn. It seemed wrong to want Thorne in any way, but it didn't *feel* wrong. On the other hand, it felt like she was betraying Gemma all over again, even knowing she'd lied about her relationship with the devil and tried to kill Chey.

"I'm sorry for this," Thorne said, breaking through the mental battle she'd been fighting. Blinking in confusion, she watched as he traced a light finger over the scar on her sternum. "I wish..." He trailed off, a frown of concentration curving his lips as though he struggled to find the right words.

Chey took his hand in a light hold with every intention to push it away, but she hesitated. She wasn't a comforting type, nor did she enjoy being on the receiving end. Even so, she squeezed his fingers in what she hoped was reassurance. "Don't go there," she murmured. "Nothing we wish for will change the past. Trust me, I know. You'll only end up torturing yourself."

If he'd been a dog, his ears would have drooped. Instead, it was his shoulders. "Maybe I deserve some torture. You've gone all these years suffering this pain and resentment for me, while all this time I never even knew. It's like I got off easy. And it's not just you. The nymph who took my horn? I never gave a damn about who might get hurt because they decided to get attached to me, but now I can't help but wonder how many others there are. How many lives were altered or ruined because I fucked up, intentionally or not?"

When he met Chey's gaze, she swore her cold heart melted a bit. There was nothing but sincere remorse in his eyes, a drastic change from the mild annoyance or humor that usually lit them. It revealed a touch of compassion she hadn't thought him capable of, yet there it was.

"You know," she said, resisting the urge to cringe when she fingered both of her scars, "sometimes you have to reopen the scars of your past in order to heal them properly."

He fixed her with a disbelieving stare, then snorted in derision. "Yeah, which lame-ass drama did you steal that line from?"

Chey couldn't stop the grin splitting her lips. "I'm not telling you."

Sighing, he shook his head and stood, then held out a hand to help her up. "As corny as it is, it's a good sentiment. Come on. The pizza's getting even colder."

Chapter Eleven

"Holy shit," Chey murmured as Thorne neared the parking garage that was as big as his entire apartment complex.

In all her years, Chey had always heard about the infamous building that was so large it was physically impossible to capture its size in just one image, even from afar. The main building and its grounds stretched at least a mile in all directions, and if the jaw-dropping width wasn't enough to gawk at, the damn tower of the main building extended so far up into the sky that she got vertigo just from trying to spot where it ended.

"As you can imagine," Thorne explained, humor in his tone, "the space is necessary in order to accommodate the number of employees needed to keep up with the constant arrival and departure of souls. It's hard to believe that before this place was built centuries ago, the Lucifers hadn't relied on hiring people to do the work for them."

Chey turned her stunned attention to him as he parked. "You mean your family used to...what, count the souls themselves?"

He chuckled. "Count, document, fetch, release—everything. It was literally work-work-work every minute of the day."

"You're kidding." He shook his head in denial, making her scoff out a short laugh. "How? You have...what? At least a few thousand employees, going by this garage alone. I can't imagine there were an equal number of Lucifers, not to mention that your sister corporations wouldn't have been given to the Levis and the Dagons back then."

"No, but they had a completely different type of system, one that worked well for them but wouldn't thrive in modern times. With EUC founded, along with Hippieland and CEP, the soul collection industry has never been better."

"Wow, you almost sound...passionate."

His prideful smile turned sheepish as he stepped out of the car. "I love my job. Just don't go around telling people that. Gotta keep up appearances."

Snorting with humor, she followed behind him toward a bank of elevators that she could only assume led to the main building. As they waited for one to arrive, she turned at the rapid clack of heels striking the ground. Two women approached them—one with long pointed ears and a clubbed tail that swished with every step, the other with skin a deep shade of red and small random patches of iridescent scales that shimmered in the overhead lights.

The red woman glanced up, her eyes going bright. Giggling, she purred, "Good morning, Thorne."

The elevator arrived, and the four of them stepped onto the spacious platform. "Hello, ladies," he greeted, allowing them to step on before him. He pressed three of the dozens of buttons lining an entire panel.

Chey was nudged aside as the two women crowded around Thorne, each pressing one of his arms between their breasts. In a not-so-subtle display, the one with the ears curled her tail around his calf, stroking him through his denim in a suggestive manner. They took turns pouting about missing him in his absence. His wide eyes met her blank stare, though she turned her back and pulled up her Critter account on her phone.

For reasons beyond her understanding, there was an odd sort of pressure in her chest, though she refused to believe it was something as petty as jealousy. If she was envious over other women publicly groping him in such an intimate way, that meant she didn't feel quite as casual about him as she should.

And despite how her hateful opinion of him had changed overnight—more so in the frequent bouts of sex they'd had after dinner and shortly after waking up—she knew firsthand that nothing good could come from falling in love with Thorne Lucifer. The women who chose to walk that dangerous path never came out unscathed.

"Hey, enough of that," he scolded them. "We've talked about this before."

Chey tightened her grip on her phone. She shuffled into the corner, as far away as the spell would allow. The elevator dinged, and the two giggled, "See you later, Thorne," as they stepped off.

Alone, the silence between them felt even more awkward than their first night sleeping together. She didn't look at him. She *couldn't*, really. She was reluctant to feel that flare of pain again, the alarming signal that she'd already crossed into the uncharted jungle of feelings that shouldn't exist.

It was Thorne who spoke first. His voice was uncertain, as if he could feel the tense air too. "Chey, I...I'm sorry you had to see that."

Shrugging, she leaned her hip against the railing, still unwilling to glance up from her phone. "No need to apologize. You didn't do anything wrong."

"No, don't do that." He closed the distance between them, though he didn't touch her. "It's that female thing where you pretend like nothing's bothering you, yet secretly you're pissed."

In the most casual tone she could muster, she asked, "What is there to be upset over? I'm just scrolling through my feed."

From the corners of her eyes, she caught him running a frustrated hand through his hair. "Yeah... All right."

The remainder of the ride was spent in a near-choking cloud of discomfort. Chey was grateful when halfway through, a half-dozen other people stepped on, causing Thorne to move away or be crushed by a seven-feet-tall minotaur's backpedaling ass. A handful of buttons later, the two of them strode onto a loud floor that immediately reminded her of entering a subway station.

Despite the early hours, there were dozens of demons roaming back and forth in a hurried motion. Not a single one of them stopped or slowed their pace for a second, yet there was the occasional, "Good morning," or "How about that game last night?" There were even a few who rushed across the floor and somehow managed to balance a phone between their ear and shoulder, a pile of folders in one arm and a coffee tumbler or breakfast sandwich in the other hand. It was quite impressive.

Thorne led the way through the flow of pedestrian traffic. He stopped to turn down a carpeted hall with a set of security enhanced doors at the end. With a swipe of a green keycard, the doors opened to a separate floor that was just as busy yet much quieter. Three corners later, they were passing through an entire room full of perfectly lined desks, each about four feet apart.

Annoyance forgotten, Chey cocked her head in curiosity. The men and women seated at the tables were all dressed in the same uniform — a black cloak with a semi-pointed hood drawn over their heads. Continuing onward, they passed another room where more demons were dressed in a different fashion. They looked like everyday deliverymen, most of them wearing either a navy-colored jumpsuit or knee-length shorts with matching shirts.

"Those are our some of our charons who are about to take first shift," Thorne explained at her inquisitive stare.

"Is that really their uniform?"

"Yes. They're our transport crew."

She nodded in the opposite direction. "What about those guys?"

"Reapers." He swiped the card against another keypad. The door opened up to a warehouse-style room. One wall had head-to-waist glass windows where over two dozen tellers sat on the opposite side, clicking away at their computers or handing out clipboards, black orbs and gadgets that looked like tiny flashlights to the triple number of demons standing in lines. Another wall had more metal doors needing security clearance to pass through, though each one had a guard standing next to it.

"The left half of the doors are for our drivers," Thorne said to her. "The reapers go through the right side. Once they clock in, the charons are assigned a route for the day. The reapers head over there to the clerks to get a list of mortals on the brink of death. They're given those orbs to tag and collect souls before dropping them off with the charons."

Chey tried to imagine how such a thing would look. She'd never seen a soul before, but she pictured Casper-style apparitions floating around the human world while the reapers absorbed them into those tiny spheres. With a grunt, she shook her head. "*Ghostbusters* is all that comes to mind."

One corner of those sinful lips curved into a sideways smile. "Something like that."

She nodded at two passing reapers with their hoods drawn. As they walked away, she spotted their backs bearing the logo of a scythe. "Why are they dressed like that?"

"The cloaks are enchanted to make them invisible to living mortals."

"No, I get that. I mean why *that* style? Surely you could have come up with a something less cheesy."

At that, his smile turned amused. "Oh, that. It's just for appearances. When the humans die, their souls are confused and sometimes reluctant to accept what has happened. Humans have always recognized their image of a grim reaper as a symbol of death. When they see our guys dressed in the same fashion, they have a better understanding of their fate.

"Mortals are so delicate, mentally and physically. Immediately after their living form dies, they become terrified and lost. Even though it seems like a costume, our system ensures that they are comfortable and at peace until they reach their final destination, whether it be Hippieland or CEP."

"That sounds oddly considerate."

He pondered her words for several moments before shrugging as if he didn't care. However, she didn't miss the slight rise of color to his cheeks that gave away his false nonchalance.

She followed him a to large circular bar in the middle of the floor, where a handful of receptionists tended to the demons standing in their individual lines. "I can only assume you're referring to The Meadows by saying 'Hippieland'."

"It used to be called Gehenna, but apparently that was too disturbing of a name for a place that was supposed to bring peace. Now the Levis all have this obsession with spreading love and serenity and butterflies all across their region. Gods be damned if that crap doesn't give me cavities just from thinking about it."

With a humorous sound, she ignored the sneers and glares from nearby demons when she and Thorne skipped to the front of one line. The receptionist glanced up from her computer screen, then sat a bit straighter upon seeing Thorne. With a fond smile and dreamy look in her catlike eyes, she flat out disregarded the reaper she'd been assisting. "Good morning, boss."

With a small nod, Thorne replied, "Morning. I need you to call for someone. It's urgent."

Her smile stretched a bit too wide. In a tone with an underlying wicked promise that was impossible to miss, she drawled a sultry, "Anything for you, Thorne."

Chey was almost unable to restrain herself from gagging. Instead, she once again edged backward as far as the spell would allow. When it fastened around her neck just enough to warn her that she was close to her limit, she paused. Having felt it as well, he whipped his head around in concern.

Though it was a pitiful move that must have seemed petty to him, the distance was necessary for Chey. She didn't trust these new feelings that had developed, and she sure as hell wasn't interested in keeping them.

She didn't hear him sigh, but she caught the rise and fall of his shoulders just before he stuffed his hands in his pockets. He fixed her with a concentrated stare, one that was so unnerving, and yet she couldn't help but wonder what was going through his head.

Just as swift as the thought appeared, she forced it aside and focused her attention elsewhere. The clerk's sultry voice echoed through the overhead speakers as she called for a Tomas Pesci to approach the central floor. Thirty seconds later, a reaper with dark gray skin and slanted oblong eyes rushed toward them, his face set in grim lines. He twisted his lips in displeasure at the sight of his boss.

"Can we make this fast?" he demanded, the sour frown making it clear that he was in a rush. "There was a massive mine collapse in eastern Europe, which means I have to go digging through an assload of tunnels. I'm trying not to fall behind on my work."

"This won't take long," Thorne assured him as he walked past. "We'll take this to my office."

As it turned out, Thorne's private office was exactly what Chey had pictured in her mind the entire trip three floors up—one huge mancave, complete with a mini bar shining under a neon light on one side and a flat screen TV with several game consoles wired on the other. It was almost similar to his condo in a way that made her think this office was just as much as his comfort zone as where he rested at night.

Wasting no one's time by relaying every detail about what had happened in the last couple of nights, Thorne explained simply and clearly what he needed from his employee. He finished with, "So, do you think you can break this spell?"

Having absorbed everything, the man pondered the question while glancing between him and Chey with suspicion. "Is...Is this some kind of joke? Some test to prove myself or some shit?"

Thorne rolled his eyes, but Chey was the one to respond. "This is a serious matter. Can you help or not?"

"I mean...if it's just a binding spell, yeah." He shook his head. "What do I get out of it?"

"What?"

He shrugged in nonchalance. "Surely I get some kind of reward for not only being late for my shift, but also using my power—which I spent years studying, mind you—to help you two."

Chey scowled, but Thorne sighed in exasperation, as if having already expected as much. "What do you want?"

The man didn't even hesitate. "Two weeks' free pass topside."

"No," Thorne said just as quickly. "A ticket for one day topside is far too much a price, let alone two weeks."

"Then I want my own parking spot. All the decent ones are always taken before I can even—"

"Not under my control."

"Then...a week of paid vacation?"

At that, Thorne pretended to ponder the request. "Three days, and I won't tell Laura you're the one who threw up in her purse on New Year's Eve."

Tomas' eyes flew wide, a deep red blush staining his cheeks as he sputtered. "How did you... Ah, fuck. Fine, you have a deal. All right, let's get this over with. Show me this spell."

Just as they'd done for Quin, Chey and Thorne stepped as far apart as they were allowed. Tomas showed no emotion as he studied the invisible tether. He poked at it a few times, then flicked it as though testing its durability. Moments later, he drew in a deep breath and began murmuring words too muffled for Chey to make out.

The entire process didn't take any longer than twenty minutes. There was no dramatic flourish of the hands, no flash of magical light, not even so much as a tingle. Tomas finished by dusting off his hands and heading toward the door. "I want your authorized approval for three days off left in my locker by the time I clock out."

"Whoa, whoa," Thorne called after him. "Is that it? I don't feel any different."

Tomas waved that aside and continued onward. "It's done."

And that was it. The man exited the office, leaving the two of them alone. Chey peered up at Thorne in question, who only shrugged in response. Deciding to test it out, she moved away from him, cracking a small smile when her throat didn't tighten with the invisible collar.

Likewise, Thorne felt around his neck, sighing in satisfaction. "Well, that was...anticlimactic."

"He made it look so easy," she responded. "How come Quin wasn't able to do that?"

Thorne strolled toward his desk and sat down, then pulled out a single sheet of paper. As he began writing, he explained, "Magic is a general term we use, but it's actually much more complex than just throwing fireballs or casting a binding spell. There are different branches, each where only certain races can wield. Like many others, we devils don't have a natural affinity to magic, but with years of practice, we can develop some minor skills. Quin has been studying it since his teenage years, but his skills are still limited. I was hoping he could have helped us, but apparently the spell cast on us was more...high level."

That made sense. Chey's kind also weren't born to use magic, so she'd never taken an interest in taking courses to learn more about it. Why study something she couldn't use to the fullest, after all? Even so, Quin might not have been able to break the spell, but his knowledge aided in them learning exactly what kind of demon they could find to do it. She was grateful, nonetheless.

Moments of silence ticked by as Thorne finished writing out his letter, presumably the one granting Tomas his days off. Chey realized a bit belatedly that since she was no longer bound to him, there was no reason for her to linger. She refused to acknowledge the pressure in her chest, but when she opened her mouth to say goodbye, she found herself at a loss. It was just one word, one that had never before given her pause. 'See ya' was a more casual option that she used rather frequently, but even that just felt...odd.

She and Thorne weren't friends. They'd started out as two relative strangers who couldn't stand each other, and while the bitterness between them was no longer there, that didn't exactly make them buddies. They'd slept together a few times, but she was a succubus and he was a man who enjoyed casual sex, so it wasn't like there was a romantic connection either. Walking away should have been so simple, and yet...

She shook her head. "Well," she started with an inaudible sigh, turning away, "I'll let you get to work."

The pen in his hand went still as he jerked his head up, blinking in surprise. "You're leaving?"

And yep, he just made it more awkward. Giving a stiff shrug, she lifted her hands in confusion. "I..."

Once again, words failed her. He twisted his lips and drew his eyebrows downward, as if he too didn't quite know what to say. She couldn't fathom anyone topside or in the underworld would be able to just walk away without a bit of ineptness if they'd been thrown in an identical predicament.

Laying the pen down, he rubbed the back of his neck and stood. "I...I guess I'll show you the way out."

"That's okay," she murmured, sticking her hands into her jacket pockets to prevent herself from fidgeting. "I remember the way we came. I'm sure you have a lot of work to catch up on after...this."

"Chey," he started, only to break off with a small grunt, "it's the least I can do. Please."

The sincerity in his voice gave her pause. In truth, she hadn't been totally honest. EUC was one giant maze. Even if she'd managed to make it back toward the elevators, she had no idea which buttons would take her back to the garage.

"Okay," she breathed.

The smile he gave her didn't quite reach his eyes. It was a sad tilt of the lips, though for the life of her she couldn't gauge why. As eager as she was to get back to her own job and continue the hunt for C.S., a ridiculous part of her was reluctant to leave Thorne behind, especially when she had a feeling the two of them wouldn't be crossing paths again any time soon.

Thorne made quick work of folding his letter into an envelope and tucking it inside his jacket pocket before heading toward the door. Though neither of them spoke as they walked side-by-side, the halls containing dozens of demons walking to their destination filled the silence between them.

When they made it back to the central floor where more charons and reapers were making their rounds, her steps faltered as she turned a curious stare toward the guarded doors. Four of them opened at once, revealing a shimmering portal that would presumably take them topside.

Thorne got a good distance away before realizing she'd stopped to gawk at them in fascination. Eight people were allowed entry, their bodies disappearing the moment they stepped through. Then, the doors closed again. Seconds later, the same thing happened as more were given access.

"Would you like to see what it's like?"

Startled, she turned her surprised gaze to Thorne. "You mean…topside?"

He nodded. "You seemed intrigued by the process of how we collect souls. If you want, I can show you in person."

"Is that legal?"

At that, he chuckled and gave a small shrug. "For others, no. We usually do virtual tour training for new employees to prepare them for the experience, but I have full authority here."

His tone didn't suggest he was bragging. He stated it in a matter-of-fact way, as though even if there were consequences, he couldn't give two shits.

Chey knew deep in her gut she should just say no. She'd already accepted that there was no need to spend any extra time in his presence, for her own sake. However, as her gaze once again roamed toward the opening and closing of the doors leading topside, her curiosity simply couldn't be ignored.

She'd seen videos and documentaries of human life topside. Even countless movies and TV shows she'd watched that were made by the mortals gave a clear visual of what it was like, but she'd always wanted to visit just once in her life. Not only that, but she'd been struggling to wrap her head around the entire process of charons and reapers capturing souls. A free, front row ticket to see it in action was impossible to pass up.

With an eager nod, she glanced at Thorne. "If you're sure it's okay…"

He beamed at that. "Wait right here."

Chapter Twelve

Both dressed in a solid black cloak with a pointed hood bearing the reaper's logo, Thorne and Chey stood in one of the lines to travel topside. Beside him, Chey practically bounced in anticipation. The sight made him smile.

In truth, taking her — a non-employee and first-time traveler — topside was more than enough to have his ass fried if Rhys found out. Thorne hadn't lied when he'd said he could do whatever he wanted. It was his division, after all. However, he'd never before taken anyone with him to the human realm, not unless he was traveling with his brothers to their yearly convention. It was just one of those rules that wasn't in black and white, yet no one dared to make such a bold move.

Even knowing that, should his eldest brother find out and reprimand him for it, he couldn't find it in him to care in the slightest. While he was genuinely pleased with Chey's open admiration for his department, it was the hidden desperate side of him that had formed the idea to bring her along. He was happy as hell not to be bound to her anymore, but the thought of her walking out of his office door had been... Well, he didn't want to put a name to the emotion he'd felt, but it hadn't been good. With her resentment gone, it had been so easy to grow accustomed to having her at his side. They had so much in common that he'd determined she was definitely the coolest person he'd ever met.

He liked her.

It was such a new feeling for him that he still couldn't tell what that meant for him, but he didn't dislike it. Chey was unlike anyone he'd ever met, even if he hadn't tried to get to know her on purpose. Having her walk out when he wasn't ready to say goodbye had just been...unacceptable.

When it was their turn to pass through the portal, Thorne nodded at the guard and passed the man his travel pass. He gave it a quick stamp and grunted, "Safe travels, boss."

"Are you ready?" he asked Chey.

Though her expression remained casual, she wasn't at all able to fight the twitching of her lips as she hid a smile. "Let's do this."

Chuckling, he took her hand in a light hold and pulled her through. The walls of the tunnel they stepped through held foggy patterns of gray magic, illuminated by luminescent overhead lights. Though they weren't walking, the portal had the sort of affect that made it feel as though the floor was carrying them forward. When they reached the end, they stepped through another shimmering portal, one that opened up into another giant warehouse-style area.

"Here we are," Thorne said, releasing her.

Chey glanced all around, frowning in disappointment. "This... This is topside?"

"Not quite. I'm giving you a tour, remember? This is what we call a Veil—a tiny space between Sheol and topside." He pointed on the far side of the room where dozens of blacked-out delivery trucks entered and exited a larger version of the portal they'd just come from. "Here is where the charons and reapers meet to exchange souls. While the reapers continue forward to the human world, the charons aren't allowed to go any farther. Once they make the hourly exchange, the reapers go back to collecting, while the charons deliver the souls to their next stop—EUC. The ones exiting the portal are either returning from one of our sister corporations or just now starting their routes."

"Wow," she murmured, taking in the bustling workers. "How long do they work? Do they have a fixed income or are they paid by the soul?"

"Our workers are paid hourly with the possibility of overtime. A typical shift involves eight hours with a max of five hundred souls per reaper, though it's rare that one person ever collects more than two hundred in one day. If they max out early, they get to clock out right away yet still get paid for the remainder of their shift."

"I get it. Is that so they don't get burned out?"

Thorne nodded. "That, and to keep our end of business running smoothly." He aimed the teleportation tool at a blank wall. "On to the next stop, shall we?"

When Chey tilted her head in confusion, he pressed a button to summon a separate portal that carried them forward through another tunnel, one that had a faint glow at the end that grew brighter each second. "What is that— Oh shit."

Chey recoiled when the two of them were suddenly encased in a blinding light. She shielded her eyes with her hands, wincing each time she tried to look.

Thorne had long ago gotten used to the sunlight of the mortal world, so it only took a second for his eyes to adjust. The portal had brought them smackdab to the heart of Los Angeles, California. The sidewalk they'd landed on was full of pedestrian traffic, yet not once did a passing human acknowledge their presence. Thanks to the glamour magic etched into their cloaks, they were invisible and shrouded with a spell that kept any mortal creature from bumping into them.

Glancing down at Chey, he chuckled to find her still shielding her eyes. "It'll pass," he informed her. "It only takes a few moments for your pupils to adjust, but they never will if you keep them covered."

"Why is it so bright? The movies I've seen were never this bad."

"Here." Without thinking, he took her wrists in a gentle hold and tugged them downward. She kept her eyes squeezed tight, and with a bit of coaxing on his end, she started to relax. Slowly, like a newborn blinking her eyes open for the first time, she squinted up at him until she was able to fully open them.

With the morning sun spilling over her features, all Thorne could do was stare in awe.

He found that her eyes weren't actually coal-black, as he'd always thought. They looked like twin pools of dark chocolate melting under the sun. Her lips were pinker and the highlighted points of her cheeks, nose and forehead gave a filtered affect.

All demons born in Sheol were adjusted to the permanent night sky. They could see just as well in the dark as humans could with light, even without electricity. Thorne had seen every inch of Chey both clothed and naked, and he'd known from the first night that she was a very beautiful woman. Standing before him in full illumination...

His heart throbbed, constricting his chest in a way that had him struggling to breathe.

Oblivious to his reaction to her, she took in the sights all around them. "Wow, this is...not much different than Infernal Regions. It's just as busy, and the smells are the same. I was thinking it would be more...human-y."

She continued speaking, but for the life of him, he couldn't bring himself to focus on what the devil she was talking about. All he could think about was how stunning she looked.

She must have known he wasn't paying attention, for when she finally looked at him, she frowned. "What's wrong? Is there something on my face?"

Closing his gaping mouth, he shook his head. "No, sorry. I spaced out for a minute there."

"Where are we?"

"Los Angeles, California. If we were in Elysium, we'd be on the far west coast, near the Acheron Ocean."

"Ah," she murmured in understanding, taking another look around. "So this is where all those human celebrities live?"

He smiled. "A good bit, but they're spread across the world. In this country, New York is another popular state for them in the northeast."

"Nice. So, where do we go from here?"

He pointed across the street at a large hospital. "There's actually a few about to pass momentarily, so you'll get to see what happens up close..."

At the way her eyes went wide with panic, he trailed off, wondering if he'd sounded too excited. "A hospital," she said in a hushed tone, a tremor in her voice.

All of a sudden, Thorne had a guess for where her unease had come from. He recalled her telling him about how she'd spent weeks all alone after being shot. Then, he remembered how she'd quite harshly said she'd refused to go to a clinic to get her head wound patched up. At first, he'd thought it was her being too stubborn and annoyed to bother going. Now, however, he had a feeling it was fear that made her want to avoid it.

He'd wanted to impress her by showing her how the reapers worked in person, but he was beginning to regret his hasty decision. The last thing he wanted to do was bring up those dreadful memories. "Perhaps this wasn't the best choice on my end. The good news is, mortals can die anywhere, so we can go somewhere else—"

"No," she cut in, giving a hard swallow. "This is... This is fine."

He frowned. "Chey, you don't have to. Really, there are other—"

Once again, she interrupted him in a soft tone. "Thirty years is long enough to hold a grudge against a place that's supposed to heal you...right?" At his concerned look, she squared her shoulders and nodded to herself. "I can do this. I *want* to."

Though he could still sense her nervousness, he could also tell she wasn't lying. She wanted to conquer her fear once and for all, and he respected her determination. "Okay, but if it gets to a point where it's too much, all you have to do is say the word."

She nodded once more. "Lead the way."

And so he did. Making sure she was right on his tail, he waited for a red light before strolling across the street toward the hospital. The black orb given to reapers not only allowed them to capture souls, but it also acted as a beacon to locate them. As he held it in one hand, he followed the guide up three flights of stairs and made several turns until he reached his destination.

There was a room all the way at the end of the hall where the door was ajar, but the blinds of the window were drawn open. A doctor and a nurse stood outside with grim expressions as they waited patiently for the family inside. Though his powers were dulled upon entering the human realm, he could still catch remnants of the choking sadness as the family cried over their lost relative.

Chey stood next to him and peered through the window. Though the mortal had been dead for several minutes, it was clear that from the wrinkles and aged spots on his skin that time had been the cause of death.

While the family hugged and cried into one another over the old man, a white apparition in one lone corner watched them from a distance. "Whoa, is that the soul?" Chey whispered, leaning forward for a better view.

"Yes."

The ghostly figure waved its arms and opened its mouth as though to try to get anyone's attention, though it was clear from its features that it was utterly confused as to why it was being ignored.

Turning his head, Thorne spotted one of his reapers rushing down the hall, his gaze fixed on his clipboard. As he neared, he stopped to scowl at the two of them. "For the love of the gods. Don't tell me I just ran up all those stairs for nothing."

Thorne snorted at his worker. "We're just here to watch. The soul is all yours."

The man sighed in relief and slipped inside the room. He withdrew the black orb and approached the soul. It turned confused eyes to him. The soul glanced down at its phantom-like form, then the dead body lying in the bed.

"It's time to go," the reaper said in a solemn, apologetic tone.

The soul peered at its family, understanding finally dawning on its features. It floated across the bed toward the huddled mortals, taking turns to plant a kiss on everyone's cheek before moving toward the reaper. Then, sending its family a small smile, it nodded at the reaper, who then aimed the orb. The soul was sucked in, and within seconds, the reaper opened a portal and disappeared.

Thorne gazed down at Chey, trying to gauge what she was thinking behind her blank expression. He'd been in the Field Division for years, so he'd long ago gotten used to the painful interaction of having to separate a soul from the life it had known. However, he still recalled those first few times he'd stepped into the field. Not even the most hardened demons could walk away unaffected upon seeing what it was like for the first time.

After several silent beats, she surprised him by giving a small smile. "Did you see the way that soul looked before he was taken away? You can tell he was…I don't know, at peace, maybe? It was like he was happy moving on, knowing he was surrounded by loved ones. Wow."

Relaxing, he nodded at her words. He didn't bother correcting by saying they referred to souls as 'it' rather than a gender pronoun. Once a mortal died, their soul was no longer male or female. Not only that, but if souls were granted reincarnation status, there was always the possibility that a male in one life would be female in the next—and vice-versa.

Instead, he responded, "It isn't always this easy, especially with younger mortals or premature deaths. However, you're correct. Though mortals have no idea what happens to them after death, there's a general hope that they will be reunited with their families again one day. This family in particular was lucky enough to be able to say their goodbyes, so even though they're hurting now, they'll never know how much that soul cherished getting to see them one last time."

With a sly smile, Chey turned to him. "You know, you talk about all this in such a casual way, but I've figured you out. You secretly really care about mortals, don't you? You're not quite the impervious badass you pretend to be."

Thorne narrowed his eyes at her. "Don't ever in your life repeat any of that to anyone else."

She chuckled and stepped away from the window. "I make no promises. Where to next?"

Grumbling under his breath, he glanced at his watch. It wasn't even noon yet, which meant they had a several hours to kill. "Well, you have two choices, detective. We can either go watch a few more reapers in action or we can go sightseeing."

At that, she raised her eyebrows in surprise. "Sightseeing? I thought you said reapers going topside wasn't like a vacation."

"I did, but neither of us are reapers, are we?" He winked. "I booked the whole day, so no one will be suspicious how we spend it."

She pondered his words for a few moments before nodding. "Okay, but if we get caught and wind up in trouble, I'm taking off running."

He laughed because he knew she meant that. "Deal." Though it was impossible to show her everything the human world had to offer, he figured he'd start by showing her his top favorite places to visit. He thought about where he'd take her first, then opened a portal. "First stop—New Orleans."

Chapter Thirteen

It had been quite some years since Chey had been able to have a full day of fun. More often than not, she was so weighed down with work that even when she managed to score some free time, she was usually too tired to do anything.

Since venturing topside, she'd had a wave of exhaustion wash over her, which Thorne had explained was expected. When Sheolic demons went outside of their realm, their powers and senses were dulled. It was the excitement she'd had for exploring such a foreign world that had kept her wide awake. Thorne had taken her to so many cities and countries that she couldn't remember the names of them all. Their final stop by far had been her favorite, though.

She still didn't care much for the sun. However, as she stood on the edge of a pier overlooking the Gulf of Mexico in southern Florida, she could almost understand how the mortals thrived under its blinding light. The last of its rays cast a shimmering yellow glow over the gentle waves, and though the beach was still crowded with tons of humans enjoying the weather, there was a certain serene beauty to it all.

"I've got to hand it to you, Lucifer. Today was pretty fun."

Thorne fixed her with a look of exaggerated shock. "Was that an actual compliment? From *you*?"

Chey rolled her eyes. "Don't get used to it. You're still an ass—just a tolerable one."

He grinned, humor lighting his eyes. "I'll take that."

Tipping her head back, she drew in a deep breath, taking in the scent of fresh air and salt water. She closed her eyes and savored the warm breeze caressing her skin. "If I had the funds, I wouldn't mind vacationing here every few years," she commented.

When Thorne didn't respond, she peered up at him, only to find him staring down at her with yet another stunned look. She frowned. "What's wrong? Spaced out again?"

He blinked, but he didn't say a word. Instead, he stepped toward her. Confused and unsure what to expect, she stiffened when he took her chin between his fingers and kissed her.

Like the night before, it was just a soft, tentative touch of the lips, but there was no hesitancy on his end. He was patient and unmoving as he stood there waiting for her to respond.

And so, she angled her head in a way that allowed them both to lean into the kiss. She closed her eyes. Something stirred deep within her, but it wasn't the usual lust that simmered when it came to Thorne. No, this was...different. Her heart fluttered and blood rushed to her cheeks, making her feel light-headed and weak. It was the kind of feeling that made her sigh against his mouth. She could spend days standing right there on the pier, his arms curled around her waist while they held on to each other.

Words that had always escaped her in the past popped to the forefront of her mind, hanging on the edge of her tongue, threatening to spill.

And right at the moment, panic flared, so sudden and profound that he pulled away from her with wide eyes. However, it wasn't her own reaction that had her shocked. As she stared up at Thorne, she took in the evidence that it wasn't *her* fear that had killed the mood between them. It was *his*. She could see it clear as day. Though devils couldn't read minds, they could read emotions, and there was no way in hell he hadn't sensed that four-lettered word she'd almost said aloud.

Honestly, she shouldn't have been surprised that he would freak out, but she hadn't counted on the stab of hurt upon realizing she'd gone against her own warning about not falling in love with Thorne Lucifer.

"Uh, it's getting pretty late," he muttered, rubbing the back of his neck and avoiding eye contact. "Maybe it's time we head back."

Ouch. Fucking ouch.

Salvaging whatever bit of pride she could muster, she nodded and edged away from him. "Yeah, that's a good idea."

Without another word, Thorne opened a portal. The entire trip back to EUC didn't take more than five minutes, but it may as well have been an hour, for the awkward silence between them hadn't diminished one bit.

In her mind, Chey kicked herself a thousand times for wanting to cry. She wasn't a sappy-ass wimp. She'd had her heart broken before — twice, actually — back in her younger days, but she'd shaken it off and kept busy until she'd moved on. However, the raw feeling of rejection burning a hole in her chest left her with a desire to barricade herself in her own bedroom, hide under the covers and shut out the rest of the world. She'd thought nothing could ever top the pain that had come from Gemma betraying her, but damn if seeing that look on Thorne's face hadn't been a close second.

Shaking her head, she hid a sigh of relief when they stepped back into EUC. The room was just as crowded as it had been earlier in the day, for which she was thankful. The rapid sounds of computer beeps, typing on keyboards and endless chattering from dozens of employees filled the silence.

Walking behind Thorne, she mirrored his actions as he took off his cloak and tossed it in a passing janitor's cart. Then, she kept to herself all the way until they made it to the bank of elevators. Just as one opened, there was a woman wearing a tight mini-skirt and a low-cut blouse who came rushing down the hall. "Yoo-hoo, Thorne!"

Chey rolled her eyes even as a wave of jealousy rolled through her. That had to have been the fourth woman in one day. She did her best to shove it aside and ignore the giggles and flirting as she and several others stepped on. Thorne glanced at her, but she refused to meet his gaze, instead choosing to sidle away and allow three others to fill the space between them.

The woman's sultry laughter taunted Chey, so when the elevator opened, she didn't even care if it was the wrong floor as she rushed out at the last minute.

"Chey —"

The closing of the elevator cut Thorne off. She glared at the metal doors and stormed away, unknowing and uncaring as she roamed through the wide halls. She hadn't a single clue where she was going, but she trusted in the mounted signs to guide her to the parking garage.

It took a good half hour until she found a flight of stairs, and another ten minutes before she found the correct level where Thorne had parked her car. By the time her vehicle came into view, her calves were burning with the need for her to sit down. As she walked, she dug into her pockets for her keys. She'd just gotten the driver's door unlocked when she caught someone rushing toward her from her peripheral vision.

Of course, it had to be Thorne. She made a rather obvious attempt to pretend she didn't see him and rushed to slide into her seat. She almost had the door closed before his large hand prevented her from slamming it shut.

"Chey, stop," he growled. "Where are you going?"

Sighing, she gripped the steering wheel and stared straight ahead, refusing to let him see the pain she knew would be lurking in her eyes. "Home. I have things to do."

"Okay, but why did you run away? I was going to walk you to your car."

Her knuckles turned white. "No need."

"Damn it. I'm trying to talk to you, so why—"

"Talk about what?" Finally, she turned a scathing glare on him, unable to hide the disgust and anger she felt. "You didn't have shit to say after that kiss, so what could you possible want now?"

He winced and gave a helpless lift of his hands. "It just...threw me off."

"It was just a kiss," she scoffed. "A kiss *you* initiated."

"It was more than that and you know it." He glanced up and rubbed his neck before returning his attention to her. "You felt something. I saw it."

Chey cranked up the car, but she didn't put it in drive…yet. With the way she was feeling, she wouldn't think twice about speeding off and hitting him in the process. Okay, she *would*, but it was tempting. "Yeah, well you know what I saw? Fear. You were terrified upon realizing how I felt about you."

He shifted his weight first to one leg, then the other. "Chey, it's not like that. It's not you. I just—"

"Please do not give me that bullshit 'it's not you, it's me' line."

"You're making this harder than it has to be." Groaning, he scrubbed both hands over his face in frustration. "Look… Last night was fun, right? We both had a good time. There's no reason we can't continue hanging out without throwing complicated feelings in the mix."

A near-suffocating silence fell between them. Chey had to force herself to breathe, to remember that she had no right to be so surprised and hurt by his words.

Shaking her head, a humorless, bitter laugh fell past her lips. She released the steering wheel and angled her body in the seat to face him, hoping he'd grasp onto the gravity behind her next words. "Succubi have a short lifespan for a reason, Thorne. We only have fifty years to find a mate—thirty, actually, because most of us don't reach maturity until age twenty. Everyone knows what happens to us once we reach our prime."

She gave him a pointed look, waiting for a sign that he understood before continuing. The only indication was the hard swallow he gave, making her nod. "I'll be forty-nine years old in a few months, which means I only have little over a year before I turn into one of those mindless freaks. I no longer have the time to entertain anyone who's only looking for a temporary fuck buddy."

Another long stretch of silence descended. Somewhere in her mind was a voice urging her to just drive away. There was no need for them to even be having this conversation. She should have never allowed herself to give into that damnable soft side of her heart, the one that was hoping he'd tell her that he felt the same way.

Funny. Just a few days ago—hell, even the day prior—she would have bolted out the door the moment Tomas had broken the spell. She would have gone straight to work to continue onward with her life of hidden bitterness and self-loathing. So much had changed in such a short amount of time that it had felt way longer.

Something in her had changed since crossing paths with Thorne again, though it wasn't all bad. Learning the truth about Thorne and Gemma had ripped open the jagged scar that had formed over the years, and while it would take some time to finally let it all go, at least she would be able to heal properly this time around. She had Thorne to thank for that.

With that thought in mind, she heaved a long sigh. "You're right. Last night *was* fun, but I have to look out for my best interests. I'm not asking you to give up your single life to be with me. I know it's not something you want, but I have to draw a line." Then, in a quieter voice, she added, "Before I can't see it anymore."

Thorne's face fell, and it took a great deal of effort for her to turn away from him. "Chey..."

She shook her head. "Goodbye, Thorne." With that, she closed the door and drove forward. She didn't glance at him in the rearview mirror. She *couldn't*, actually.

She and Thorne had started out as two relative strangers who couldn't stand each other. That spiteful state of mind was gone now, instead replaced by mutual infatuation and respect. While he may not have followed her as she'd tumbled over the border between like and love, she knew he cared for her in some way. He'd just made it painfully clear that he was unwilling to take it any further beyond good sex.

When she'd told him about the threat hanging over her head, she hadn't been lying. Her prime was right around the corner. She refused to wind up like another untamed succubus, mad with desire and unable to control herself around anyone with a penis. She'd live the rest of her days screwing anyone and everyone without stopping—not to rest, not to bathe, not even to eat. If she didn't die of starvation first, there would certainly be the mate of some male she'd screwed bent on killing her.

Chey refused to go out like that. It was the primary reason she'd even moved back to Elysium. Finding a mate to prevent that horrible fate was a huge priority.

She could no longer deny that she cared for Thorne on a more intimate level than she ever had for anyone else. She was in love with him. It hurt to drive away from him because it would be the last time they'd ever see each other. Getting even more involved with him was just setting herself up for heartache. She just couldn't do that to herself.

However, she couldn't and didn't judge him for his reluctance. It was unfair to hate him for not wanting to become anything serious. The anger and shame and bitterness she felt was only directed at herself. She'd known better. She'd reminded herself over and over and over again that falling for Thorne was just a heartbreak waiting to happen. She only had herself to blame.

Using one sleeve, she swiped at her eyes, refusing to let a single tear fall. When she turned onto the highway and EUC was no longer visible in her rear view, she cranked up her radio on full volume to drown out the sound of her heart racing.

It's over, she whispered in her mind. *It's in the past.*

Between hunting down a serial killer in the city and trying to put an end to the hormones that would eventually consume her, she couldn't afford to dwell on the agonizing hole spreading through her chest.

Chapter Fourteen

After a long night of tossing and turning, Chey got up and dressed hours before her alarm went off. She hadn't had much of an appetite in the last two days, so she settled for downing a protein shake for substance and energy. Unfortunately, it couldn't do a damn thing to rid herself of the feeling of loneliness, but before she sank back into the pit of misery, she snatched her keys off the counter, grabbed her tote bag and strolled out of the door. She checked to make sure the locks were in place before getting into her car.

She lived over an hour away from their office headquarters, but she didn't mind the long commute every morning. It gave her plenty of time to gather her thoughts and strengthen her mind before returning to a case she'd gotten nowhere with in years.

Vaughn and another detective had gone to interview Alexius' sister in her stead, and all they'd managed to get from her was that he didn't have any enemies that she knew of. Despite being an incubus, Alexius took dating seriously and had been looking to settle down. He'd called her the night before he'd been killed and mentioned that he'd met someone who seemed like a good match, so he'd wanted his sister's help in finding a nice outfit to wear.

Hearing that from Vaughn had caused Chey's heart to clench in pain. While she couldn't say she'd developed feelings for the man on the spot, she had been looking forward to their date to see where it would go. There was no way she could have predicted he'd be killed the very next day, but that hadn't stopped her from feeling a grand amount of guilt over his death. A cruel voice had taunted that had she not tried to help Thorne at the bar that night, she and Alexius would have gone home together, and he wouldn't have been murdered.

Chey gave a sharp shake of her head and gritted her teeth. Months of having the 'never let a case become personal' rule drilled into her mind back at the academy had flown right out of the window the moment she'd recognized Alexius' tattoo. It was hard to keep a level head when every day C.S. roamed free was a day she'd failed to do her duty. She had to remind herself that even if it cost her own life, she'd find C.S. and make the bastard pay. If nothing else in her life went right, she'd make sure that was the one thing.

With that determination in mind, she took the next exit and drove another ten minutes before pulling into the parking lot of the station. It was already half-full, which meant she wasn't the only early-bird today. *Good.* The lack of silence would keep her thoughts from running wild, an issue that hadn't existed before she'd woken up bound to Thorne.

As she walked through the building, she received a few 'good mornings' before making it to her desk. However, she didn't take a seat. Instead, she unlocked one of the drawers to pull out the case folder. Then, she gathered a few more supplies before heading toward the private room where she, Vaughn and a handful of other detectives would convene to go over details.

There was already a large board with images of each victim pinned to it, along with key details about their identities. Though there were only five deaths, a separate panel held pictures of nearly a dozen men with their faces beaten until they were unrecognizable. Those were the living victims from Asphodel—seven men who'd been hospitalized after being attacked by C.S. She hadn't been leading the case back then, so all she had from those victims were their written statements about the attacks.

Placing her stuff down on the table, she eyed the board with five men. Only the second one didn't have a name by his picture, for they still hadn't found out his identity, nor had anyone come forward to file a missing person's report. It always filled her with remorse when they couldn't ID someone. Not only had his life been stolen from him, but no one cared. No one had been there to claim his body and lay it to rest.

The memory of it made her shoulders droop in sadness. While it had been improper, she'd anonymously paid with her own money to buy the man a gravestone and have him buried. She hadn't done it for any kind of reward or attention, however. In truth, she knew that her chances of finding a mate before her prime were becoming less and less of a possibility. Death was practically peeking around the corner, and in all her years, there wasn't anyone she knew who would do the same for her.

She'd receive a respectful ceremony due to her service, of course, but not a single person who'd attend would be someone she considered a loved one. She didn't have any family. The two friends she could claim were Vaughn and Alber, but even then, those were work friendships. She trusted them both to an extent, but it wasn't like they were besties who hung out on a regular basis. She was just...alone.

It was a fact she'd accepted years ago, but as the inevitable end drew closer for her, she couldn't help the fear and resentment over how the world had done nothing but shit on her all her life.

A gentle knock at the door drew her attention toward Vaughn as he stepped inside carrying two cups of coffee. "Looks like you could use one of these," he stated, handing one over.

Grateful for the distraction, she took the drink. Drawing in a deep breath, she smiled. He'd fixed it just the way she liked it—more cream and sugar than any genuine coffee lover should have. "Thank you. I don't suppose you've had an epiphany and figured out who C.S. is."

"Unfortunately, no." He moved to take a seat in the chair near where she was standing. Stretching out his legs, he peered at her over the top of his drink. "I'd ask how you're holding up, but I have a feeling the answer is pretty obvious."

"No kidding," she muttered. "I'm sick of not knowing a damn thing about this perp. Five years later and not one slip-up."

"Traveling between regions requires wealth and partiality from one of the Big Four, yet we profiled him to have some kind of military background."

"Yes, but that still leaves an endless list of names. At this rate, we're just running in circles. We're missing something." She leaned her weight onto one leg and took another sip while staring at the victims' images. "He began with pummeling random men on the streets and escalated to beating their skulls in. Yet between the last hospitalization and the first death, he went silent for almost a year. Why? What was he doing? What was the stressor that made him snap?"

She tilted her head to one side. The case had been given to her like an old puzzle box with a third of the pieces missing and no printed image to use as a guide. Just when she thought she'd managed to fit two fragments together, she'd spot another that fit just as perfectly, making it difficult to determine which one to use.

As it was, all the crime scenes had been in public, yet secluded areas, which meant C.S. hadn't just run up to them. Instead, he'd lain in wait, or perhaps even followed them until he found the perfect time to attack. He was patient and organized, which suggested he was a power killer — someone who sought to gain control of his victims.

However, Chey wasn't convinced, despite her peers' disagreement with her opinion. Besides the selective hunting, C.S. lacked all the signs of a classic controller. He didn't take souvenirs, nor did he linger after killing. She'd once thought he was a thrill seeker for leaving his initials carved into the victims, but he hadn't tried to reach out to the media or sent any kind of taunts to the police to shed some light on himself. If anything, it was almost like he had a personal reason for choosing those men, and whatever that motivation was, it was full of anger.

They knew where he chose his victims, but not how or why. Once they managed to figure that out, they'd be a step closer to catching him. However, no amount of digging into the victims' private lives had revealed any kind of crossover. As far as she knew, all twelve men could have been from completely different worlds.

Chey focused her attention on the second dead victim — John Doe. She had a feeling deep in her gut that perhaps he would be the key to finding the mysterious link — if it even existed — but as far as any of them knew, it was a lost cause. John Doe had no identifying marks, no prints in the system, no previous dental records and no record of his DNA anywhere. Furthermore, C.S. had beaten his face so badly that putting his image out in the hopes that someone would recognize him had been completely off the table.

"Cheyenne."

Blinking, Chey turned a confused gaze to her partner, who watched her as though expecting a response. "What? Did you say something?"

He shook his head. "It appears I just had an entire conversation with myself."

"Oh," she grunted. She hadn't even realized she'd zoned out, having grown lost in her musings about the case. "My bad."

He watched her for several long seconds, though not for the first time, she couldn't guess what he was thinking about. The man had a pro poker face. She blamed it on his blood. Before modern civilization had taken place, the naga had been notorious for being hunters with endless patience and the ability to strike their prey with lethal precision. They could be in plain sight, but no one would ever know they were in danger until it was too late. "I see you finally got rid of that devil asshole. I hope that's not what's got your mind all over the place."

She grunted again, glancing away. "He wasn't all that bad."

"You're defending him now? You've spent years hating his guts."

"I'm just saying he's...not what I thought he was. I learned the truth about what happened with Gemma."

"Bullshit. He's still a bastard who can't keep his dick in his pants and fucks anything with a hole and a heartbeat."

Turning to him with a dry look, she drawled, "Succubus over here who fucks anything with a horn and a heartbeat."

Folding his arms, he leaned back in his chair and grouched, "Not everything, apparently."

With a sigh, she sank into the chair next to him. "Careful. Green isn't the most flattering color on you."

"I'm allowed to be jealous." His knees bumped into hers as he faced her. He set his drink down on the table and fixed her with the most solemn look she'd ever seen on him. "I've made jokes in the past, but I want you to know they were all serious. There's no one else in this world who could ever understand you the way I do. Forget about this whole dating scene and give me a chance."

"Vaughn—"

"No, listen to me. Neither of us have ever needed to sugarcoat anything, so I'm going to tell it to you straight. You've been trying to find a mate, but you don't have much longer. We've known each other for years, and in that time, we've come to respect and trust each other. That's what mating is about. It's two people who care about each other and want to spend their lives together — not meeting a random guy on the street to keep from turning into a hollow sex shell. I know you've been keeping me at arms' length because of our job, but if transferring to another precinct or turning in my badge is what I have to do to get you to say yes, then so be it. I'm willing to do anything to make this work between us."

To say Chey was shocked was a huge understatement. As Vaughn had mentioned, he *had* joked around in the past about the two of them being together, but she'd thought that was all it was. Jokes. There'd been several times when he'd offered to take her to dinner or give her a ride home or even help quench the pain whenever she'd gone too long without sex. He'd shown her that he cared for her, but not once had she actually thought that his feelings went beyond those of just being close work partners.

She wasn't a romantic, but the honesty and sincere emotion swirling in those hardened gray eyes would have won her over had he been someone else. Specifically, a one-horned devil with a wicked smile and molten brown eyes that stared back at her every time she closed her eyes.

A fresh stab of pain twisted her heart as she glanced away from Vaughn. His words were everything she didn't want to hear at that moment — not while she was still trying to cope with Thorne's offhand rejection, not while she was drowning in guilt over not bringing C.S. to justice and, most importantly, not while she was still trying to make sense over her muddled feelings toward both Gemma and Thorne. She was a fucking mess, and the last thing anyone needed was to be thrown into her world of conflicting emotions.

Mistaking her silence for denial, Vaughn made a disgusted noise. "It's Thorne, isn't it?"

Surprised, she jerked her head up in confusion. "What?"

The sneer he gave her was full of malice, though it was hard to say if it was directed at her or himself. "You've been acting different ever since you two crossed paths again. He's on your mind right now, isn't he?"

Taken aback, she straightened in her chair. "Ever since Alber told you what happened to me at the bar the other night, you've been fixated on making it seem like I can't function because of him. What's your issue?"

"You tell me. After everything he put you through, you're still defending him."

"That's because you're talking shit about a man you don't even know," she snapped. "I spent years despising him when he wasn't even the one at fault. Wanting to move on from the past and not spend the rest of my life being bitter doesn't mean I'm in love with him."

"No, but I saw the way you two looked at each other the other day—and now you have this heartbroken look all over your face. It's clear that you do have feelings for him." When Chey fell silent, unable to deny the accusation, he shook his head. After a beat, the anger on his face once again morphed into that blank poker face. Though it was an unnerving trick, she'd always envied ability to wipe his expression at the drop of a hat.

"Look," he continued in a calm tone. "I'm not trying to argue. All I'm saying is I've known you long enough that I can see when something is bothering you. This has nothing to do with the case. Whatever he did or said to you, I would never hurt you, Chey."

Chey rubbed a hand across her face. Frustration, confusion and a touch of discomfort warred through her. "Vaughn, just...stop. Do you realize how big of a bombshell you just dropped on me?"

"Come on," he said with a humorless laugh. "After all these years, this can't be the first time you've realized how I feel about you. You must have sensed *something*."

"Yeah, but I never thought it was...*that*. Gods below."

As if I don't have enough shit on my plate, she thought, feeling as though another weight had been added to her shoulders. It was miraculous she was even still able to stand.

"I've done everything imaginable to try to get your attention. I can't believe it has been going right over your head all this time."

She peered at him in question, wondering what he meant by that. She tried to think back on any attempt he might have tried, but to her, everything had just seemed friendly—a bit overprotective at times, especially when it came to her dating life, but always friendly. Shaking her head, she frowned. "I'm sorry, Vaughn. I really had no idea."

"Wow," he said with a snort, though there was no animosity in his tone. All she could detect was bewilderment. "Well, now you know. My offer still stands."

"I'll have to think about it, okay? Right now, it's just... It's a bit much."

His eyes darted back and forth as he stared into hers, though she couldn't guess what he was searching for. What she *did* know was that he was sure her reluctance was based on Thorne, and while that was true to an extent, there was far more to it than that.

At last, he gave a single nod. "I've waited years to get this off my chest. A little while longer won't hurt."

He reached out to tuck a stray curl behind her ear, and Chey tried not to wince at his touch. It wasn't that she found Vaughn repulsive — quite the opposite, in fact. He was handsome with the sort of rugged good looks that would have left her younger self pining for him. However, the intimate feel of his fingers gliding across her cheek left behind an icy trail that instantly made her want to recoil. Had he been anyone else — as in, someone she hadn't known and trusted for years — she would have trusted the feeling in her gut to move as far away from him as possible.

But this was Vaughn. She blamed those daunting alarm bells on her lingering feelings for Thorne, trusting that they would pass sooner or later.

* * * *

Even though the workday had ended two hours prior, Thorne remained in his office at EUC. He sat on the couch, watching reruns of an old comedy show while downing shots of liquor from his private stash in the mini bar. On any other given night, he would have been out at a local bar or a club looking for some entertainment in the form of beautiful curves and wicked smiles. However, ever since Chey had left him behind, he hadn't been in the mood to do shit else besides stay inside.

He was avoiding going home for the simple fact that everywhere he looked, he was reminded of her. His bedsheets still carried her scent, as did the couch — and the bathroom, and the patio. One glance at any surface in his condo brought forward memories of all the sinful deeds they'd done their last night together — as well as the morning after.

Going to work had been just as bad. He couldn't focus on even the simplest tasks without his train of thought going back to her. More than once he'd spotted a full head of dark spiral curls and perked up in excitement, only to realize it wasn't her. Even earlier in the day he'd heard that familiar, soft laughter in the distance and followed it around a corner, just to be once again disappointed upon finding someone else.

His mood had been just as shitty as his attention span, too. It was a daily occurrence for a good bit of the female population in EUC to approach him with offers to slip into a nearby closet or the elevators. While he would have been more than tempted just a week ago, the mere thought of having any other woman touching him was just…wrong. He'd shocked and pissed off a handful of people at his rejections over the last two days, but it couldn't be helped.

Sighing, he downed another shot and laid his head on the back of the couch when his vision began to waver. The alcohol was by far the strongest he'd had in a while, which had been precisely why he'd chosen it. He'd hoped it would cure him of his sour temperament.

He wondered what Chey was doing, how she was feeling. Her breed of succubi needed sex at least once every day to survive, so he knew she wasn't going without. He couldn't fault her for how she was created, but it certainly created a bitter hole in his chest. There he was wallowing in self-pity, unable to even look at a single female without thinking about Chey, while she was probably out there doing whatever to whomever.

Is this what a breakup feels like? Not that he and Chey had been exclusive in any way, but in the brief time they'd spent together, he'd developed an attachment to her far greater than anyone else he'd ever been with.

A sharp knock at the door sounded, followed by the knob being turned right away. "Knock, knock," his sister-in-law announced in a chipper voice. "Anybody home?"

Instead of responding, Thorne sank into the cushions, not wanting to be bothered. However, his inner wishes were ignored as both of his brothers and Remi entered his office and made themselves comfortable around him.

"Oh, gods," she said in a not-so-subtle loud whisper. "He looks terrible."

Thorne stabbed her with a lazy glare. "What the hell do you guys want? I'm trying to watch a show in peace." Well, that was what he'd meant to say, but the words came out slurred and toddler-like.

"That's why we're here," Rhys grunted, throwing his arm over his mate's shoulders. "You've been acting weird."

"What are you talking about? I've been minding my own business in here."

"Precisely. It's seven in the evening but instead of humping your way through downtown, you're here moping. What's this about?"

"What's this, some kind of invention... internshion...intervention?" He scoffed. "Leave me alone."

Remi flashed her ever-so-innocent smile at him, though the mischievous twinkle in her eye was far from pure. "Would your foul mood perhaps have something to do with that pretty succubus I heard about the other day?"

Narrowing his eyes, Thorne peered at all three of them. Judging by the humor each of them failed to contain, he knew exactly what this was about. As expected, they'd come to mock him. "All of you can kiss my ass."

Quin chuckled. "Polite pass on that. What happened to Chey?"

Thorne poured himself a shot. "None of your damn business."

"Ah, well I'm making it my business. Can't say I've ever seen you down this bad."

"Ditto," chimed Rhys.

Annoyance slid through Thorne at his family sticking their nose in his business, but it wasn't like he didn't deserve it. He couldn't count how many times he'd gone out of his way to wriggle his way into his brothers' affairs simply for the hell of it. Back when Rhys had been struggling with his feelings toward Remi, Thorne had practically threatened the man into making a move on her. Though he wasn't sure if they were there to help him cope or to just irritate him, he knew they wouldn't leave him alone, no matter what he said.

"It's nothing," he grouched, focusing his gaze on the television while he drank more of the bitter liquid. "We broke the spell and she left. That's all there is to it."

"If that were the case," Remi drawled, reaching to snatch the bottle away when he went to pour himself another shot, "you wouldn't be trying to drown your feelings with this…this…" She squinted at the logo typed in an old language, then sniffed at the opening before gagging. "Whatever the hell this is."

"Strong stuff," he muttered.

"The strongest in your stash," Rhys commented. He took the bottle from his mate and poured himself a glass. "The kind you only break out when you're trying to get over some terrible news."

"Wow, so it's true then. Are you really heartbroken? I didn't even realize you've been seeing someone. What happened?"

Quin shook his head. "Did you ever find out how you two met in the past?"

Rolling his eyes, Thorne heaved a sigh of disgust. "If it will get everyone off my back, fine. Chey and I got the spell broken and I took her topside with me to see how the reapers and charons work." He ignored the horrified expression on Rhys' face and continued. "At the end of the day, I kissed her, and I saw how she felt about me. Instead of telling her I felt the same way, I froze and took the pussy's way out by offering for us to just be fucking friends with benefits. She shot me down and that's the last I heard from her."

Remi frowned in confusion. "A succubus turned down free sex?"

He shook his head. "A succubus who will be at her prime in about a year."

Rhys drew in a sharp breath and Quin winced, both spearing him with looks of pity. Remi merely fixed him with a disbelieving stare for several seconds. "I don't get it. She's in love with you. You're in love with her. Instead of pursuing a relationship, you're just going to sit in here and cry about it?"

Thorne glared at her. "Did you not hear a word I said? She said no. She doesn't want me."

"I heard you loud and clear, buddy. It sounds like she *does* want you, just not your half-assed suggestion to be a temporary fling. I think the problem is you don't know what *you* want."

He opened his mouth to growl some choice words, but after a beat, he crossed his arms and settled for glaring down at the coffee table.

"See?" she continued, a fine layer of disgust coating her words. "You can't even admit it. You're, what, eighty-seven years old? You've encountered dozens upon dozens of women in that time, and no one has ever held your attention for more than a few quick pumps. The moment the gods decided to shine in your favor and send you the one woman you fall head over heels for, you just let her walk away. Why?" She laughed, but there was no amusement in the sound whatsoever. Just...bitterness. "You think Rhys and I were looking for love when we first met? Hell no."

Looking beyond offended, Rhys cleared his throat, making her turn to him with a sheepish smile. "No offense, babe, but...come on. You even told me in the beginning that you'd prefer if we kept things—and I quote—'*purely physical*'."

He snorted. "I don't recall anything of the sort."

"The point is, can you imagine where either of us would be if we hadn't decided to give each other a chance? He'd be bitter and depressed in some political marriage while I..."

A haunted look crossed over her features, and Rhys tightened his hand around the glass so hard that he had to set it down when they heard a little crack. Thorne's irritation dissipated as he recalled how close they'd come to losing her. Graham Belial, current ruler over Abyssia and descendant of the Lucifers' biggest rival, had hatched a plot to kidnap Remi and hold her against her will until he could force a mating on her. If not for Thorne, Rhys and Quin arriving just in time, she would have been taken and there was nothing any of them could do about it.

She shook herself, as though trying to be rid of the haunting memory of what had almost become her fate. "All I'm saying is when the gods offer you a blessing, take it before those bastards snatch it away. They're quite fickle that way."

"You don't understand," Thorne muttered, glancing down. "I'm not a relationship-savvy man. I don't do those rose petal baths and candlelight dinners. I don't do the random bouquets at work or the sweettalking my way out of an argument. Romance just isn't my cup of tea."

At that, Quin laughed. "Perhaps it's because I was only there for less than an hour, but nothing about Chey gave me romantic vibes. Hell, you two had been watching a horror movie when I showed up."

Thorne thought it over and realized his brother was right. Chey was the type who'd enjoy a date night full of gaming in their pjs rather than dressing up and going to a fancy a restaurant. "Fair point. But what if I have more crazy broads trying to harass her because of me? Look at this shit." He unhooked the glamour chain around his neck.

All three of their mouths parted in shock as they stared at his single horn. Then, Rhys was the first to let out a '*pffft*' noise. Remi bit her lip and slapped her own hand over her mouth, and Quin didn't even try to hide his amusement as he snickered with glee. "Bro, what the fuck happened?"

"You look like a—"

"Yeah, yeah, shut up," he grouched, putting the necklace back on. He'd only been trying to prove a point, but his buzzed state of mind had overestimated the depths of their compassion in trying to help him. When they managed to compose themselves, he flipped them off. "It's not funny. The nymph who drugged me took my horn, and Chey got dragged into it. She was the one to wind up hurt with a huge gash in her head. You guys remember Gemma? That girl who lived next door to me and made my life hell?"

His brothers nodded and Remi tilted her head in question, so he gave a brief explanation. He finished with, "They were best friends, but in the end, Chey was shot and left for dead. It's like no matter what happens, she keeps getting hurt because of me. How can I possibly offer her a relationship when I can't even protect her?"

"Ah, so that's where the true reluctance comes from," Rhys announced, sounding pleased. He leaned back in his chair and slid one hand into Remi's. "That's the thing about love, brother. No matter how much time has passed, the anxiety of losing your mate will never disappear. You can be at their side twenty-four-seven, and it's still not enough. That fear will always remain, but it only makes you cherish what you have while you have it."

Remi flashed Rhys a loving smile, and he returned the gesture by kissing the back of her hand. The sight made Thorne want to puke, but he recognized the flare of envy in his heart. Though he'd never in his life thought he'd admit such a thing, he wanted what they had. Ever since his eldest brother had mated Remi, he'd smiled far more in the past two years than he had in...well, for as long as Thorne could remember.

He wondered what it would be like to have that kind of relationship—not all the mushy shit, but to wake up every morning and see the face of someone he loved, to walk around grinning like an idiot due to the euphoric feeling brought on by the bonding ritual, to come home after a bad day of work and be greeted by the warmth of his mate instead of a cold, empty condo.

There was no denying that he loved Chey. Hell, according to his brothers and Remi, it was pretty damn obvious that he was devastated over her. All his life he'd been reluctant to settle down—terrified, actually. He'd convinced himself that being a bachelor forever was such a sweet gig that he'd never wanted to give up that title.

However, being with Chey had made him see that there was more to life than just casual sex with nameless strangers. Growing close to her had led to him discovering a woman who was so unique and unlike anyone else he'd ever met that he wanted to know more. Likewise, he wanted her to learn everything about him—his favorite places to go, his secret hobbies, his deepest fears and everything in between.

He pondered all their words of advice and began to wonder if perhaps there really was hope for the two of them. He couldn't picture himself with anyone if it wasn't Chey, nor could he bear the thought of her binding herself to another man—a man who could never understand her on an intimate level. He'd never know why she walked with her chin so high or why she *had* to be so strong. No other man could ever comprehend that beneath her hardened shell was a woman who'd been broken and betrayed so horribly that it was damn near impossible for her to open up to anyone else again.

And if by chance she ever did give a man that opportunity, he'd be a fucking idiot to simply let her walk out of his life.

Thorne pushed to his feet so abruptly that he had to hold his arms out for balance. The shots of liquor he'd downed had been stronger than he'd anticipated. Without thinking, he grabbed hold of Quin's arm to steady himself, but his brother recoiled hard enough that Thorne went tumbling back down into the couch.

"What the fuck is your problem?" Quin growled, pacing away to put his sanitizer to use. He squirted a large dollop into his palm and slapped it all over his bare arms. He peered down at the arm Thorne had grabbed, repulsion causing him to crinkle his nose. "Now I have to burn this shirt. Thanks, man."

"It was an accident," Thorne grouched, trying once again to stand, albeit a bit slower. "Bet if I had red hair, you wouldn't mind one bit."

At that, Remi chuckled and made her way to Quin. She dug through her purse and passed over a pack of wet wipes. "Jealous because your brother likes me more than you?"

Quin muttered a thanks. "Unlike you, I've never seen her drop a piece of bacon on the floor only to pick it up and continue eating it."

"There's a five-second rule for a reason." Comfortable enough to stand on his own, he headed toward the door. "I'm out of here."

"And where the devil do you think you're going?" Rhys called after him.

He didn't break stride, though he stumbled over his own feet and nearly fell again. "To find Chey before she starts to hate me again."

In the blink of an eye, Rhys was standing before him with his arms crossed, glaring with that annoying big-brother frown that used to make Thorne want to piss himself. Of course, that was before he'd hit a growth spurt and surpassed both him and Quin in his teenage years. "I hope you called a cab. You're in no condition to drive."

"Get out of my way, man. I can drive just fine." When he tried to step around, his brother just as easily blocked him again. "Move."

"Let him go, Rhys," Remi drawled from across the room. "So what if he wants to risk death by driving under the influence. It's not like he has a young nephew who will grow up wondering what happened to 'Unky Thor'. Oh, wait…"

Thorne shot her a glare. Well, he tried to. All he could make out was her blurry figure framed by a blotch of red hair. "That's a low blow."

"So is you endangering your life, as well as anyone else who is on the road tonight."

"I'll drive him," Quin announced, though he didn't sound happy about it. "Can't turn down having front-row seats to watching you make an ass out of yourself."

Pursing his lips in irritation, he conceded with a loud sigh. It appeared he had no choice but to accept his siblings' meddling once more. "One day, all three of you are going to wonder why I suddenly started making your lives a mortal's view of hell."

Chuckling, Remi gave him a quick peck on the cheek before taking her mate's hand and walking toward the door. "Awfully bold of you to threaten the grand-daughter of the most powerful god in the underworld."

"Not to mention the wife of the future ruler of Elysium," Rhys added, nothing but pride in his tone as they exited.

Grumbling under his breath, he turned to Quin as he approached with a mix of amusement and annoyance on his features. "Those two really make it hard to feel sorry for starting a food fight at their wedding."

With a snort, Quin walked ahead of him as they left the office. "Reason number twenty-seven for why you'll never be invited to mine. Let's go."

Chapter Fifteen

Showered and dressed in an oversized tee, underwear and fuzzy socks, Chey fixed herself a glass of wine and settled on the floor of her living room. Spread out before her on the coffee table were the images of the dead victims, a notepad and a folder containing the details of the case.

She'd managed to go two days without sex, but her lack of taking care of her needs was beginning to catch up with her. Cramps wreaked havoc in her lower abdomen, but it was thankfully not so severe that she needed to find release right away.

As irresponsible as it was on her end, she just couldn't convince herself to find a random man like she'd always done. Thorne's face would pop up in her mind each time, making her put it off for as long as possible. She knew she wouldn't be able to go much longer without it, but she hoped that by then she'd be too drunk with lust to be filled with regret. For the time being, she patted herself on the back for managing it well.

And by managing, she meant pouring all her energy and focus into studying the case file laid out before her. She'd read and re-read all the pages so many times in the past few years that she could recite everything word-for-word from memory alone. Unfortunately, her impressive recollection hadn't served a single bit in helping her finding a break.

C.S. was as big as a mystery as he'd been before she'd tied all the victims to him. The only thing she knew about him was that he was a tall male with enough strength to overpower ripped men like Alexius. He wasn't after a specific type of demon, for the victims ranged from incubi to shifters to even an elf, all from different races and ethnic backgrounds. Also, he had to belong to a high-ranking family in society, for he had enough money and political influence from one of the Big Four to be able to travel through regions.

While Chey and her team had dug up information on dozens of families with that type of power, all the men and women with the initials of 'C.S.' had wound up being dead ends. Half of them had solid alibis while the others had gotten lawyers involved with threats of suing if SPD didn't back off. While it was clear those particular individuals were guilty of something, the investigations for her case had ended there.

Heaving a deep sigh, Chey glanced at her phone when it started to buzz. She checked the caller ID before answering. "Never in my life would I have expected you of all people to call me from an actual phone."

On the other line, Alber made a disapproving *tsk* sound between his teeth. "Well, I tried calling on the crystal, but as usual, someone didn't bother answering.

Let me guess. You either lost it or it's hiding somewhere in your sock drawer."

Despite the weariness weighing her down, she smiled at his dry tone. "Neither, actually. I happen to have it right in front of me." As she spoke, she stood and rushed toward the kitchen. As silently as possible, she picked up her keys and stepped outside.

"I hear a door opening," Alber drawled. "It's in your car, isn't it?"

"Not at all." She tiptoed across the pavement and unlocked her car door.

"Right. So, what's all that noise in the background?"

It took quite a bit of shuffling her hand around blindly before her fingertips grazed the jagged piece of rock. She grabbed and straightened to gently close the door back. "No idea what you're talking about. I'm holding it as we speak."

Alber snorted. "You insult my intelligence with your terrible lies, Cheyenne."

As he dove into another one of his speeches about the importance of keeping communications nearby at all times, Chey headed for the porch. However, she slowed her steps as an odd prickling sensation touched the back of her neck. With narrowed eyes, she went on high alert, recognizing the feeling of being watched. It was one of the most basic survival instincts she'd developed years ago, one that had her glancing all around like a gazelle looking for signs of a predator nearby.

There was nowhere close where anyone could be hiding except for the boarded-up house sitting across the vacant lot next to hers. It looked as eerie and secluded as ever, but she scanned every visible door and window to make sure each opening was still sealed off.

Then, from the corner of her eye, she spotted movement. Turning so fast that she almost got whiplash, she reached for her waist holster, only to remember she'd taken it off after showering. However, the need for a weapon was unnecessary, for the cause of her alarm was a harmless raccoon scurrying across the road.

"By the gods. Cheyenne, are you even listening to me?"

Sighing, Chey used her free hand to rub her eyes. "I'm sorry, Alber. I really think I'm starting to lose my shit. I'm over here about to go to war with a raccoon."

"So, you admit that you *are* outside. I knew it." Alber grunted. "Would your distracted state of mind perhaps have something to do with your newfound love triangle?"

Chey groaned and continued walking toward the porch. She cast one more wary glance at the vacant house before stepping inside and locking the door. "I guess you heard about what happened today?"

Alber snorted. "There isn't much gossip I don't hear these days, my dear. How do you feel about it?"

Returning to her seat on the floor between the couch and the coffee table, she took a deep drink of her wine. "Honestly, I don't know. I mean, it's *Vaughn*. I've never thought of him as anything more than my work partner. It just feels...odd."

"Yeah, I don't blame you. I always joked about him having a thing for you. I never knew it was more than that."

She shook her head in dismay. "Can we change the subject? I've had enough of emotional roller coasters in one week."

"Understood." In the background, his chair squeaked as he moved around. "The reason I'm calling you is to let you know I might have found the name of our John Doe."

Shocked, Chey raised her eyebrows and reached for her notepad. "You could have started with that."

"The keyword here is 'might'. I'm currently waiting to hear back from forensics, but I thought you should be the first to know."

"Let's hear it."

"Elliot Miller. Born and raised in Asphodel's capital city. Sole owner of a small, yet popular wood crafting shop, but his business went down the drain little over two years ago after over a dozen customers attempted to sue him for buying his products but not receiving them. He never showed up for any of the court cases. Not only that, but I dug into it a little more and found out that around the same time, he completely disappeared. He stopped paying his bills, but there's been no signs of him running away. His bank account is still active and hasn't been touched since. And finally, while his cell phone service has been disconnected, his last known location was somewhere in the vicinity of where John Doe's body was found — the exact same night."

As Alber spoke, Chey jotted down every detail. "Alber, you dorky genius. You are the best."

"Naturally," he chirped. "Nice to know someone appreciates my skills."

"I always do. Wood crafting, huh? That explains the callouses on his hands. The coroner said it was possible he could have been a construction worker or something along those lines."

"Close enough. I went through his website, and his work is really quite impressive. He hand-carves furniture. Tables, chairs, dressers — everything. He even creates these really intricate patterns that give it an antique feel. Sucks that such talent went to waste."

Chey gave an absent nod as she continued scrawling notes. "Three years to finally put a name to his face. I wish we could have..." She trailed off and stopped writing as a memory flickered in her mind. Frowning, she read over her own notes before digging through her tote bag.

"You should really see someone about your short attention span," Alber joked.

Ignoring him, Chey pulled out a stack of business cards tied together by a rubber band. A good bit of them were hers, but most of them were from random companies she'd acquired over the years. She shuffled through all of them until she found a laminated one that had a solid brown background and a swirling logo that read 'Miller Custom Woodworks'. She flipped it over and saw the handwritten phone number on the back.

"Alber," she started, her blood running cold, "what's the name of Elliot's business?"

"Hmm? Let's see..." He made a few clicks on his computer. "Miller Custom Woodworks. Why?"

Chey pulled the phone away from her ear and pulled up the keypad, then typed in the cell phone number on the back of the card. Sure enough, a contact popped up — Elliot the Wood Guy. She switched over to her messages and scrolled back a few years to find he was one of the men she'd contemplated dating back when she had been living in Asphodel. Shortly before she'd moved back to Elysium, they'd gone on a nice date but that was the last she'd heard from him.

Just like the others.

With shaking fingers, she picked up the image of John Doe and stared at it. She tried to dredge up the image of Elliot, a handsome shifter with pitch black hair and dark eyes. He hadn't had any tattoos, but she remembered he'd had a cute star-shaped birthmark just under the left side of his jaw. As she studied the picture of his battered face, she spotted ruffled black hair and that exact same mark below a bruised cheek.

She thought of the other men she'd dated, only to wind up being ghosted, even after the dates had gone well. There'd been an elf. She didn't usually go after fae, but they'd bonded over their shared love of classic video games. Picking up the image of the fourth dead victim, tears stung her eyes as she began to notice the similarities between him and the elf she'd met. She picked up another image and all the pieces started to fall in place.

She'd thought Alexius' death had been an unfortunate coincidence, but after looking over all five victims with fresh eyes, she knew better. Even as she looked over the men who'd been left alive, a few of them looked familiar, though the ones she recognized hadn't been anyone she'd tried to get close to. They'd been random hookups before she'd started to take her dating life seriously.

C.S. hadn't been targeting random men at all. He was after the ones *she'd* been with.

Hell, C.S. weren't even the perp's initials. They were *hers*. She could see that now. Cheyenne Sidney Wilcox. All that time he'd practically been taunting them with such a vital clue, yet not once had any of them ever considered that the initials were for someone else.

Bile rose in Chey's throat, making her slap a hand over her mouth to keep it down. Still, she was powerless to stop the tears from falling as a fresh tidal wave of guilt filled her, threatening to drown her with its intensity.

Five years. She'd been hunting C.S. for five fucking years, trying to find the connection between victims, when it had been her all along. Whatever C.S.'s motive was, she was the primary reason seven innocent men had been hospitalized and placed in ICU while five others had been murdered in cold blood.

As she sat there sinking in despair, a distant buzzing sound made her realize that Alber was still on the other end of the phone, calling out her name. It took several hard swallows and a few deep inhales before she could find her voice, but even then, it was a struggle to get the words out.

"Alber, I need a favor. Send me Thorne's number."

His annoyed grumbling stopped right away. Perhaps hearing the distress in her voice, his became filled with worry. "Why? What's going on?"

"Just...please." With that quiet plea, her words broke and a small sob escaped.

"Damn. All right, I'm sending it now."

Chey only nodded, even knowing he couldn't see it. She disconnected the call without another word. As promised, a text message came through to her phone not even a minute later.

Fingers still shaking, she dialed the number. However, she didn't hit send right away. Instead, she took several minutes to try to compose herself, a feat that wasn't at all easy. She cleared her throat, and when she felt her voice would be strong enough, she made the call.

She hadn't expected him to answer, but disappointment still slid through her when she got his voicemail. She thought about leaving a message, but before she could, another call came through. "Hello?"

There was a pause. "Chey? Is that you? How did you get my — You know what? It doesn't even matter." He gave a small, awkward laugh. "I'm glad you called. I was actually on my way to your — "

"Thorne, it's me," she said, unable to hide the tremor in her tone. "C.S. has been targeting men because of me. Alexius, Elliot, all the rest. You might be next. Please be careful. He catches them off guard and — "

"Whoa, whoa," he cut in, sounding alarmed. "Wait! Back up a minute. What are you talking about?"

Drawing in a deep breath, Chey used her free hand to swipe the tears in her eyes. "I'm so sorry. All these people were hurt because of me, and now you might... You could..."

When her voice grew louder due to her rising panic, Thorne said, "Sh-h, calm down. Just breathe, Chey. Tell me what's going on."

Chey closed her eyes as her heart gave a painful squeeze. Then, she did her best to explain everything to him, from the moment Alber had told her about Elliot, to her figuring out the details in between. When she finished, Thorne blew out a loud breath. "Gods below. Are you home right now?"

"Yes."

"Good. Stay inside and lock the doors. Don't let anyone in, okay?"

"But — "

"Chey, please," he urged. "This bastard could be anywhere. Even if he hasn't tried to attack you before, I don't want to take that chance. Promise me you'll stay inside until I get there."

His concern for her was touching, so much so that it almost eased some of the apprehension in her heart. Almost. "I promise."

He released a sigh of relief. "Thank you. I'll be there as soon as I can."

After hanging up, she made another call. Unlike Thorne, Vaughn answered on the first ring. "Hey, beautiful. Have you thought about my offer?"

"Where are you?"

"Ah, I'm still at the station. Is everything all right?"

She glanced at a hanging clock. It was still rather early in the night, but he had a tendency to pull all-nighters. There'd been times when she'd left work and gone in the next day to find he'd never left. His dedication had always run deep. "I know how all the victims are connected." As she gave him the same explanation she'd given Thorne, she found her words trailing off toward the end when she realized he hadn't made a single sound. "Vaughn, are you there?"

In a tone far calmer than she'd anticipated, he asked, "Who else have you told about this?"

Taken aback, she frowned. "I was just about to call Shade to—"

"No, don't. You can't tell anyone else yet. If they learn you're the reason behind these murders, they'll bring you in as a suspect."

"Yeah, I know, but it it'll help finally catch this bastard, I'll go voluntarily."

"No, just..." He made a slight sound of frustration. "Just wait. I'll be there in a bit. We need to weigh your options before taking the next step."

With a huff, she felt her shoulders sink. "Fine, but I'll only give you an hour to convince me."

He grunted a response and ended the call.

Sighing, Chey moved to sit on the couch. As she waited, she wondered why she'd chosen to call Thorne before Vaughn. Vaughn was her partner and just as invested in the case as she was, so by all rights he should have been the first to know about this new information. Despite that, all thoughts had propelled her into calling Thorne to warn him that he could very well be the next target on C.S.'s list. Hell, even a piece of her had worried that it would have been too late.

Another thought crossed her mind as she pondered why she'd hesitated in letting Vaughn know that she had, in fact, told someone else about her findings. Both he and Thorne were on the way to her house, so he would learn the truth in just a little while, but something about the way he'd asked had given her pause.

Which was ridiculous. Right next to Alber, Vaughn was the closest thing to a friend she had. He'd never given her a reason to not trust him. She blamed her wariness on his recent confession to her, but she just as quickly scolded herself. Her career came first, so there was no reason for her to treat him unfairly.

A sharp knock at the front door rattled her from her musings. She glanced at the clock again and noticed that only ten minutes had passed since her phone calls. At the same time, her heart raced in the hopes that it was Thorne. She hadn't had time to ask why, but he'd stated he was already on the way to her house. It was possible he'd already been close by.

With that thought in mind, she rushed to the door. She peeked through the peephole and felt disappointed upon seeing that it was her partner instead. "Vaughn?" She reached for the deadbolt, only to pause in suspicion with her fingers on the cold metal. "How did you get here so fast?"

Through the tiny round hole, confusion flitted across his features. "What? I was already nearby."

Her heart began to race as a lump of coal settled in her gut. "You told me on the phone that you were still at the station. It takes an hour to get here, even without traffic."

He brought his lips together in a straight line as his expression went blank. He stepped toward the door and stared at her as though he could see through the peephole. "Cheyenne, let me in. Please."

"Not until you tell me why you lied. Where were you?" A thought crossed in her mind, and she dropped her hand. "How did you even know I would be home? I didn't tell you that."

Though his face maintained that cold, stony mask, those faded scales began to line the base of his throat and edge ever upward toward his temples. The fine hairs along the back of her neck and arms stood on end. "Open the door."

She glanced past him and saw that her car was the only vehicle parked on the street. Not only that, but he lived in an apartment closer to the station, so there was no way in hell he could have walked or even jogged.

When he continued watching her in that eerily soulless way, alarm bells went off inside her head. She recalled just recently when she'd gone outside and had felt as though someone had been watching her. She'd brushed it off and convinced herself that it was just paranoia, but she was beginning to second-guess it. Her gut was never wrong, after all, and at that moment it was screaming that the man standing on the other side of the door was not the person she'd thought he was all these years.

"He shows several signs of being a thrill seeker, but it doesn't look like he's killing for the media's attention. Maybe he's doing it for someone specific? It just seems like these kills are...personal."

Her own words rang through her mind, followed swiftly by Vaughn's.

"I've done everything imaginable to get your attention."

Chey broke out in cold sweat and edged away from the door. "I need you to leave."

She heard his heavy footfalls as he stepped even closer to the door. "Cheyenne, open this door right now. I just want to talk to you."

Through the barrier separating them, she picked up on the way his voice had dropped in tone and he drew out the 's' sound in his words. It was a sign she knew meant he was gearing up to strike.

Studying her surroundings, she tiptoed toward the kitchen. She had a few guns stashed away in secret hiding spots, the closest being in one of the cabinet drawers. She'd seen Vaughn in action plenty of times to know she had to move faster than she ever had in her life. Otherwise, she'd never be able to outrun him.

A loud boom sounded as he kicked her door. The deadbolts held fast, but the splintering of wood warned that the next kick wouldn't hold him off. She dashed toward the drawer, and just as she slid the magazine in place, the door gave in. She whirled around and flicked the safety off just in time to fire off a shot to his thigh.

Vaughn growled but didn't falter as he knocked the gun from her hands. Chey landed a few punches and one solid kick before he caught her by the back of her neck. He spun her and used his grip to slam her head face-first into the countertop. Pain reverberated through her skull and her vision wavered for a moment, but she didn't give up. She threw her elbow back and caught him in the nose, making him bark and loosen his hold enough for her to escape. She kneed him in the stomach and shoved at him, causing him to lose balance.

Using the moment to slip away, she ran for her bedroom where another gun was hidden. Blood dripped from her forehead to her eyes, temporarily blinding her as she slammed the door shut behind herself. She used all her weight to lean into the wood paneling when Vaughn crashed into it. All the while, she cursed herself for choosing not to use steel doors when she'd had her home remodeled — that, and her stubbornness in overestimating her ability to defend her home without the assistance of a security system.

She used her forearm to swipe her eyes, allowing her to see a bit better. The gun was in her nightstand, already loaded and ready to shoot. She judged the distance and questioned if she'd be fast enough to get to it in time. Vaughn rammed into the door again, that time almost overpowering her. She was sure that it was a losing battle on her end, but she'd be damned if she went down without a fight.

And so, she decided to risk it.

Darting forward, she snatched the drawer opened at the same time Vaughn came crashing inside. Unlike in the kitchen, she stood no chance as he had his forearm around her neck before she could even grab the gun. He hauled her away, tightening his arm when she began kicking and flailing her arms, doing everything she could to land some kind of blow.

Chey dug her nails into his arm to pry it away in order to draw in some air, but he held fast. Blackness crept along the edges of her vision as she fought to breathe. "Why?"

Though the question came out as a pathetic wheeze, he understood perfectly as he pressed his lips against her ear and growled, "Because you're *mine*."

With those dark words delivered, she felt the sharp pain of his teeth sinking into her neck. The paralyzing effects of his venom coursed through her veins at a rapid pace, turning her muscles to jelly until she couldn't even stand on her own.

Vaughn tossed her over his shoulder and carried her away toward her car. She had no idea what was going to happen to her, but it wasn't the fear of death that caused terror to seize her chest. It was the knowledge that she knew full well that her partner was going to go off the grid. It had taken five years for her to finally find a connection between the string of murders and only one other person knew about it.

However, even if Thorne made it her house and had the mind to call the police, by the time they pulled DNA and figured out Vaughn was the one who'd attacked her, their trail would be long gone. And if Vaughn truly had been C.S. all along, he had all the resources in the world to disappear without a trace, leaving behind no way of tracking him.

He was going to get away with everything if she didn't find a way to escape or fight back. That is, if the venom didn't kill her first.

Chapter Sixteen

"Gods below," Quin whispered.

As he pulled to a stop in front of Chey's house, a lump of despair settled in the pit of Thorne's stomach upon seeing her door wide open and hanging off its hinges. He didn't even wait for his brother to shut the car off as he jerked his seatbelt off and shoved the door open.

He smelled her blood long before he stepped inside, but it did nothing to prepare him for the sight of what looked to be a nasty fight. The small kitchen table was overturned, and several dishes lay in broken shards all around. A pool of blood soaked the floor, and another — Chey's blood, to be exact — stained the edge of the counter. There was a gun that had been thrown across the floor, and a quick glance at an opened drawer told him that Chey had been unable to get to it in time.

"Chey? Cheyenne!" Of course, he didn't get a response. Still, he scanned every corner for some sign of her.

He followed a trail of blood through the hallway, but when he spotted her bedroom door kicked in, panic flared. Her room looked just as bad as the kitchen with the bed in disarray, a busted lamp lying on the floor, as well as more blood staining the walls.

Thorne shoved his hands through his hair. Though it was clear she'd put up one hell of a fight, she'd lost far too much blood. His temper rose, but at the same time, devastation hit him with the force of a semi that he'd been too late in reaching her. "Fuck!" he shouted as he shoved his fist into the nearest wall.

Behind him, Quin placed a firm hand on his shoulder, but Thorne shrugged him off. "Don't touch me! That bastard got her."

With a sympathetic gaze, Quin took in their surroundings. "Yes, but he didn't kill her. Their blood is still fresh, meaning they couldn't have gotten far."

Snarling, Thorne turned a glare on his brother. "How the fuck am I supposed to track her when I don't even know who the hell took her? Her car is gone, so they're not on foot, man. They could be anywhere."

Shoving past him, Thorne made his way to the front door, but he paused when he heard vibrating. There on the coffee table was Chey's cell phone. He glanced at the caller ID and read the name Alber. "Hello?"

There was a short pause. "Who the hell is this? Where's Chey?"

"Is your name Alber? Chey told me you were a coworker of hers. Is that true?"

The man's suspicion was tangible through the phone. "Who wants to know?"

"Thorne Lucifer. She called me little over an hour ago saying she figured out that C.S. was attacking men she'd been with. Someone got here before I could. There's blood everywhere but no bodies and…and I don't know the hell I'm supposed to do. She said you're the computer guy. Is there's any way you can track her car or hack some traffic cameras or something?"

"Bloody fucking shit," the man growled through the line. There was a chair squeak, followed by rabid keyboard clicking sounds. "Tell me everything that's happened from the moment she called you."

Thorne did as instructed, doing his best to relay every detail. Alber typed away as he listened, only interrupting to mutter a curse once or twice. When Thorne finished, the man let out a long sigh. Though he tried to speak in a professional manner, he was unable to disguise just how worried he was for Chey's sake. And in all honesty, while he'd never before met Alber, hearing him sound so worked up didn't leave him feeling any type of relief.

"That's why she freaked out earlier," Alber murmured when he finished typing. "When I told her about Elliot, she kind of zoned out on me and wouldn't explain what was wrong. Dammit, so if she is the missing link, that explains why victimology has been all over the place. Then, again, that doesn't make sense. She's a succubus, so if C.S. was attacking everyone she'd slept with, there would have been way more deaths. So, what made him target these specific men?"

As Alber rambled on to himself, Thorne was growing impatient. He walked toward the coffee table, only then noticing the images spread out. "Does any of that really matter right now?"

From the corners of his eyes, he saw Quin edging around the kitchen talking to someone from his cell phone. "Actually, yes, it does. Figuring out why C.S. chose these specific men might be the key to figuring out *who* he is."

Thorne tapped his foot, unable to bite back his annoyance. "This has been an active case for five years, and according to Chey, you don't even have one suspect on the list. How the hell are we supposed to figure out who he is? Even if your people came in to sample the blood here, it could take days to process it. By then Chey could... She could be..."

Damn, but he couldn't even finish the sentence. The thought of her out there at the hands of such a savage murderer made him want to tear the city apart to find her. She'd already faced death once before and he hadn't been able to do a damn thing about it. He hadn't even known it was happening. There was no telling what that asshole was doing to her right now, but to know he'd been just a little too late in reaching her in time left him feeling raw on the inside.

"Now is not the time to freak out on me, Lucifer," Alber snapped. "Unlike before, we have new information. We know that C.S. has been after Chey all along, which means there's a greater chance in narrowing it down to who he is."

Closing his eyes, Thorne drew in a deep breath to steady his nerves. He sank onto the couch and picked up the picture of Alexius, the victim from the crime scene Chey had taken him to. "She mentioned that something was off about the last guy's death. C.S. had shown a lot of anger in killing him." He looked over the other images and thought about her explanation over the phone. "These men that were killed… She'd gone on dates with them or at least considered it."

"That's right," Alber muttered. "Because of her prime, she's been trying her luck at the dating scene. She said they all ghosted her, though. When she'd try to reach out for another date, they'd just not respond. And now they're dead."

Thorne peered them over. "She told me she was running out of time. When did she first start trying to find a mate?"

Alber was quiet for a moment as he thought about the question. "It was shortly before she moved away from Asphodel, so…three, maybe four years ago."

He glanced at Chey's notes taped under the image of a man with the number one written at the top corner. "Marcus Bishop was the first murder. Twenty-fourteen, so that was four years ago."

There was brief shuffling of papers before Alber responded. "The victim before him was placed in ICU just under a year before the first kill. What are you thinking?"

"It seems more than a coincidence that the first murder happened around the same time she began looking for a mate."

Alber drew in a short breath. "That could have been the cause of C.S.'s stressor. Succubi mate for life, so if she managed to settle down with anyone else, she'd be completely off limits to him. That is, *if* jealousy is his motivation."

Thorne's heart thundered in his chest. "If that's the case, this guy either followed her everywhere or knew enough about her private life to know who she was seeing." Alber didn't respond, so Thorne continued. "For him to have been stalking her for this long, it could be someone she knows, whether personally or in passing. She also told me that this guy is able to travel through regions, so he's likely connected to one of the Big Four. How many people with that kind of political power has she been close to?"

After a beat, Alber's voice was quiet as he murmured, "No one."

His short answer made Thorne scowl. "There must be *someone*. Maybe there was a one-time thing or an acquaintance or..." He trailed off as something Alber stated had questions popping up in his mind. "Wait a minute. You said, 'before she moved away from Asphodel'. Chey is from Elysium."

Alber fell silent for so long that Thorne had to check the phone to make sure the man hadn't hung up on him. "Hello?"

A long sigh came from the other end of the line. "I could lose my job if anyone found out I told you this. Chey has been on the force for over ten years. For those who show a certain type of skill and dedication in their work, in very rare cases they may get drafted to our elite program. To outsiders, it just looks like a special promotion, but it's more to it than that. This program allows our detectives to move between regions without having to go up the political ladder for consent. Sometimes they can put in a request to transfer, other times they're sent to help with...er, *difficult* cases. Chey was one of the rare few able to transfer because of her 'promotion'."

That was news to Thorne. He could feel the way his face was pinched with confusion as he struggled to absorb Alber's information. He'd never before heard of such a thing. Traveling between regions was so complex that even Thorne had only been able to do it a handful of times in his life, and even then, it was only due to his family visiting the Dagons or the Leviathans for some kind of formal, aristocratic event. He wondered if even his father or Rhys knew about the capabilities of the so-called 'elite program' in SPD.

He shook his head and decided it didn't matter at the moment. Rescuing Chey and ensuring she was safe in his arms was all that mattered. "So, what are you saying? The killer could be one of your people?"

"As much as any of us would hate to admit it, it would certainly explain everything. Like how even with the very first attack, C.S. knew when and where to strike, cover his ass and still remain undetected all this time. I could look through our files and pull up everyone who'd transferred from Asphodel to Elysium around the same time as Chey, but that could be at least a few dozen. And since they all go to the same training school, she would have met almost all of them."

That was definitely not what Thorne had been hoping to hear. He rubbed a frustrated hand through his hair. "Let's say this guy is one of your special cops. Chey recognized the last victim from the bar she and I were drugged at. According to her, they'd only exchanged numbers, so he must have been watching from a distance. How many people knew she would be there that night?"

"Me and just about everyone in her jurisdiction. They were all given... Hold on a moment."

Alber didn't even give Thorne the chance to respond before he put him on hold. The cheery elevator music didn't do a damn thing to ease his worry over Chey. As he stood to pace, Quin pocketed his phone and approached him. "Rhys is on the way with the cavalry," he said, referring to the Lucifers' private regiment.

Every family in the Big Four had their own personal security team, though with the modern, mostly peaceful times, there was hardly a need for them unless in times of absolute emergencies. "He wants us to stay put until they get here."

Thorne rolled his eyes but before he could utter a response, the shitty music stopped and Alber picked up. "Fuck me. I can't get ahold of Vaughn and I can't track his phone."

"Vaughn? Her partner?"

"I'm going through his file now. They'd gone through training together as partners, but they got sent to different precincts upon graduating. When Chey was sent back to Elysium, he put in a request shortly after. It took a few months before he got approved, but once he did, they wound up as partners again."

"That son of a bitch," Thorne growled, gripping the phone so hard that it cracked. He loosened his hold, but it took some effort. "I knew there was something weird about that bastard. I couldn't read him, but the way he'd stare at Chey was just... Shit. How can I find him?"

He didn't miss the hesitancy in Alber's voice as he explained, "Look... Maybe you should leave this to the professionals, Lucifer. This group I told you about? It isn't anything to take lightly. Each member is trained to use their natural abilities as their biggest weapon. Chey is able to use her pheromones to compel just about any unmated male to do her bidding. It's why she's one of our best interrogators and undercover agents. Vaughn is half naga. His greatest strength lies in his ability to attack when you least expect it. Not only that, but he's a strong son of a bitch. If he's been C.S. all along, then you've seen just what kind of damage he's capable of doing."

"You're not as smart as I thought you were if you believe any of that shit is going to stop me. All I care about is finding Chey before it's too late. She may not have the time to wait for your people to gather and come up with a plan."

"I knew you'd say something like that," he sighed. "I'm still required to call this in. Like I said, Vaughn's off the grid right now, so I can't track him. He wouldn't be so foolish as to take her back to his apartment. I can maybe check through the traffic feed to see direction he was heading, but it could take some time. The nearest camera to Chey's neighborhood is over a mile away, and that's only if he even turned onto a main road."

Thorne gritted his teeth. It was on the tip of his tongue to snap and take his frustration out on the man, but he swallowed the inappropriate words. "Fine. I'm keeping this phone on me, so call if you find anything."

"Same goes for you."

At that, Thorne pocketed Chey's cell and shoved his hands into his pockets. Regardless of his impatience, Alber *had* been helpful. There wasn't a doubt in his mind that Vaughn was the culprit behind everything. Thorne had known that bastard had been weird. Back at the crime scene, and even in the following hours when they'd driven to the police station, the man had kept a laser-focus on Chey. Anyone would have to be blind to have not noticed the longing in his eyes or the possessive way he stood over her every time Thorne had gotten too close.

Thorne had found mild amusement in the pathetic display at the time, and so he'd opened his senses to get a reading on him, only to come up to a blank wall. Very, very few demons were able to block themselves off to a seasoned devil, let alone one with the powerful Lucifer blood in their veins. He'd found it odd but hadn't questioned it. Now, however, he kicked himself for not trying harder. Perhaps if he'd put more effort into it, he would have sensed *something*.

Shaking his head to clear the guilt threatening to swallow him whole, he turned to Quin and found him leaning over the blood pooled on the kitchen counter. Though his germaphobia had to be eating him up inside, his gloved hands were steady as he used a white cloth to sweep through the thick fluid.

"What are you doing?"

Quin didn't look up as he remained concentrated on his task. "This is Chey's blood. Since it's still fresh, I may be able to conjure a tracking spell."

Hope flared to life in Thorne's chest as he rushed to his brother's side. "Really? You can do that?"

Pinching the cloth between thumb and index finger, he handed it to Thorne with a grunt. "Take this." He then peeled the gloves off and dropped them onto the counter before taking out his sanitizer and scrubbing it between his hands. "If I can get this to work, we're going to have to move fast, meaning we won't be able to wait on Rhys. The spell will only be active for an hour."

Not caring one bit about the red staining his fingers, Thorne clenched the rag and nodded. "How does it work?"

He followed Quin out to the car. He waited as the other man popped the trunk and began pulling out a few items from a tote bag—candles, a small journal, some kind of white powder and a smooth black stone. "Once activated, the blood will slowly begin to evaporate. So long as you're holding it, you'll be able to essentially see an invisible trail that will lead you to Chey."

Quin closed the trunk, but instead of heading back inside the house, he spread everything out in a semicircle around Thorne. He handed him the black stone before lighting the candles one-by-one. "Is this safe?"

With a small sound of amusement, Quin began flipping through his book. "Do you want to find Chey or not?"

Thorne grunted, but he didn't ask any more questions. Hell, even if the spell required some kind of drastic sacrifice and scorched half of his body, it wouldn't matter. He was a desperate man who'd do and suffer anything at that moment if it meant saving her.

Squaring his shoulders, he drew in a deep breath. "Get on with it."

* * * *

At some point between being shoved in the trunk of her own car and being driven around for a good bit of an hour, Chey had felt her heart rate slowing to the point that she'd lost consciousness. While she struggled to open her eyes, her other senses made her aware that wherever she was, it was warm and silent. She also had a splitting headache, but the cramps in her abdomen greatly outweighed the pain.

Groaning, she squeezed her eyes before trying once more to open them. She was lying flat on her back, giving her a view of an open-beam ceiling. It took a great bit of effort to tilt her head slightly to one side, letting her know that the venom was still in her system, but it was slowly beginning to wear off.

So, he chose not to kill me after all, she thought. Naga venom was potent enough to completely paralyze just about anyone with a single bite, and depending on the type of demon, it could cause death if one didn't take an antidote soon after.

Chey took in her surroundings. The room she was in looked like a basement turned into a livable area. It was a huge open space with a wall built on the far side. The converted bedroom had several pieces of furniture, including the bed she was lying on and a nightstand holding a bowl of water with a damp towel. There were no windows, and only two doors that she could see. One was partially opened, revealing a walk-in closet, while the other was closed. However, judging by the sound of running water coming from the other side, she assumed it was a bathroom.

She narrowed her eyes on that door and tried to sit up. However, not only was she still mostly paralyzed, she found her wrists were bound to the bedposts above her head.

First the hotel, now this, she thought with a scowl. She'd had enough of waking up tied to beds that weren't her own. Twice in one week was far more than she was willing to deal with.

The door opened and Vaughn stepped out, wearing nothing more than a pair of low-hanging sweatpants. His short hair was damp, suggesting he'd just gotten out of the shower. Upon seeing her awake, he grinned and moved to her side. The bed dipped as he perched on the edge.

"I thought you'd be asleep much longer than this," he murmured. He picked up the towel and wrung the excess water out. She flinched when he reached for her, making his smile waver. "There's no need to be afraid."

She pulled her eyebrows together in disbelief. "Don't. Touch. Me." It took quite some effort just to form those words, but the fact that she was able to get her jaw and lips to function was a good sign that she was gaining control of her body.

He tilted his head. Instead of responding, he ignored her repulsed expression and proceeded to dab the cloth against her forehead. Though she could hardly feel a thing, she could tell he was being gentle so as to not hurt her.

Ha! A little late for that, don't you think?

When he finished cleaning her skin, he dropped the towel back into the bowl and made himself more comfortable by lying next to her. He used one hand to prop his head up and studied her. "You know, I've waited a very long time to have you in my bed like this. I just wished it had been under different circumstances."

The way he spoke in such a casual manner disgusted her. "You're C.S."

As usual, his expression gave nothing away. He didn't even blink at the accusation in her voice. "*You* are C.S., actually. I merely did you a favor."

She scoffed. It turned her stomach to look him in the eyes, but she held his gaze while she worked on getting some feeling back into her fingers. "Murdering innocent…men is a favor?"

"Yes." When he used his free hand to tuck her hair behind her ear, she recoiled, though he didn't seem to care. She still felt numb, but she could have sworn her skin felt cold to the touch where his fingers had grazed her. "I still remember the first day we met at the academy. You were so beautiful, so fearless and confident. I knew from the very beginning that you were meant to be mine. If you would have given me a chance back then, none of this would have had to have happened."

Chey wished like hell she were free. Rage burned in her gut along with nausea at the notion that she'd spent years putting her trust into a literal cold-blooded murderer. "You're blaming...me for...your crimes?"

With that same hand, he trailed his fingers along the curve of her ear, down to her jaw. There was no remorse in his eyes, no sorrow over what he'd done, only fascination as he watched her. "You are a succubus. Over and over again I had to sit back and watch you screw any and every man who came your way, yet not once have you ever spared me a glance. I changed my hair, the way I dressed — everything, yet nothing I did would make you see me."

"You—"

"Yes, yes. You don't sleep with coworkers," he mocked as he rolled his eyes. "A commendable policy you stuck with for over a decade, but even after you made it to the top, you still turned me down. What did they have that I didn't? What more could I do to get your attention? Do you know how many nights I stayed up asking myself that?"

It was a rhetorical question, so she remained silent while he continued. "It wasn't easy, but I resigned myself to simply be patient until you came around. I would have waited an eternity if that's what it took." His eyes darkened, and for the second time since looking at him through her peephole, she caught sight of the true monster that had been hiding under her nose for years. "But then everything changed when you started looking for your forever mate."

Chey concealed her relief when she felt tingling in her fingers. Ever-so-slightly, she flexed them, stretching and curling them over and over until they were no longer numb. "Why did…that change?" she asked, more to keep his attention on her face and not her hands.

"That's rather obvious, isn't it? Your people mate for life. How could I possibly risk letting someone else steal you away?" Once more, he began trailing his knuckles across her skin, a smile that didn't reach his eyes playing at his lips. "I realized I was running out of time and… Well, you know that old saying — drastic times, desperate measures. I didn't expect you to start your hunt so soon, but when I saw you out on that date for the first time, I just knew I had to act fast. After that" — he gave a casual shrug — "I did what was necessary to protect you from making a mistake. If you think about it, everything I did was for you. No one will ever be able to love you the way I do, Cheyenne."

Chey closed her eyes. While she continued trying to ease her wrists free of the bindings, she had to fight another wave of nausea at the notion that the man she'd called friend could be so twisted. He truly believed in his cause, and the idea that all those men had suffered because of her own ignorance at seeing the truth was sickening.

A mountain of blame threated to crush her beneath its force, but she battled to keep it at bay. Her biggest concern at the moment was breaking free and getting the hell out of there, yet overpowering Vaughn was impossible, even at her strongest. As much as she wished to believe she was capable of throwing a good enough punch to knock his lights out, she was no match for him.

At least, not physically.

Her strengths always tended to lie in her cunning. Vaughn might be deranged, but he wasn't unintelligent by any means. However, if she played into his sick fantasy, it could be just the perfect distraction she needed to escape. It repulsed her to her very core to act the part, but if she had any hope of putting a stop to his madness, she'd endure it.

With a hard swallow, she opened her eyes to peer at him with the most sympathetic look she could muster. "You did all this...for me?"

His touch softened as he glided his fingers down her cheek toward her mouth. "Yes."

"Because you love me?"

He swiped the pad of his thumb across her lower lip. "More than you know," he murmured. "Cheyenne?"

Forcing her lips into a small smile, she eyed him through lowered lashes. With deliberately slow movements, she flicked her tongue across his thumb before drawing the digit into her mouth, eliciting a sharp hiss from him. His gaze smoldered with heat, and the only thing in the world that disgusted her more than his actions was her response to his lust. The twitching of his nose told her he sensed her arousal, unwilling as it might be. However, she spotted the moment their potent effects hit him.

He clenched his jaw as a haze of lust clouded his eyes. It was the only warning she had before he rolled on top of her.

Chapter Seventeen

It was sheer luck that Thorne and Quin made it to the seemingly abandoned farmhouse located in the middle of fucking nowhere just as the tracking spell wore off. Thorne had called Alber to give him the location, but he'd tossed the phone just as the man had begun to warn him of the potential dangers inside once again.

He couldn't care less if an entire nest of naga demons were waiting there. He'd single-handedly fight through them all to get to Chey. Fortunately, he'd grabbed her discarded gun from the kitchen while Quin had his own piece, as his brother snuck around the back of the house. They didn't really have much of a plan, but the urgency of the situation had him relying on blind hope for the first time in his life.

The front door was locked, as expected. Drawing in a deep breath, he gave the thick panel a solid kick and rushed inside, gun drawn and eyes sharp as he scrutinized the place. White sheets covered the living room furniture and carboards boxes took up nearly every corner, though the house was surprisingly clean compared to the outside. It was clear that someone had been in the process of moving in or out, though he had a sinking suspicion that Vaughn was not the true resident.

With light steps, he cleared the living room, kitchen and a small bathroom. Quin met him around the stairs, though his brother signaled he would check it out while pointing toward a sealed door near the kitchen.

"Basement," he mouthed.

Thorne nodded and the two of them split up once more. As he neared what he could only assume led to the basement, a familiar scent tickled his nose, sending goosebumps along his skin. It was Chey. Her pheromones were thick in the air, compelling enough to make him falter for just a moment to gather his bearings.

Bracing himself for the full impact of her cogent scent, he eased the door open and slipped inside.

She's here, he thought, his heart swelling with relief upon knowing she was still alive. Still, he wouldn't allow himself to relax until she was in his arms and far away from her psycho bastard of a partner.

Thorne tightened his grip on the gun and eased down the wooden stairs, careful to not make a sound. When he was halfway, his eyes adjusted to the inky darkness. The bottom floor was made of concrete, the walls covered in soundproof vinyl. The basement was just as large as the main floor upstairs, though the furniture laid about revealed it to be where someone had turned it into their living quarters.

As he rounded the corner where he heard hushed rustling, he narrowed his eyes upon spotting a king-sized bed with a lone figure bound to the posts. It was Chey. She had one hand free from the binds and was working on the other. Turning to him, her wide gaze met his, and his heart gave a wild flutter when he saw relief fill her eyes.

"Chey," he whispered on an exhale, lowering the weapon as he temporarily forgot about the posing threat.

Her mouth was taped over, and she was unable to speak. Instead, she gave a vehement shake of her head. He frowned when she looked past him.

He didn't sense any shift in the air, yet her silent gesture gave him just enough time to avoid the swipe of a knife that had been aimed at his head. He dodged, though not quite fast enough as he hissed when the blade sliced into his upper arm. Before he could react, Vaughn launched himself at him, sending them both knocking into a dresser with enough force for Thorne to lose his grip on the gun. It went sliding across the floor near the bed, too far out of reach.

Their fight was a series of flying fists and growls, and it soon became very clear to Thorne why Alber had been so persistent about not going against Vaughn alone. He was nothing more than a blur as he landed blow after blow, his punches jarring as they met Thorne's jaw and cheek. Thorne kicked out, sending the man stumbling backward. He used the brief opportunity to tackle the big bastard, simultaneously grabbing the wrist where he still held a knife.

Vaughn bared his fangs and rolled them, gaining the upper hand as he pushed downward. "She's mine," he sneered, plunging the blade to the hilt in Thorne's shoulder.

Thorne snarled at the same time Chey gave a muffled scream. Vaughn wrapped both hands around Thorne's throat, squeezing so hard that his blunt nails dug into the skin.

Just as the corners of his eyes started to bleed gray, a loud shot rang out, echoing off the walls. Vaughn went still, a look of confusion twisting his face. With jerky movements, he turned to glance over his shoulder.

Cheyenne was slumped onto the floor, one elbow bracing her weight as she aimed her gun at him. Her eyebrows were pulled together in anger, though her eyes held a sheen of tears.

"Cheyenne," Vaughn choked, his voice tight with disbelief. He released Thorne and stood. "How could...?" He shook his head. Growling low and tensing as though to pounce, he took all of two steps before Chey let off three more rounds in his chest.

He dropped to the ground at the same time Chey's arms fell, as though no longer able to support her own weight. Gripping the hilt of the knife still embedded in his shoulder, Thorne held his breath before jerking it out. He then double-checked to make sure Vaughn was down for good before moving to Chey's side.

"Chey," he breathed, helping her shift into a sitting position. As gently as he could, he peeled the tape off of her mouth. He then slid his good arm around her and held her tight, burying his nose into the top of her hair while she shuddered. "Gods below, I was so worried."

She hugged him back, though it was weak, making him realize she must have been drugged or poisoned. The thought had him gritting his teeth, wishing like hell he'd been the one kill Vaughn.

"You're so stupid," she half-murmured, half-cried.

Thorne smiled and hugged her tighter. "So I've been told."

Footsteps sounded in the distance, rapid beats against the stairs as someone descended. Chey tensed, but Thorne merely relaxed when he recognized his brother's scent. He waited until Quin rounded the corner and flipped on a light switch before shooting him a lazy glare. "Where the hell were you when I was getting my ass kicked?"

Quin took in Vaughn's dead body and chuckled. "Letting you get your ass kicked." He peered over both of them. "You two straight?"

Thorne's left eye was almost swollen shut, his shoulder was on fire and he was certain his jaw may have been cracked. "I've seen better days, brother." He tilted his chin down to take in Chey's features. Besides a bloody bruise on her temple, she didn't appear half as battered as him. "Are you all right?" he asked anyway.

"Venom," she replied.

Nodding in understanding, he returned his attention to Quin. "Mind lending a hand?"

Though his face was frowned in discomfort, Quin reached down to gather Chey into his arms. "Let's get...the hell out," she grouched.

Thorne had to brace himself on the nightstand to push to his feet before following his brother up the stairs. Just as they made it to the main floor, they were surrounded by dozens of officers all donned in black gear. "Freeze! SPD!"

Someone gave a dry snort of humor. "A bit late to the party, fellas," Quin murmured.

* * * *

After forty-eight hours of processing, giving statements and undergoing a double round of antibiotics to cleanse her system of naga venom, Chey wanted nothing more than to curl in her bed and sleep for at least the next week. It wasn't so much that she was physically tired. The last two weeks had been so draining that she hadn't even tried to fight against her boss' insistence for her to take a temporary leave of absence. In truth, she'd turned in her letter of resignation, but he'd simply handed it back to her with the suggestion to take some time to clear her head before making such a brash move.

As much as she wanted to push her argument that she didn't deserve to be on the force, she accepted that she could use a break. Perhaps she should get out of the city, go visit the countryside. Better yet, she could make a trip down to the coast. It was warmer down south compared to the northern city of Infernal Regions. Mimosas on the beach while listening to the endless waves crashing against the shore might do her some good.

Sighing, she glanced down at her watch as she headed for the lobby. It was just after noon, which gave her plenty of time to get home to start planning a getaway.

"Heard you were trying to retire early," a familiar voice called out behind her.

Slowing, Chey turned to spot a man she'd never seen approaching her. Well over six feet tall, he looked fresh out of the military with his dark hair styled in a crew cut and bulging muscles peeking from a pressed cotton tee. His hands and arms were lined with enough colorful tattoos that it was impossible to spot a single inch of bare skin.

It took several confusing moments for her to realize he'd directed the statement toward her. "Do I know you?" she asked with a frown.

The man fixed her with an incredulous stare. "Really? Nearly a decade of keeping your ass out of trouble, and this is the thanks I get? Unbelievable."

Dumbfounded, Chey shook her head when she recognized the accent. "Alber?"

"The one and only," he drawled. Then, a grin split his lips.

Chey was beginning to realize that she really sucked at her job. She'd never once met Alber in person, never so much as seen picture of him. He'd always been the faceless friend on the other end of the phone who she'd come to adore. "You're...taller than I imagined." That was an understatement. He was the complete opposite of the computer geek she'd pictured so many times.

He chuckled. "If I had a torq for everyone who said that." He nodded at the small box tucked under her arm. "Are you really leaving?"

With her free hand, she tucked a lock of hair behind her ear. "I...haven't decided. Honestly, I don't deserve to be here, Al. For five years, a murderer has been right under my nose and not once did I know."

The humor left his eyes, turning them sympathetic. "None of us could have known, Cheyenne."

She gave a bitter scoff. "Yeah, but he was *my* partner. My friend. How can I possibly stay here in good conscience after knowing I could have saved —"

"Listen to me," Alber cut in, placing his hands on her shoulders. "You and I both know that if you keep dreaming up what-ifs and what-could-haves, that shit will eat you up for the rest of your life. I had unlimited access to Vaughn's entire life story, and not once did it cross my mind that he was our guy. And not to shit on your IQ or anything, but compared to mine it's..."

Chey elbowed him in the gut, making him chuckle. "What's your point?"

"My point is you can't blame yourself. There's no telling how many other lives you saved, and I can assure you the families of the victims will be at ease knowing justice has been served. You're a damn good detective, Chey. We need you."

She thought his words over, letting them sink in until she found a bit of comfort in his faith in her, senseless as it may have been. She flashed a gentle smile. "I'll think on it. *After* my much-needed vacation."

Alber grinned down at her and threw one arm over her shoulders as he guided her through the lobby doors. "Any idea where you're going to go? I hear the south is lovely this time of year."

"That's what they say," she agreed. "What are you doing here anyway? I didn't think you ever left the bat cave."

"I don't normally, but I wanted to be here in person to drop off a gift. I don't trust the postal service to deliver this." Once outside, he took the box from her and traded a blank envelope.

Suspicious, Chey peeled it open and pulled out two shiny gold slips, both marked with some official-looking stamps. She frowned up at him. "Tickets? What, am I going to the Chocolate Factory or something?"

Alber laughed. "Or something." As she recognized them for what they were, she parted her lips in shock, making him chuckle. "Just don't ask me how I got them." He winked and nodded his head past her.

"There's your ride. Promise to give me all the details when you come back." With that, he turned to stroll back inside.

Still struggling to comprehend what was happening, Chey faced the parking lot. Something fluttered in her chest at the sight of Thorne leaning against a blacked-out SUV, his legs crossed at the ankles. He waved at her from across the distance.

Biting her lip to hide her smile, she made her way toward him. They hadn't spoken much since he'd rescued her. They'd been kept in separate rooms at the hospital. She'd been released a day before him, but she'd had to go straight to the station and haven't had the chance to see him since.

"You're supposed to be home resting," she chided, stopping a few feet away from him. She shot a pointed glance at the sling his arm was braced in.

He flashed a crooked smile. How he looked so damn adorable, even with a dark bruise under his eye and one horn nothing more than a small nub, was beyond her. "I'm sure that was just a suggestion. Besides, it's just a scratch now."

"Right," she drawled. "What are you doing here?"

"Oh, I was just in the neighborhood..." When she raised a dubious brow, he chuckled. "Okay, fine. I wanted to see you. How are you holding up?"

"If I get asked that one more time, I'm going to turn violent."

"Fair enough." His smile softened as he looked her over. He pushed from the car and placed a hand on her shoulder. A shiver danced over her skin as he used his thumb to caress her neck. "I've missed you."

Sighing, Chey turned her nose into his palm. "Careful, Lucifer. You sound like you're getting attached."

"What if I am?"

The question gave her pause, making her stiffen in surprise. She glanced up at him in uncertainty. "If you are, I'd say you have terrible taste. My life is a shit-show."

His expression didn't change. Instead, he continued to watch her with those soulful brown eyes threatening to be her undoing. "So is mine. I'd say we're perfect for each other."

Chey's chest became tight even as she frowned. "What are you saying?"

Thorne closed the short distance between them and took her chin in a light hold. "I'm saying I love you, Chey. I've known it for a while, and I want to throttle myself for being too much of a coward to say it sooner. And when I almost lost you…" His throat bobbed on a hard swallow as he glanced away, but moments later, he returned his attention to her. "I know we started off on a rough patch, but I want you to know I'm willing to do whatever it takes to prove to you that my feelings are genuine."

Chey was pretty damn certain that the way her heart was pounding under her breasts was not normal by medical standards. She'd never, ever considered herself as an emotional person, but she had to cover her mouth to stifle her gasp as he sank down on one knee.

He took her hand and held it. "Marry me, Chey. Say you'll be my mate."

Chey dug her fingers into her cheeks, but it was futile as a surprised laugh bubbled past her lips. It didn't help that Thorne managed to look offended, no doubt thinking she was laughing at him.

"Get up, you idiot," she giggled, using both hands to tug him to his feet.

"Wow," he grouched, perplexed. "Two days of studying how to propose via chick flicks, only to have you laugh at me. Those movies had it all wrong."

When her chortling wound down into a wide grin of amusement, she squeezed his hand in reassurance. "Thorne, I'm touched. I love you, too, but... Come on. Look at everything we've been through in just a week. Do you really think either of us are ready for a lifelong commitment right now?"

His shoulders deflated and a cute pout touched his lips. "Yes." At her dry look, he heaved a deep sigh and pulled his hand away to rub the back of his neck. "Er, I guess you might be right. I don't exactly have the best track record when it comes to relationships."

She nodded in agreement. "And I don't even need to remind you of my oh-so-cheerful love life. I want to be with you. I really do, but right now, it's a bit much, don't you think?"

He reared back, his eyebrows drawn together in confusion. "Wait a minute. Are you friend-zoning me?"

Chuckling, she gave him a playful slap on his good arm. "No. Instead of just jumping into anything, let's take it slow. Spend some time together, get to know each other... That sort of thing."

"So...dating?"

"Yes, dating. We can be together and build an organic relationship, then somewhere down the line we can both see where we stand."

Thorne's expression turned thoughtful as he considered her proposal. While she was thrilled to have him admit that his feelings matched her own, it was evident that they both had a lot of self-healing to do. They both had troubled pasts full of insecurities and doubt to face, so she hoped he'd see her reasoning behind wanting to take things slow.

After some minutes of quiet contemplation, Thorne finally looked at her with a pleased smile, one that had her relaxing into him as he pulled her in for a hug. "Don't get used to me saying this, but I think you might be right."

Chey went on her toes to place a lingering kiss to his lips. "If you plan on sticking around for a while, I'm afraid you'll be saying it more often than not."

Chuckling, he slid his hand to rest on her lower back. "There's no *if* about it. You're stuck with me now and forever, Chey."

"We'll see about that. In the meantime, what do you think about having our first date somewhere up north?" She waved the two tickets under his nose.

"Topside?" he asked in disbelief. "How did you... You know what? I don't even want to know. I have a few places in mind I'd like to show you."

She pressed more firmly against him, using her hip to tease the stiffness poking back at her. "First things first. My place or yours?"

The devilish grin curling his lips had liquid heat pooling in her panties. "Why wait? My windows are tinted."

Locking her hands behind his neck, Chey nipped at his lower lip. "Then let's go for a ride."

With the way his eyes darkened with hunger, she knew he'd caught on to her wicked suggestion. "Gods, you're going to be the death of me," he breathed, just before pressing his lips to hers.

Want to see more from this author? Here's a taster for you to enjoy!

The Royal Gordanos: A Royal's Touch
Makayla Roberts

Excerpt

Humans are such mundane creatures. They carry on with their lives, unaware of just how vast the world truly is.

They're unconscious of the immense number of demons roaming through their cities, living secret lives among them. Demons hide behind magical glamour spells to make themselves invisible to mortal eyes, but many of them just blend in with only the subtlest indications of their natures. Vampires have stunning, heart-wrenching beauty – shifters, the sweltering heat of their skin that is far hotter than a human's and trolls have impenetrably thick skin and a brief flash of red in their eyes when they grow angry.

That was one of the things Ava loved most about humans. They were simple-minded. Where her world was filled with danger, darkness and children of the underworld, humans were oblivious to the mystical existence around them.

She envied that about them. To be able to live their lives with no clue that they were always surrounded by creatures that go bump in the night. It was miraculous how blind they were.

Yes, envious indeed. Yet, at the same time, she couldn't help but admire them.

To have a demon strolling past them every day, even serving the food at a restaurant they frequented — *cough, cough* —yet never even knowing... She only wished to trade places with them. Maybe then she'd be able to get a full night of sleep.

"Don't tell me you're daydreaming again, Ava," a friendly, yet gruff voice called out.

Ava turned a smile on her boss, who was raising a bushy gray eyebrow at her through the small square window separating them. Though he was a rough-looking old man with a perpetual scowl, he had a heart of gold. He'd give the clothes on his back to someone in need.

A trait lacking in the majority of demons.

"Sorry about that, Mr. Tommy," she said. She picked up a thin white rag and tasked herself with wiping down the countertop. The diner she worked in was fairly empty at this time of the morning. The early morning rush had ended, but there were a few customers seated at the tables, finishing off their meals.

Tom's Place wasn't anything special, but there was a certain charm about the diner that made Ava feel comfortable working there. A gray-and-white checkered tile floor complemented baby-blue booths and metal tables. The walls were the same blue, with aged pictures from the diner's first opening in the twenties hanging on the walls. The windows had a faint tint on them to keep the inside cool and shaded, which was perfect for Ava.

She had a mild allergy to the sun's rays.

In all honesty, she didn't need this job. She'd managed to save up a considerable amount of wealth over the years to keep herself comfortable for a while.

However, as a waitress, it was a great way to interact with humans. She enjoyed studying them, learning more about their ways. She'd been sheltered from them until she reached adulthood. When she'd gone off into the world to discover for herself what was out there, she'd developed a substantial fascination with the fragile beings.

It had quickly become her small bit of joy in life — *which is rather…bizarre, isn't it?*

They were a puzzling race. The smallest of incidents could be fatal for them, and they were foolishly driven by their emotions rather than their minds. She didn't understand it in the slightest, but she wanted to. It was intriguing.

But no matter how much she enjoyed watching humans, she couldn't get involved with them any more than that. She'd never forgive herself if anyone was hurt because of her carelessness.

Especially not *that* human. There was one in particular her body craved like no other, which was a very, very dangerous thing in her predicament.

The bell above the diner door rang and the delicious scent of sandalwood filled her nose. *Speak of the devil…* She frowned to herself and looked up at the two men who took a seat at the diner bar, right in front of her. As always.

They were both dressed in uniform and both as handsome as could be. However, it was the one to the right who made her heart skip a beat. The human cop was so good-looking it was almost painful. In all her hundred-plus years of living, she'd seen her share of handsome men. But this one? He took the cake.

He had a crew-cut hairstyle, his hair cut close to his head on the sides, while the remaining dark hair on top was longer and neatly brushed backward. His eyes were a bright golden color, framed by thick, dark lashes that were long enough to make any woman seethe with jealousy. He had a thin, straight nose and a chiseled jawline so sharp that only a master craftsman could have sculpted it with such perfection. And his lips? Full, flawless and made to please a woman.

And when he smiled…

Good gods, when he smiles. His teeth were even and white, his cheeks bearing the deepest set of dimples she'd ever seen. Add to that his six-foot-three muscular build and he was a walking sexual invitation affecting women within a five-mile radius. And Ava was no exception.

Which was what frustrated her more than anything. She couldn't get involved with anyone right now — least of all a human — no matter how much her body ached for his touch.

"Good morning, Aaavaaaa," Marc drawled, those dimples flashing when he grinned.

Ava kept her face blank at the lazy way he drew her name out, but inside her heart was pounding. Even his smooth voice had her shifting her feet as heat began to pool in the pit of her stomach.

She gave him and Duncan a simple nod, ignoring her body's reaction to the sexy male. "Good morning," she responded, avoiding Marc's simmering gaze. "Edith will be over to take your orders shortly."

His dimpled smile never wavered. "Ahh, still too shy to talk to me, are you? It's been how many months now?"

Ava didn't respond as she turned to walk through the door to the kitchen area of the diner.

Too shy to talk to him? Gods. If he knew how bad she wanted him, he'd be running in terror until he reached the Atlantic Ocean.

Shaking the thought from her head, she headed toward the stock room where the other waitress, Edith, was gathering a few items.

She looked over at her. "I was *not* expecting that morning rush today," the aged woman said. "I know it's Friday, but golly."

Ava nodded in agreement. "Right? I have no idea where that crowd even came from. Is there some sort of special event going on in the city?"

Edith's gaze turned thoughtful. "If there is, I haven't heard about it. Chicago is pretty big, so there's no telling."

"Hmm. Well, your favorite customers are here. I'll finish stocking while you take their orders."

Edith blinked in surprise, her wrinkled gaze turning dreamy. "Marc and Duncan?" She let out a little happy squeal, dropping her handful of straws and condiment packets. "Oh, cripes," she muttered, crouching down to pick them up.

Ava got down to help her. "Don't worry about it. I'll get these. You go on."

Edith gave her a small frown. "Ya'know, Ava, I've been wondering for a while now… You're so nice to everyone that comes in but you always avoid those two. Why is that?"

Ava felt her cheeks heat just a bit. *Damn those old eyes of hers.*

She kept her head down, focusing on picking up the dropped items. "No reason," she mumbled. And damn herself for not being a good liar. What was the purpose of being a demon, known for their manipulation and cunning mental prowess, if she couldn't even master the art of telling a lie?

She knew that pathetic excuse wouldn't stop the other woman from prying. She was like a fluttering grandmother, always attempting to piece things together.

"Child, they're both drop-dead gorgeous," the woman continued. "They're cops, and neither of them has a ring on his finger." She paused for a second. "Wait! Could it be *because* they're cops? I know some people who tend to avoid the law at all costs. Is that the reason?" She looked around suspiciously before lowering her voice to a whisper. "Are you on the run from the authorities? Are you worried about getting deported? Don't. I won't rat on you."

Ava let out a small chuckle. In the few months since she'd been working there, she'd learned how much of a chatterbox Edith was. She voiced all her thoughts and opinions without a care in the world. Half the time Ava was sure the woman didn't even realize it. "Deported?" she asked, smiling.

Edith nodded, tapping a bony finger to her wrinkled cheeks in thought. "Yes, deported back to Mexico where you came from."

Ava shook her head. "I'm Italian, Edith, not Mexican. Two completely different countries on two completely different continents."

Edith waved that away. "Whatever. I'm not so good with all these different accents. Too many of them sound alike."

Ava only continued to smile. Despite Edith's claims, Ava's Italian accent was very faint. She'd spent a great number of years all over America, so she often picked up on their ever-changing lingo. The only time it became noticeable was if her emotions surged, which had yet to happen since working here.

"There are plenty of other police officers who come in here, and I have no trouble talking with them," Ava responded. "Honestly, I don't have an issue with either

Duncan or Marc. Let's just say I'm fairly shy around men who look that good." It was a lie, but she couldn't very well tell the woman she didn't talk to Marc because his very presence was enough to make her body tingle with desire. *Talk about embarrassing.*

"Oh well, I suppose that makes sense. Ever since you started working here, you would clam up and act all shy with only those two. Especially Marc. *That's* the one you need to shag."

Ava shook her head again. "Shag? What does that even mean?"

The woman stood up, raised a brow and put a bony hand on her hip. "You know what I mean. He's young and virile. You're young and gorgeous. You're both single. And I see the way you look at each other when no one's looking." She winked at that. "If I was just a few years younger, I'd mount that stallion in a heartbeat."

Ava bit the inside of her cheek to keep from laughing out loud. *A few years younger? Yeah, right.* They both knew full well that Edith was in her seventies — wrinkles, gray hairs and all. "Polite pass, Edith. I'm just not interested in seeing anyone right now."

That much was true, at least. Dating or even purely sexual relationships were impossible for her. *Hell, with my bad luck, it'll probably always be that way.*

"Oh well, your loss then, honey," Edith said, shrugging. She smoothed the front of her apron and straightened her thin shoulders. "How do I look?"

Ava rose as well, smiling warmly. "Fabulous."

Edith grinned and made her way back to the front, putting a little sway in her steps. Ava shook her head, still smiling. *That woman is really something else.* She was living proof that anyone is only as old as they feel. Well, to humans anyway. Time had no meaning to most demons.

She'd grown quite attached to the woman and her husband, Mr. Tommy. Though they had incredibly different personalities, they were both so sweet and generous. There'd been a few times when she'd seen them take people off the streets, offer them a hot meal and warm bed, clean them up and give them a job at the diner before helping them find something better. There weren't very many demons, if any, who would do such a thing without expecting something in return. It was the kind of pure, human love that made them want to help each other.

She placed the fallen items into the trash and washed her hands. She then pulled on a fresh pair of latex gloves, grabbed more condiments and went back to the front, where Edith's flirtatious giggling could be heard.

Ava hid a smile and began stocking the bins underneath the counter a few feet away from them. The woman was married and old enough to have great-grandchildren, yet she still flirted away with the younger men. It was fairly amusing, and the guys all went along with it.

As always, she was aware of Marc's presence. Over the smell of grease, butter and the other employees and customers, his scent stood out the most. It was a mix of his aftershave and his own personal aroma that filled her senses, making her head spin. That alone was enough to drive her mad with want.

And it was such a nuisance. She loved humans, but he stood out like a sore thumb—a very sexy, enticing sore thumb. And it was bloody frustrating because she didn't even know why. Why was it just him she felt so enamored with? Why did she feel such an intense reaction? Why did her heart jump every time her eyes met his? Yes, he was extremely attractive. Then again, so was his partner and several other men she'd come across. *So why only him?*

Speaking of his partner, she looked over at the Scot out of the corner of her eye.

Duncan looked normal enough, but he wasn't human. Oh, he very much smelled like one and did well to hide it, but she knew better. Demons could always sense another demon's presence.

Unlike Marc, Duncan's reddish-brown hair was longer and brushed back, the tips curling around his ears. His face was clean-shaven with a faint scar running from his chin up to his ear. However, it did nothing at all to take away from his handsome features. If anything, it gave him more of a gruff, sexy look, like those proud Highland warriors she'd seen on the covers of romance novels. But there was just something in the air around him that was demonic — a deadly, powerful aura that never failed to make her wary.

Oh, she wasn't afraid of him. She could hold her own against most demons. She did, after all, possess the blood of Royal vampires, some of the strongest demons to ever walk the earth.

However, Duncan was… Hell, she didn't know. His eyes were dark green with flecks of yellow around the pupil, but they held a predatory gleam that hinted at his demon side. It was like he was always searching for his next meal. That made her think he was some sort of shifter. Whether it was canine, feline or something else, she had no idea, but either way, he'd be a dangerous adversary.

Duncan was talking to Edith, making her laugh. When the woman turned away to place their orders, he looked over at Ava out of the corner of his eye, catching her watching him at bay. He winked and gave her a knowing smile. He knew she was a demon as well. It had been evident when they'd first met each other months ago, though neither of them had ever once mentioned it.

And why should they? Most demons were naturally private creatures. It wasn't like they often sat around a campfire holding hands and singing songs about peace and love. The thought made her give a soft snort.

Still... More than once she'd wondered what kind of demon he was and why he was parading around as a human cop. The intelligent look in his eyes told her he was far older than he appeared. He was a demon who'd lived a long life and had many stories to tell.

She gave another small shake of her head. *Oh well.* No need for dwelling on such trivial thoughts. Even if she had the answer to that question, it wouldn't change anything. As much as it would be nice to have demon friends she could feel comfortable around and let her fangs down with once in a while, so to speak, she would just have to keep dreaming. She wasn't the safest person to be around. And Marc...

He was a human. Getting involved with one was something she'd sworn to never do. She'd interact with them, even take their blood when she needed it. But with Marc, she wanted him in a way she hadn't ever felt before.

That in itself was dangerous. She would have to keep her distance from him. She feared that once she gave in to her carnal desires, it would be hard to stop.

And she would never forgive herself if something were to happen to him, all because she'd brought him into her world.

"Hey, Ava, come listen to this story," Edith suddenly called out. "It's intense."

Jarred from her thoughts, Ava bit back a sigh. *Damn you, Edith,* she thought. She was a character, but she was nosey as could be—nosey, and always trying to play matchmaker between her and Marc.

Ava picked up a clean blue towel and slowly walked over to them. The closer she got, the more Marc's scent clouded her mind. He was smirking as if he knew the effect he had on her. *Damn him too.*

Even as she silently cursed him, she was powerless to fight the way her body clenched in response to his look. *I'm worse than a harpy in heat, for crying out loud.*

"Thanks for joining us," he said playfully. Ava shrugged, annoyed that her tongue was dry. The more she looked at him, the more drawn she became. He was undoubtedly human, but he had a certain pull about him that could rival that of a full-grown incubus.

She began to dry the already-dried coffee mugs under the counter, setting them in their proper places as she listened.

Duncan was the one continuing the story. From what she'd learned from Edith, he had been born and raised in Scotland up until he'd been a teenager, then he'd moved to the US where he'd become a full citizen. He still had a thick accent when he spoke.

Although, with him being a demon who probably aged much more slowly than humans, it was no doubt just a cover. Not that he wasn't Scottish... The thick brogue and powerful aura gave him a warrior's presence that couldn't be faked. However, he could have spent several centuries in his homeland before coming here. *Who knows?*

"Anyway, one day we got a call about this drunk guy running down the street in this old neighborhood. It's broad daylight and he's just running, screaming at the top of his lungs. So we answer the call and roll up on this guy, expecting him to be high as shit. When we found him, he was rolling around in a field of grass screaming '*They're inside of me!*' This wasn't the first nut case we'd come across, so the procedure was pretty standard."

While Duncan continued with his story, a prickling sensation slid down Ava's neck, causing her to look up. She glanced around the room, but none of the patrons were out of the ordinary. The feeling became stronger and it was one she was all too familiar with. She narrowed her eyes, peering out of the large, shaded windows. She trusted her senses more than anything, and right now they were telling her something sinister was nearby.

She was never wrong.

Sure enough, across the street in the narrow alley stood a lone, cloaked figure. Even with the daylight outside, it was still dark between the two buildings. The humans on the other side of the street continued walking, completely oblivious to the danger standing within feet of them. To anyone who could see it, it would look like an ordinary person dressed for the changing weather.

To Ava, the figure stood out. It wasn't a human. It was hidden deep in the shadows, but she could make out two glowing-red eyes from under the hood it wore. Even with the distance, her enhanced eyesight allowed her to see the creature open its mouth in a wide grin.

Found you, it mouthed.

Her heart raced in her chest as she broke out in a cold sweat.

Damn, damn, damn. She'd known it might only be a matter of time before she was discovered, but she'd been too reckless. She'd hoped she had finally shaken the ghouls off her tail and had allowed herself to get too comfortable. *Curse it all.*

There was the sound of glass breaking, followed by a sharp pain in her hand, but she didn't even flinch. She glanced down at the shattered cup she'd grasped too tightly, watching as her blood flowed onto the sink and countertop.

She hissed, quickly running the water and holding her hand under the faucet.

By the gods. Now, with the scent of her blood in the air, it'd be even harder to make an escape. She'd just dug her own damn grave.

Edith appeared at her side, trying to help Ava with her wound, even as she was beginning to panic. Even Marc and Duncan look alarmed, and she could see Duncan's nostrils flaring, his eyes widening as he caught her scent.

Shit and double shit.

She had to make a quick escape.

Though most ghouls preferred night over day, there were a few who were strong enough to withstand the burning sunlight for a certain amount of time — like the one across the street, for example. And they were definitely not afraid to kill any humans who came between them and their target. If she stayed much longer, no doubt everyone in the diner would be injured…or worse. They would be collateral damage.

Wrapping her hand in the blue cloth towel, she turned to the small square window separating her from Mr. Tommy. She clutched her bleeding hand to her chest. "Sorry, Mr. Tommy, but I've got to go." She didn't even wait for a response. She took off her apron and sped out of the back, ignoring calls from her coworkers. She burst through the door and raced down the street. She knew the ghoul was following. She could feel it moving swiftly through the streets and alleys, following her scent. Her superior speed was near blinding compared to the ghoul's, but even then she didn't have much time. Once one of those creatures caught a scent, it was damn hard to get rid of them.

She only prayed her sudden departure would cause the creature to avoid harming anyone near the diner.

Home of Erotic Romance

Sign up for our newsletter and find out about all our romance book releases, eBook sales and promotions, sneak peeks and FREE romance books!

About the Author

Makayla's love for reading began at the age of twelve when her mother introduced her to the world of mystical creatures. From then on, she discovered a talent for turning her own imagination into words. From fanfictions to short stories to full-length novels and novellas, if she wasn't focused on school activities, she was either reading or writing.

Raised on the coast of Mississippi, Makayla juggles her everyday life between work and being a mom. In her free time, she enjoys binge watching criminal suspense shows, shopping, painting, wood burning, and of course, working on her books.

Makayla enjoys writing stories with strong elements of romance, adventure, and paranormal. Vampires, shifters, fairies, dragons—she loves them all!

Makayla loves to hear from readers. You can find her contact information, website details and author profile page at https://www.totallybound.com